Out of Love

JEWEL E. ANN

Copyright © 2020 by Jewel E. Ann
Print Edition
ISBN: 978-1-7345182-8-3

Cover Designer: © Sarah Hansen, Okay Creations
Formatting: BB eBooks

Dedication

To Jack and Jill, thank you for telling me your story.
It will always be my favorite.

Chapter One

Livy Knight Age Fifteen

"E THAN SAID YOUR dad's a psycho."
I slammed my locker door shut and scowled at my best friend. "You can't be serious."

Maggie's nose scrunched. "I know. Your dad is way better than my dad. And he's hot as fuck. My dad … well, you've seen him. It's not pretty."

"Maggs … yuck! You know I hate it when you talk about my dad like that. He's a computer geek and *my dad*. Please stop saying *as fuck* in the same sentence as my dad."

"He has tattoos and knows martial arts." Maggie ambled toward algebra. "And he doesn't have a dad gut. And he doesn't make rude bodily noises around your friends. That makes him hot as—"

"Lalalalala!" I covered my ears and then fell into a fit of laughter. "Seriously, lots of people have tattoos. And martial arts? Whatever … he's all talk. I mean … he teaches a community education self-defense class. He knows how to break someone's nose if they try to steal his wallet, and he gets pepper spray at a discount. I'd call that paranoid, but not psychotic."

Maggie gripped the straps to her backpack and shrugged. "Ethan said he was risking his life by telling anyone, but he swears your dad was waiting for him last night when he climbed out of your bedroom window."

"My dad wasn't home. Ethan's full of shit." I grabbed a sports drink from the vending machine.

"He's telling people your dad threatened him. Said he could either play football with two functioning legs or date his daughter from a wheelchair."

I coughed on my drink. "No. He didn't say that."

"I'm just telling you what Ethan's telling everyone. But seriously, Livy … what was Ethan doing in your room?"

I smirked, opening the door to the classroom. "Just stuff."

Livy Knight Age Sixteen

"DAD! STOP!" I chased after my dad as he stalked up the sidewalk after Brendon. Poor Brendon wasn't wearing pants or a shirt, just a red pair of boxer briefs and the most terrified expression I had ever seen. His clothes remained scattered on my bedroom floor—abandoned—just like his car across the street because … his car key was in his pants.

"Livy Eloise Knight …" Dad pivoted toward me when Brendon's half-naked body took a right at the street corner. "Get. Inside. The. House."

My bare feet slapped the concrete in the ordered direction, pounding the rhythm of my displeasure with each step—a retreat to my prison. "You are such a hypocrite!" I spun around as soon as the front door clicked shut behind him. Crossing my arms over my chest, I canted my head and squinted at the overprotective warden.

His gaze inspected every inch of me. The transparency of his thoughts fed my anger. He didn't like my tight, ripped jeans, my pierced belly button, or the thin fabric of my top. I hoped he could see the transparency of my thoughts too. *It's my body.*

"Bring me his clothes and his car key." The muscles along his jaw flexed as he clenched his teeth.

"You're ruining my life!" I balled my hands into fists.

"Livy ..." His eyes narrowed at me.

"Were you a virgin at sixteen, Dad? Huh? Were you?"

He didn't flinch.

"That's what I thought. So ... whose dad tried to kill you when you screwed his precious little daughter? Did you, Mr. Rule Abiding Jackson Knight, get chased up the street in nothing but your underwear?"

Still no reaction.

"I miss Mom," I whispered on a sigh and fled to the solace of my room.

Livy Knight Age Seventeen

"I'VE HEARD RUMORS ..." Garrett said as I slid his shirt over his head.

It wasn't ideal, but the back seat of his SUV had enough room to do what we couldn't do at my house or his. Four out of seven of the lights in the vacant parking lot were burned out. And I was a week away from turning eighteen.

Two weeks away from graduation.

Three months from starting college.

"What rumors?" I tossed his shirt aside.

"About your dad." He unbuttoned my blouse.

"You can't believe everything you hear."

Garrett moved to San Francisco at the end of the previous semester. It was pretty shitty of his parents to make him move to a new school one semester shy of graduation.

"I heard dating you is a bad idea."

"Who said we're dating?" I smirked as his gaze fell to my breasts barely hidden behind white cotton lace.

"Is this …" He scraped his teeth along his full bottom lip, eyes drunk on the sight before him.

"Is this what?" I reached around to unhook my bra.

"Your first time." His jaw relaxed, drawing in a shallow breath.

"First time in the back of a vehicle?" My bra shifted a few inches, fully exposing my chest.

"First time … you know … having …"

"Sex?" I brought his hand to my breast, letting my eyes drift shut when he gave it a gentle squeeze.

"Y-yeah." Garrett's voice trembled, and his hand shook as if he was afraid my boob might break like a water balloon. His whole body vibrated beneath me.

My eyes flew open, unblinking with realization. "You're a virgin?" I whispered.

His gaze slid up to mine. "Not … necessarily."

"Garrett …" I blew out a slow breath while biting my upper lip. "You've been accepted to Stanford. *Not necessarily* isn't a real or intelligent answer to your virginity status."

His hand fell away from my boob as all six feet of him deflated, leaving me perched atop a heap of bones, muscles, and shriveled confidence. I'd seen videos of him playing lacrosse—taking and giving hits so big my own lungs gasped for air. What a really terrible assumption I made, relating sex and sports. Any working dick could have slid into a vagina.

"You're not a virgin?" he asked with a pensive expression.

"Well, it's hard to explain." I grinned, leaning in to kiss him.

Knock. Knock. Knock.

We turned to the window and the angry fist rapping it three times.

"Who the hell is that?" Garrett asked.

I sighed, pulling my bra back on and buttoning up my blouse. "I'm going to get out on that side. You get out on the other side."

"Why? Do you know him?"

"How fast can you run, Garrett?"

"What? Why? Livy, who is that?"

I slid off his lap and unlocked the door. "My dad. Now run, Garrett!"

"Livy Eloise Knight. Get your ass in the car."

Chapter Two

Livy Knight Age Twenty-One

"LIVY, YOU'RE A walking disaster." Aubrey glowered when I rushed into the kitchen with my shirt half on and the handle of my backpack cutting into my hand.

I dropped it to the floor and fished my other arm through my shirt while stealing a slice of Aubrey's bread and plopping it into the toaster. "I'm late."

"No shit. And you left the peanut butter out last night—lid off, spoon still in the jar."

"Oops …" I wrinkled my nose. "Sorry, I was *starving* when I got home last night." After depositing my water bottle into the side pocket of my bag, I shoved my feet into my white sneakers sans socks.

"Surfing isn't an excuse for leaving messes *or* being late for your first day of classes."

"It's my last year." I grinned. "They can't fail me now."

Aubrey rolled her eyes while slicing veggies and fruit for juicing.

She was starting her junior year as a sociology major with no clue what she planned to do with that degree. I was a senior in political science—President Livy Knight … after law school, of course.

She acted thirty, making daily chores schedules for all four of us in the house while I played the part of a sixteen-year-old, putting surfing above all else.

She was responsible. I was fun.

We made it work.

Hooking my bag over my shoulder, I snatched my toast and winked at Aubrey. "Muah! Bye, bae. Have a great day at school. Don't forget to take your teacher an apple."

I didn't have to glance over my shoulder to know she wore a scowl and secretly had fantasies about a shark devouring me. Responsible people hated fun people. They also got ulcers, died of heart attacks, and remained virgins well into their thirties. In all fairness, the two-story Mediterranean style house with a red roof, white paint, and teal arched front door belonged to her parents—ageless hipsters who worked for an animation studio but lived in a posher house in Santa Monica. They kept the house close to campus just so Aubrey had a place to live while going to school. I never fully understood the uber-wealthy, but if knowing them meant cheap rent, my own room, and a pool … then I wasn't going to judge.

The second scowl of the morning came twenty minutes later when I arrived late to my first class. Two minutes … I wasn't sure that truly counted as late, like less than five over the speed limit never resulted in a ticket. Professor Patel paused her opening statement, curling her pale lips around her veneered teeth as she waited for me to take a seat. Of course, all of the open seats were in the front row, but I'd have sat on some dude's lap before I walked down several flights of stairs to the front row.

A nice, non-glaring student moved over one seat to let me sit on the end of the third row from the back. I stepped around the German shepherd perched at the end of the second to the last row to get to the open seat. After shrugging off my back-pack, I made a quick glance over my shoulder while easing into my seat. The owner of the service dog eyed me, delivering the third scowl of my morning.

Turning back toward the professor, I begged with an apologetic smile for her to keep talking, diverting the room's attention from me to her again. Once she started speaking, I stole another peek at the guy behind me.

Why did he seem so pissed off? Two minutes. I was two fucking minutes late. And why did he have a dog in a college lecture? If he were blind, he wouldn't have seen me walk in late.

I tried my best to focus on Professor Patel and her overview of the snooze fest clean energy and technology course, but I caved to my curiosity, sneaking another glimpse at dog guy. He had to be new, a transfer, a drop out coming back.

It wasn't that I knew everyone in my graduating class. However, sexy, scowling guy with a German shepherd would have snagged my attention long before my last year.

After class, I grabbed my backpack and turned to strike up conversation with dog guy and maybe to apologize for being two minutes late—and see if he'd let me love on his German shepherd.

"Where'd you go?" I mumbled to myself, lifting onto my toes before fighting my way up the stairs and through the crowd. There was no way he got away that quickly. He must have ditched class early which made him infinitely more mysterious and appealing.

"Way to show up late." Karina elbowed me as we spilled out of the building with the rest of the herd.

"Hey." I grinned while we navigated down the mountain of

stone steps. "Two minutes."

"Last year, bae … are you ready for this?"

I slid my arm through the other strap of my backpack. "Hey … did you see the guy with the dog?" My gaze continued to survey the area.

"Uh … yeah. He was the topic of whispered chatter from the moment he walked into the auditorium until class started … *two minutes* before you arrived."

I rolled my eyes. "And?"

"Slade Wylder. He would have been a senior our freshman year, but he disappeared for a few years. Not sure why or where he went. Anyway … he's back, and he lives across the street from you—maybe three or four houses east. Someone said he's renting the firehouse that was condemned."

"Dickerson's?" My head whipped toward her.

"Yep." Karina's lips popped.

Patty Dickerson's husband kidnapped a freshman girl the year before I started college. He kept her drugged in their dungeon for six months without Patty having a clue. Patty was in a wheelchair from some degenerative disease, so she never knew. There were some rumors that Patty didn't even know they had a basement/dungeon—they weren't exactly common in SoCal.

The one beneath the firehouse was small and sounded creepy as fuck: dark, windowless, and accessed by a trapdoor. A bunker for sick bastards to hide their victims. The girl managed to start a fire after Professor Dickerson—yep, he was a psychology professor, go figure—left a lit cigar near her.

The girl died. Patty got out. Professor Dickerson went to prison.

Someone bought the place and fixed the damage from the

fire, but it had sat vacant with a *For Rent* sign out front ever since I'd lived on the street.

"How is it he has a dog in class? He's not blind."

"Someone said he's deaf."

I wrinkled my nose. That didn't make sense.

"I suppose he reads lips." She shrugged.

"Then he should sit in the front row, where he can actually see her lips."

"I don't know. Maybe it's an emotional support dog."

"When did they start allowing emotional support animals in classes?"

Karina laughed. "I don't know anything about any of it. I'm just telling you what people were saying before class started. I'm this way." She nodded to the right.

"Okay. I have an hour break." I yawned.

"Nap?"

I nodded, still yawning.

"Set an alarm. See ya."

I found my tree, but it wasn't vacant on the east side in the sun. It was always vacant because … My. Tree.

Black tee.

Black jeans.

Black leather boots.

German shepherd.

Dog guy took my spot.

"I wouldn't," his deep, clipped warning prickled along my skin.

I liked it.

I liked the angle of his shadowed jaw and his prominent cheekbones—sharp like his tone.

I liked his deep brown hair trimmed close on the sides and

long and messy as fuck on the top, as if he didn't give it more than a quick comb through with his fingers before stumbling out the door.

My hand paused. I wasn't petting the dog, just letting it smell me. And how did he know I was there? He mimicked a log, his head resting on his bag, legs stretched long and crossed at the ankles, hands interlaced on his chest.

Unmoving.

Eyes closed.

"Are you deaf?"

He didn't move—not a flinch, a peek of one eye opening, a flutter of his long eyelashes.

I took that as a yes.

Then he must have seen me coming, felt my presence or the vibration of my footsteps.

Dropping my bag to the ground on the opposite and sunless side of the tree, I retrieved a pear from my backpack and took a bite while settling onto my side, resting my cheek on the bag. Something rustled behind me, and I glanced back. The German shepherd shifted to face me.

"Jericho," Mr. Stole My Spot warned.

A couple girls veered off in our direction. "Oh my god! What a beautiful dog." One leaned down to pet him, and he growled. The girls jumped back. "Whoa ... okay." They skittered off just as quickly as they'd detoured toward the tree.

Spot-stealer reached over and gave Jericho a scratch on his head as if to praise him for growling at the girls. However, Jericho's gaze remained affixed to the pear in my hand.

I took another bite of pear and slid the chunk out of my mouth. Then I tossed it in front of Jericho.

"Leave it."

I smirked at the gruff voice.

For a deaf person, he missed nothing. I peered in that direction again. Maybe he sat up and saw the piece of pear.

Nope.

He just knew.

The dog released a slight whine and dropped to the ground with his snout resting on his front paws.

Scooting my body and my bag a few inches toward the tree trunk, I reached my arm over my head, grabbed the piece of pear, and flicked it closer to Jericho.

I gasped as a shooting pain radiated from my wrist to the socket of my whole damn arm. Unforgiving fingers imprinted on my skin, and my hand tingled, losing all feeling.

"Feed my dog again, and I'll break your fucking arm."

"Whoa! Let. Go. Of. Me!" I ripped my hand from his grasp and scrambled to sitting, rubbing my wrist. By the time I glared over my shoulder to give him a few more choice words, he and his dog were ten yards away, heading up the stairs. His voice wasn't what I expected. Agitation bled through in his abrasive tone, but it also held perfect inflections—not so common for deaf people. Or so it was my experience.

"Asshole," I mumbled with my own perfect speech inflection while frowning at my pear that had fallen to the ground when my arm came under attack.

I breezed through my next two classes without gaining any real knowledge. Tall, dark, and one hundred percent asshole kept my mind preoccupied. After chatting with friends outside of my last lecture hall, I hopped on the first available scooter and headed home. Parking the rental on the main street, I trekked up the small hill to my house, slowing as I passed the Dickerson home. It looked similar to Aubrey's house. The whole street was a little too cookie-cutter for my taste.

After making a slow pass by the house, I picked up my pace until I heard a car behind me. As I turned my head, a black Volvo SUV with tinted windows flew into the driveway. My brute enemy climbed out and opened the back door for Jericho. His gaze shot in my direction for a split second before he shut the door. I held my breath as if doing so would make me invisible.

Slade Wylder reminded me of the Grim Reaper—minus the scythe—cloaked in black, right down to his car and its windows. Eyes so dark they appeared hollow from a distance.

My mom said my dad had a mysterious dark side to him when they met. Maybe it's why I'd always been drawn to men my father wouldn't find worthy of his baby girl. I felt certain he hadn't slept a day since I left for college. He was lucky I stayed in-state—a six-hour drive south of LA instead of the East Coast, where I seriously considered going to escape the warden.

Before Slade Wylder had a chance to take another sip from the cup of my blatant curiosity, I shot him a half smile—the one I loved giving to my father—and sauntered to my house.

"Dude! Guess who moved into the firehouse?" Kara nearly choked on her soda, wiping her mouth as I dropped my backpack by the front door.

"You're not supposed to sit on the kitchen counter. If Mommy Aubrey catches you ... you'll be evicted."

Kara leaned back against the white cabinets, hiking a knee to her chest, resting her foot on the edge of said white granite countertop. Bare feet on the kitchen counter would have sent Aubrey into a disinfecting frenzy. "This is hers." Kara held up the can of diet soda shit and smirked before taking another sip.

"And it's the last one. I'm already in deep poo poo with Mommy."

"You really are. And … yes. I know who moved into the firehouse. And he's just as creepy as the rumors we've heard about Professor Molester Dickerson. Slade Wylder. He's in my first class. And he has a dog." I grabbed a glass and filled it with water from the fridge.

"He's deaf. And really fucking hot. That's what I've heard. Is he?" Kara's eyes widened in question.

I took a few swallows then rubbed my lips together. "Hot or deaf?"

"Both."

"I don't know if he's deaf. It might explain the dog. He's definitely hot. But sadly … a jerk of epic proportions. I tried to give his dog a piece of my pear, and he grabbed my wrist and threatened to rip my arm off if I ever do it again."

"Whoa … that fits then." Kara tapped the edge of the can against her bottom lip and curled her straight black hair behind her ear.

"Fits?"

"Yeah. Missy's up in her room, but we were talking about him before you got home. She heard from Cory that Slade's a little shady. Maybe dealing. No one knows for sure. Apparently, he's been seen on the regular coming home at all hours of the night. I guess he started his last year a few years back. A week into it, someone thought they saw him at a bar with his face totally fucked-up and his arm in a sling. He never returned to school … until now. I bet he owed someone some major cash but didn't have it."

I nodded. "Probably. I'm surprised he came back to finish school."

"I'm sure he's just using it all as a front to deal whatever shit he's dealing. I'd stay away."

I continued to nod slowly while staring at the marble tile floor between us. It seemed a little odd that someone clearly interested in the law would have a side job breaking said law.

"I'm serious, Livy. Don't put yourself in danger just to piss off your dad."

My gaze snapped up to Kara.

"Don't give me that look, Liv. Your favorite pastime is making your dad mad." She wasn't wrong.

"Well, his favorite pastime is worrying about me way too much. Let's get going." My head jerked in the direction of the stairs.

"Way ahead of you." Kara lifted her tee, revealing her bikini. "Think Aiden will be there tonight?"

I smirked. "God ... I hope so. My favorite OG. He's fucking brilliant."

"And old, as are all original gangsters." Kara hopped down from the counter. "It's creepy the way you flirt with him."

"Dude, I don't flirt with him. He's older than my dad. It's called admiration and respect." I left her with a disapproving scowl then changed into my bikini, grabbed my wet suit, and waited by the door for the rest of the crew.

We surfed until the night extinguished our glorious sunshine. My annoyingly responsible friend fished me from the water to get home for classes the next day. As much as we wanted to slap on a few glow sticks and hang with the twilight crowd, Missy convinced Kara and me to pack it up.

"It's like you're totally trippin', watching them out there." I gazed at the water and my diehard friends glowing as they rode the night serpent.

"Like UFOs." Kara laughed.

With our surfboards secured to the top of Missy's SUV, we cruised home with the windows down and Maren Morris's "To Hell & Back" blaring from the speakers. I wasn't a country music girl until I met Kara. Our freshman year, she converted me in a matter of months. Missy took a little longer to convince, but we all eventually got there. Except Aubrey … she didn't surf—and she despised country music.

Chapter Three

I ARRIVED AT class the next morning with two minutes to spare *and* my mint green tea with a generous amount of honey from my favorite tea and crepe cafe. No time for crepes, but I had a tiny food orgasm while I waited in line at the pickup counter. Oh the torture … as plates of decadent French goodness strode past me on trays for customers who didn't have an eight o'clock class with a professor who had no issues shaming late arrivals.

Blackberries.

Whipped cream.

Chocolate drizzle.

It wasn't fair.

Instead, I grabbed a prepackaged energy ball at the checkout counter. Almond butter, spirulina, coconut, and dates didn't have the same effect as ooey-gooey crepes.

Slade Wylder and his mystery service dog snagged my attention from their spot in the middle section about halfway down the stairs of the theater-style lecture hall. Two seats behind him were available. Any woman with a sense of self-preservation would've picked the farthest possible seat from him. Too bad I wasn't just any woman.

I claimed a seat behind him and one to the left so maybe he'd see me out of the corner of his eye. When he didn't offer a single glance, I sipped my tea and cleared my throat.

Nothing.

He's deaf, stupid.

After my invisible face-palm, I crossed my legs and not-so-accidentally kicked the back of his chair. He slowly glanced back at me. I shifted my tea to my left hand and made a fist at my chest with my right hand, circling it clockwise—sign language for "sorry."

His deep-seated frown didn't budge. It only intensified, indenting the space between his thick, serious eyebrows.

Pinching my drink between my knees, I used both hands to sign, "I said sorry. No need to break my leg off." Unavoidable pride bent my mouth into a grin while I waited for him to acknowledge my ability to communicate with him. Tiffany, my best friend from kindergarten until eighth grade, was deaf. She taught me sign language. Well, she taught me some sign language. My dad taught me the most. He also taught me to speak some German and Russian. Before he decided to be a computer engineer, he had considered working with the government as an interpreter.

Slade answered my performance with one slow blink. How could he be so unimpressed? Seriously … how many students did he encounter who could sign?

I didn't give up. My hands quickly worked my next thoughts. "I think we got off on the wrong foot. I'm Livy Knight." I punctuated my signed words with a smile. My Aunt Jessica said after my mom died, I punctuated everything with a smile. She knew I was trying to show everyone that I was okay. I didn't want anyone to feel sorry for me.

But god … *I* did. I felt so damn sorry for myself. And my father. He never recovered. I always sensed his love beneath the thick armor of overprotectiveness, but it was like a light went out when she died. Dark and heartbreaking. Every smile held a jolt of his pain. I couldn't do anything but smile bigger, trying to lift him out of his dark hole. *You can't hold on to her. She's gone.*

Slade blinked a second time. Unimpressed.

"Good morning," the professor silenced the room.

My gaze shifted to her for one second, and by the time I returned it to Slade, he'd faced forward again. He managed to go the entire lecture without so much as a stolen glance over his shoulder at me. I couldn't say the same. My stolen glances were to the front of the room. By the end of class, I could have sketched every detail of Slade Wylder's side profile. Every prickly whisker shadowing his face. The permanent downward turn of his mouth. The soft sweep of his eyelashes on his high cheekbones when he rested his eyes or maybe took a few seconds nap—I couldn't tell. The rest of his body remained statuesque. No note taking. No body shifting like the rest of the uninterested prisoners of the professor.

Nothing.

He just ... didn't move until five minutes before the end of class. Then in one fluid motion, which startled me out of my heavy inspection, he and Jericho made a stealthy exit from the lecture hall.

"Shit," I whispered, cringing at the spilled tea pooling by my feet as I scrambled to shove my laptop into my bag and bolt toward the door. After depositing the empty cup into the trash just outside the room, I pushed through the main doors and scurried down the wide stone stairs. "Wait!" I chuckled at myself. "He can't hear you," I mumbled.

I slowed my jog and stretched my strides to an impossibly fast walk when I caught up to him. He halted like a soldier snapping to attention, but he didn't turn toward me.

Pivoting to face him, I presented my kindest smile. "What's your next class?" I signed.

Nothing.

"I'm sorry about yesterday. He's a service dog. I get it. I should have kept to myself."

His gaze remained affixed to mine. I dropped my hands to my sides. Such a dark, unreadable soul. Maybe he'd recently lost his hearing and didn't understand sign language. So many thoughts went through my mind as I waited to find a way to communicate with him, until …

"What the fuck are you doing?"

My eyebrows inched up my forehead. "You're not deaf."

"Brilliant observation. Are we done here?"

When I hesitated for more than one second, he brushed past me.

I pivoted one-eighty. "PTSD? Bipolar disorder? Panic attacks? Suicidal thoughts? Is he an emotional support dog?" My voice lowered to a whisper when his confident pace increased the distance between us. "Okay. That went well."

"Did Livy Knight strike out?" Karina nudged the heel of my shoe with the toe of hers before sidling next to me.

On a laugh, I nodded. "Royally."

"Maybe he's gay."

I lifted a shoulder. "Maybe. I wasn't hitting on him. He just makes me … curious."

A throng of students from the dismissed class swallowed us, forcing us forward.

"Well, he's definitely mysterious."

Tipping my chin up, I searched for him, but he'd already disappeared. "Yes. Mysterious. Sure wish I didn't like mysteries so much." I smirked. "But I can't help it. I do."

"Liv ..."

"What? I'm just..." gathering my blond hair off my neck, I rested it over my right shoulder and absentmindedly braided it "...curious why he has that dog in class. He's not deaf or blind. And I want to know why he's renting the firehouse—seemingly by himself. And everyone ... I mean *everyone* knows it's haunted. I don't see how he can afford it unless his family's rich or he is, in fact, a drug dealer."

"Or he's a serial killer and thought a haunted homicide house would be a great fit. He could have bodies stored in freezers in that dungeon they call a basement. Ever think about that?"

I nodded. "You know me. Of course I've thought that."

We laughed in sync.

"I have to go. See ya."

"K." I shot her a conspiratorial smile as she veered off to the right while I headed to my next class.

Deep state.

Conspiracy theories.

Corruption.

Serial killers.

All forms of crack for me. My mom used to say my overly curious and highly suspicious mind came from my dad. However, I never equated his overprotectiveness to CSI or government espionage.

After my usual scooter drop-off at the end of our street, I made one pass in front of the firehouse, turned around, and made another pass. No black SUV. No signs of Slade Wylder.

Just a quick peek. I fed my obsessively curious side with the very drug it needed to avoid. The guy threatened to rip my arm off, and I hadn't completely forgotten his rumored drug dealer status. Yet …

Yet I made a sudden right-left glance and sauntered up the driveway like I lived there. Closed shades obscured any chance of me getting a peek inside the firehouse. If Slade Wylder owned houseplants, they were going to die. Was the dungeon of death still there? The trapdoor covered by a rug?

Slade didn't seem like the kind of guy who'd have rugs. Or houseplants. Or cookies in a jar on the counter. My mom always had cookies in a jar for me. After she died, my dad tried to fill the jar with store-bought sandwich cookies. I turned my nose up at them and his pathetic attempt to fill my mom-void with store-bought cookies.

I'll-rip-your-fucking-arm-off Wylder felt more like a dirty-black-boots-in-the-house kind of guy. I imagined him coming home at a werewolf's curfew, taking a piss, leaving his jeans unfastened, peeling off his shirt, and collapsing onto an unmade bed with his boots on—one leg dangling off the side.

Finding no luck getting the tiniest glimpse into the house from windows and doors, I snooped around the detached two-car garage. The side access door had a window, but it was painted black … and it was locked.

"You know what happens to trespassers?"

"Jesus!" I jumped, whipping around and pressing my back against the door like a fly nailed with a swatter. As I swallowed, coaxing my thundering heart back down into my chest, I clenched my hands. "I'm … I'm not trespassing."

"My property. You weren't invited." His frown deepened. "Trespassing."

On an eye roll, I mimicked his intolerable facial expression. "So?" I shrugged. "Call the cops." My gaze dropped to Jericho.

He smiled at me. For real. My mom used to show me pictures of Gunner smiling at her. She said only the people German shepherds loved the most could recognize their subtle smile. I refrained from breaking the news to Slade that his dog already loved me more.

"Fine." Slade's one-word response shifted my attention to his cell phone heading toward his ear. "I need to report a trespasser on my property. The perp refuses to leave. Yeah, the address is 803 Sun—"

"Oh my god! I'm leaving …" I held up my hands in surrender while taking two steps sideways before pivoting and pounding my feet down his driveway. The nerve … I was not trespassing. And *perp*?

I didn't glance back until I made it up the street and crossed over to my house, where I had a good view of the firehouse. Slade and Jericho were nowhere in sight. My jaw continued to hang open, and I choked on the shock of him calling the police on me.

"What's that look about?" Missy asked, tossing her phone beside her on the espresso-colored leather sofa by the front window.

I inspected her gray fitted tee. It was mine. "Nice shirt. And … no look. Well …" I dropped my bag by the stairs. "Psycho Slade caught me on his property and called the police."

"Seriously." Missy sat up with wide brown eyes unblinking and messy brunette bangs swooping across her forehead.

Sprawling out on the plush, gray and white area rug, I pulled my knees to my chest to give my lower back a stretch. "Total dick move. There's no way he really called the police. I didn't see his phone screen, but I did hear the mumble of someone on the line with him. Probably an equally asshole-ish friend playing along."

"Do you think Slade Wylder *has* friends?"

My body vibrated with laughter. "Good point. Talk about personality deficit. Maybe his brain is damaged from shooting shit up his veins, or maybe his parents didn't love him. I don't know what his issues are, but they are severe."

"Why were you on his property anyway?"

"Duh ... because he lives in the firehouse. He takes a dog to class, but aside from his obvious personality disorder, he doesn't seem to have a solid reason to have a dog in a college lecture hall. But mostly ... I'm just curious. And pissed. The more he acts like an asshole to me for no good reason, the more I feel the need to figure him out." Straightening my legs, I laced my hands behind my head and stared at the ceiling. "I mean ... what if he's another Professor Dickerson? My curiosity could save lives."

"Or end yours. You read too many thrillers. He's not a plot to solve. He could actually be a dangerous person. For. Real. Did you ever think of that?"

"I walked around his house. I didn't go inside."

"Because the door was locked or because it was a bad idea?"

"Yeah." I grinned.

"Yeah to which one?" She chuckled.

"I mean ..." I rocked up to sitting and folded my legs. "The garage door was locked too. And that's fine ... whatever. Maybe he keeps important stuff in his garage. But the side door's window is painted black. All the shades are down in the house. All. Of. Them. That's not normal. He's hiding something."

"Drugs!" Missy ran her fingers through her hair. "If you

had drugs in your house … maybe meth residue on the coffee table and bongs haphazardly discarded on the sofa—you'd shut your blinds too."

I returned an easy nod. "True."

The doorbell rang, and Missy jumped up to answer it. I craned my neck to see who was there, scrambling to my feet when I made out the two police officers.

"Uh … Livy?" Missy turned just as I came up behind her. "They're asking about someone in this house who was trespassing down the street." With her back to the officers, her eyebrows crawled up her forehead. "I'll leave you to it."

I slapped on an innocent smile as Missy skittered off to the kitchen. "Hi."

"Miss, we received a trespassing complaint, and—"

"Whoa …" I shook my head, crossing my arms over my chest. "I was just seeing if he was home. When no one answered the door, I checked the garage. He caught me trying to look in the garage door window. That's it."

The female officer bobbed her head several times. "Well, he said you've been harassing him on campus as well. So maybe it's best to keep your distance."

"I …" My head shook. "I can't believe he reported me. You should give him a warning for wasting your valuable time. There's probably some real crime going on right now, but you're here because my asshole neighbor upped his dickhead game. His dog likes me more. That's why he's mad. And if you want a real tip … I heard he's dealing drugs."

They gave me two pained expressions. I couldn't read if they were feeling sorry for me, like the poor obsessed, stalker girl or because they realized how ridiculous it was for them to give his prank call the time of day.

"Do you have a credible source?"

I shrugged. "No. But that doesn't mean it's not true. You should search the premises … but I know … you'd need a warrant and a credible source."

The stocky officer with a graying goatee smiled. "Yes. For now, just watch yourself and keep off his property."

Not a chance.

"Absolutely." I returned a tight grin as they retreated to their car parked on the street. My gaze shifted to the firehouse for a few seconds before I shut the door and leaned my back against it.

"What the hell?" Missy rushed me from the kitchen. "Dude … he seriously called the cops on you! Wow … what did you do to piss him off?"

"I don't know. But he's not winning."

"Wait? What? No." She shook her head a half dozen times. "There is no *winning*, Livy. You've known him … and I use that word lightly … for two days. I don't think you should interpret the police at our door as a game."

Trapping my lower lip between my teeth, I slanted my head and narrowed my eyes. "What do you suppose he's doing in that house? The rent is outrageous. No one in their right mind moves into the firehouse. It's haunted. Everyone knows that. I don't care where he's been. It's just common knowledge."

Missy shook her head. "I think it's a ginormous fuck-off. If I sold drugs, could afford my own place, and wanted privacy, I would rent that place."

On a laugh I rolled my eyes. "No you wouldn't. The only person who believes it's haunted more than I do, is you."

"True. I'm saying if *I* were a hot, fearless drug dealer …

then I would totally rent the place. I bet the ghosts are freaked out by him."

"Maybe." I glanced at my watch. "I'm running an errand."

"Beach?"

I pulled my ponytail up higher on my head and twisted it into a bun. "No. I have something I need to do."

"As long as it doesn't have anything to do with *him.*"

Without making eye contact, I slid my hand into my back pocket to check for my bank card. "Pfft ..." I rolled my eyes to stress the absurdity.

Chapter Four

AFTER A QUICK trip in my Jeep to The Panting Barkery, I stood at the end of Slade's driveway, rehearsing my speech. When the words refused to do anything but fumble from my mouth, I opted to just go with whatever came to mind in the moment.

Three solid knocks later, the front door creaked open. Dark, unwelcoming eyes shot me a bored gaze.

"If I stressed out Jerry, I'm sorry." I held up a bag from the dog bakery. "I'm sure you've trained him to be a guard dog. My *trespassing...*" I made air quotes "...probably confused him. You know ... your clear anger mixed with his obvious love for me." The handsome dog appeared at his side, snagging my attention. "Hey, Jerry. I brought you treats." I pulled out a cow ear ... fur still on it.

"Place," Slade said.

Jericho whined.

"Place," he said again with the slightest edge to his tone as if he wasn't used to giving a command more than once.

I frowned when the dog disappeared into the house. "Fine. Give it to him when you see fit. Your dog. Your rules." As I slipped the ear back into the bag, the door slammed in my face. A grin quirked my mouth. It had been a while since someone caught my interest the way Slade Wylder did. Before meandering home, I left the sack by the door.

The next morning, I set off to class early enough to wait in the back corner for my favorite distraction. Just when I thought about giving up and picking a seat, Slade and Jericho slipped into the auditorium at the far door. He took his usual seat on the end of a row. Luck winked at me, bringing the empty seat beside him into view.

"Morning, Jerry." I scratched his head, grinned at my scowling neighbor, and nodded to his legs—knees nearly hitting the seat in front of him. "Excuse me, please."

Slade didn't move an inch. "Does your insurance cover prosthetics?" he asked with his eyes on the empty lectern at the front of the room, like he was talking to himself.

"Why?" I stepped over both of his legs and plunked my ass into the seat next to him.

"Because I warned you."

After depositing my bag on the floor and plucking my water bottle from the side pocket, I propped my unlaced white sneakers up on the chair in front of me and peered over at … well, quite possibly the most formidable *and* sexiest man my eyes had ever seen.

The chaotic hair.

The thick stubble shadowing his face.

The intensity of those eyes.

But the lips … so damn full.

The fact that they were pulled into a firm line of contempt for me was unfortunate but not a deal-breaker—not yet.

I refused to acknowledge his earlier threat to rip my fucking arm off. "Do you sleep well? I heard you're out until the early hours of the morning. Is it the ghosts? The firehouse is haunted." I sipped my water and rubbed my lips together. "I've read they're most active between midnight and three in the morning. Do you set an alarm? Where do you go for those three hours?"

Slade could burn me to the ground with a look … without blinking.

Not. One. Blink.

His hand, resting on his leg, flexed, accentuating the veins in his arms. Vein porn. Yeah … I liked veiny arms. Unmarked, veiny arms. My dad's tattoos made unmarred flesh my kryptonite. I had no intention of crushing on a guy like my dad, even if my family said it would happen, and my dad would suffer the ultimate karma. Whatever that meant.

"Did you give Jerry the cow ear?" I widened my eyes in question as I sipped my water again and studied the side of his face. The front of his hair stood erect while the hair above his ears swept forward, framing perfection.

"*Jericho.* Unless you want to lose your tongue too." He turned to slaughter me with those eyes.

Easing the water bottle away from my mouth, I grinned. "My arm *and* my tongue. Wow … that's a little harsh, don't you think?"

Slade Wylder hovered near me like a storm cloud, sending sparks of electricity through my veins and chills along my skin while siphoning oxygen from my lungs.

The professor cleared her throat at the lectern, stealing my attention. I continued to feel the wolf's gaze stuck to me, certain my neck detected his hot predator's breath as well. Midway through the lecture, I slid a notebook from my bag and wrote a note to Slade.

> *Have you ever torn a person's arm off?*
> *Ripped their tongue from their mouth?*
> *Do you surf? How old is Jerry?*

Would you happen to have a stick of gum on you?

Keeping my attention on the front of the room, I dropped the paper onto his lap. He read it while I squirmed in my seat. So many thoughts played tag in my head.

Have those veiny hands truly harmed anyone?

Does he just deal? Or is he an addict?

Does he play fetch with Jerry?

Would his whole face crack into a million pieces if he smiled?

What would those lips taste like pressed to mine?

That last thought jumped into the mind games without permission. I was curious … determined … not a masochist. Snatching up every douche bag just to piss off my dad was yesteryear Livy. I found his body sexy, not his attitude. I wasn't that girl. Not anymore.

"You're in over your head." He stood and escaped before I completely cleansed my inappropriate thoughts.

I chased after him, hellbent on breaking him. Saving an innocent victim. Maybe just … Just what? I didn't know. My feet carried me without giving my brain time to figure out what I was doing. It didn't matter.

He was gone.

Not a distant silhouette. Not a fading shadow.

Just … gone.

After adjusting my backpack on my shoulder, I stabbed my fingers through my hair, turning in a slow circle, surveying the sparse dotting of students milling around. "What does that mean?" I mumbled. "How am I in over my head? Unless … you're into something shady, Slade Wylder."

I skipped out early on my last class of the day, packed my Jeep, and cruised to the beach to wash away the day from my body and *him* from my mind. Hours later, when the evening breeze slithered over my body, covering my skin with goose bumps, I glanced at my phone.

Aubrey: *Is it weird that I bought a loaf of bread several days ago and I've only had two pieces, but now all that's left are heels?*

I grinned, knowing she wasn't really mad. In fact, I could easily imagine her eye roll, like when I left out the peanut butter. Aubrey had passionate dreams and possessed mad organizational skills, but she struggled in school—unlike me, who rarely had to crack a book. Another trait I inherited from my dad. If I hadn't spoon-fed Aubrey everything she needed to know to pass her hardest classes, the bread theft might have been a bigger offense.

Livy: *I'll pick some up on my way home. Grabbing dinner, then I'll be home. LY.*

"Leaving?"

I turned toward Elias, the only person I knew who spent more time at the beach than I did. He ran a hand through his wet, dirty blond hair, water rivulets sliding down his bronzed torso.

"Yeah." I leaned to the side and twisted my hair to wring out the water before slipping on my favorite wide, ripped-neck sweatshirt that hung off my shoulder. "I'm starving."

He followed me to the Jeep and helped me secure the board on top of it. "Wanna grab a pizza and go back to my place?"

I clenched my fingers around the frayed cuffs of my sweatshirt and leaned my back against the driver's door. "Yes." I tried to suppress my grin, but it only made it bigger as I felt my cheeks flush. "But I'm not going to do that."

His head cocked to the side, sexy yet adorable like a puppy. "And why is that?"

"Because you're my favorite fantasy." I shrugged, diverting my gaze to the side.

A hearty laugh spread from deep in his chest to his gorgeous, white smile. "Sounds like the *perfect* reason for you to come over."

"Nope." I forced my gaze to his, and I held up the key fob and unlocked the Jeep. "I like you best in my fantasies. And I like sharing space with you here. I like flirting with you." I turned. "You have no one to blame but yourself."

"Me? What?" He coughed with disbelief.

I climbed into the driver's seat. "I've heard you don't sleep with the same girl twice."

"So?" He lifted a shoulder.

"So … I think it's infinitely more stimulating to be the one you can't have."

His only comeback was a smirk. Yeah … he knew the chase was *everything*. "Catch you later, then."

I grabbed the door to shut it. "You'll never catch me, but I look forward to watching you try." With an equally sly grin, I shut the door, started the Jeep, and pulled out of the lot.

Since the Jeep needed gas and my stomach needed food, I stopped by a convenience store to fill up and grab an iced tea and lukewarm slice of pizza before stopping for a loaf of bread. Holding the slice of pizza between my teeth, I opened the Jeep door.

"Wallet," an angry voice gritted in my ear as the pizza fell to the ground along with the iced tea.

The owner of the angry voice slammed me into the door.

Tears burned my eyes as realization snaked up my spine. Stale cigarette-smoke breath washed over my cheek as its suffocating warmth enveloped my ear. The tip of a knife dug into my side below my ribs, already having cut through my sweatshirt.

"Make one fucking sound and I'll gut you right here. Just give me your fucking wallet."

My wallet was in my bag on the floor of the Jeep—along with my pepper spray. I had my bank card in the back pocket of my jean shorts. My dad taught me what to do in that situation. Only, I'd never been in the actual situation. And I didn't do what he told me to do. I wasn't prepared.

I was paralyzed.

And I'd parked at the farthest pump where the lighting was poor. Short of someone watching the live security footage, I was hidden from anyone who could help me. To people driving by, I looked like I was getting felt up by a frisky, horny boyfriend.

I froze.

I cried silent tears.

I choked on my breath and the acid creeping up my throat.

"It-it's in-inside … o-on the fl-floor."

"Well, that's a shame. Looks like you're going to give me something else instead."

"Please …" I whimpered and sucked in a harsh, painful breath as the tip of the knife broke my skin.

"Shh … no need to beg, princess. Now walk left and keep your fucking head down."

His other arm snaked around my waist as the knife dug a little deeper into my side. He kept his head ducked and buried next to my ear as I curled my fingers into his arm to steady myself—to try to break free without a knife lodging into my torso, leaving me there to bleed out.

I should have gone to Elias's place. Consensual sex would have been less life changing. Because … I knew. I knew in that very moment my life was about to change forever.

A plane nosediving to the earth.

A ship sinking to the floor of the ocean.

A piece of my soul on the verge of being ripped from existence.

My Aunt Jessica told me something happened to her as a teenager that changed her—irreparably damaged her—forever. Everything—good and bad—that had happened to her since that day was woven with a tiny piece of thread from that exact moment.

She said, "Either you die, or you're born again. But you're never the same."

He led me to the side of the convenience store, behind the trash dumpster—the air heavy with stench and black like the heart of the man hurting me.

The knife disappeared for a breath while he shoved me to the ground and straddled me.

"Hel—"

He extinguished my cry for help and stilled my flailing limbs with the blade of the knife poised to slit my throat.

"Shut. The. Fuck. Up."

I stilled, except for the rapid rise and fall of my chest as the headlights of a car in the distance lit his face for two seconds. He was young. Maybe early twenties like me. Clean shaven. Fair-skinned. Neatly trimmed hair like he gave a shit about something—just not me. He could have been a guy I would have said yes to for a date.

Evil didn't have a look.

And we weren't on a date. He was using his free hand to unfasten his jeans, lifting onto his knees just enough to slide down the front of them before tugging at the button and zipper to my shorts.

I was two blocks ... two blocks from home.

Evil didn't care about zip codes.

I messed up. I got too comfortable. I thought it couldn't happen to me.

"Please don't ..." I whispered again as hot tears slid down the sides of my face.

As he ripped my panties down my legs, I closed my eyes and wondered if my mom could see us. I hoped not. I hoped her afterlife didn't involve seeing her daughter being violently raped.

Then ...

The knife disappeared from my throat, and his legs brushed mine briefly before he wasn't touching me anywhere. My eyes snapped open, one hand going to my neck while my other hand reached for my panties and shorts halfway to my knees. A shadowy figure vanished, but it wasn't human. It looked like an animal. Scrambling to my feet, I swiped my hand along my leg and rubbed my fingers together.

Blood.

A lot of blood.

My other hand reached for my side; it was bloody too, but the blood on my leg was not mine. My side wasn't bleeding *that* much.

"Help ..." I croaked, but it came out as barely a whisper while I stumbled a few steps, my knees shaky and my body frail with fear.

"Help …" I said a little louder.

I kept moving toward the front of the store. A young couple getting out of their car saw me and rushed to help me.

Chapter Five

I DIDN'T CALL my dad.

I gave the police my account of what happened, and Aubrey, Kara, and Missy picked me up from the hospital after I was examined and three stitches were placed into my side to close the small wound.

My dad would have thrown me over his shoulder and hauled my ass from LA back to San Francisco. He would have locked me in the house and not let me return to school until he figured out a way to hire a bodyguard for me.

So I took the rest of the week off from school. I talked with Aubrey's therapist—on her parents' dollar. Dr. Izzy Garfield suggested I tell my family. I nodded, knowing there was no way I would ever tell my overprotective father.

I didn't rule out telling Aunt Jessica … eventually.

Just a few yards away from the convenience store dumpster, they found the man who tried to rape me—with his throat slit. As for who killed him? That remained an ongoing investigation with no witnesses and no leads. The suspicious part was they found bloody prints from a dog, but the man who tried to rape me wasn't killed by an animal. I told the police that I thought I saw a brief shadow … almost like a ghost of a dog disappearing into the distance.

"I'm not leaving you." Aubrey crossed her arms over her chest and narrowed her eyes at me perched on the sofa watching HGTV as the other girls waited at the door with their suits on, cooler packed.

"I'm fine." I smiled.

"Then why aren't you going with us? You don't have to surf. You can chill with me." Aubrey prodded. "I should call your dad. If he finds out we didn't—"

"Dude!" I pressed the heels of my hands to my temples. "I have three stitches. The man is dead. I'm fine. I just don't feel like the beach today. Is that a crime?"

All three of my friends cringed at my outburst.

I sighed, drawing my knees toward my chest and resting my chin on them, gaze on the television. "Sorry. I'm just … fine. Please go and have fun for me. One day. Give me one more day. I'm going back to school tomorrow. Can we just forget about this? Please."

After a few seconds of silence, Aubrey nodded. "Lock the door when we leave. Keep your phone by you. I'll be checking in regularly."

"Thanks, Mom." I relinquished a small smirk and sideways glance.

Seconds after the door closed behind them, I jumped off the sofa and locked it. Then I checked the back door and all the windows. After I made a sandwich, I peeked out the back windows and the front windows. "You're paranoid," I murmured to myself. Then I slowly unlocked the front door. I could sit on the porch. I did it all the time. It was safe. Nothing to fear.

Yet … all I felt was fear.

As I eased the door open an inch, I froze.

Like a stone statue, Jericho sat outside my front door. No Slade in sight.

"Hey …" I opened the door the rest of the way. "What are you doing, Jerry?" I glanced right and left.

Nope. No Slade.

I feathered my fingers over his head and back, continuing to survey the area for … anyone. "Are you thirsty?"

He collapsed into a downward position, facing the street.

"Come," I nodded toward the door.

He ignored me.

"Okay. I'll be right back. You just … I don't know. Wait for me." I grinned while disappearing into the house to fill a bowl with water. When I set it beside him, he took a few slurps before resuming his position like a guard dog.

"Are you here for me?" I sat on the stone porch in the shade next to him. "There's no way he lost you. So …" I stared at the firehouse, looking for any signs of my asshole neighbor. What if something happened to him? I wondered if I was the only other person Jericho knew besides Slade. However, Jericho didn't know where I lived. So that didn't make sense.

"You're a pretty boy. Did you know that?" I brushed my hand along his back several times. A few minutes later, I grabbed my computer and pulled a chair next to my guard dog to get some schoolwork done and respond to the texts Aubrey sent me every thirty minutes. Other than the occasional pissing in the sparse area of grass, Jericho stayed next to me all afternoon.

When the girls pulled into the driveway, he stood and trotted toward the firehouse.

"Jerry?" I called after him.

He kept going like a robot programmed to stay until they returned.

"What's going on?" Missy asked as they climbed out, hair

damp and windblown, faces freshly kissed by the sun.

I returned my gaze to Jericho who disappeared to the backside of the firehouse. "I think he sent his dog to protect me."

Kara laughed. "Unlikely. Seriously ... what was he doing here?"

I shrugged, moving the chair back to its spot. "I'm serious. I don't know. He appeared shortly after you left. Then he just ... took off when you pulled into the driveway."

"And Slade?" Missy's single eyebrow peaked.

"No sign of him."

"Do you think it was him?" Kara opened the door, and we shuffled inside.

"What do you mean?" I plopped down on the sofa with my computer.

"Do you think it was Slade who killed your abductor?"

I gazed out the window and shook my head slowly. "No. He's ... a creep. Mysterious. And maybe a druggie. But my gut tells me he's not a killer. Killers don't send their dogs to guard the doors of women they despise."

"Well, if he sent his dog to keep watch over you, I don't think he despises you," Missy said as she headed up the stairs.

"Maybe he just doesn't want anyone to kill you before he gets a chance to do it himself." Kara smirked while Aubrey gasped. Kara cringed. "Sorry. Too soon for that joke?"

My grin answered her question, which only made Aubrey huff off in a tizzy because I wasn't taking the situation seriously. Or so it seemed.

"Why would he send his dog unless ... he knows? And how would he know?" Kara continued while slipping off her tank top, revealing the sunburn from the cut of her new bikini top.

"People talk. I haven't been in class. Gossip spreads quickly."

"Or ..." She pulled the strap away from her shoulder and frowned at the red line. "He was there that night. Saving you like ... a vigilante."

I chuckled. "A vigilante?"

"We don't know his true intentions yet. Vigilante is the most we can say for sure right now. But Livy ... seriously ... what if he *killed* someone to save you?"

I stared at her, not knowing what to say. She blew out a slow breath and headed upstairs.

In reality, I was thoroughly rattled by the gas station incident. I wasn't sleeping. Keeping it from my dad weighed heavily on my conscience, and simple things like walking to the mailbox or the thought of walking down the street the next day to grab a scooter scared the shit out of me. Parking on or near campus was a nightmare, hence the reason I grabbed a scooter, but I knew I'd be Jeeping it for a while.

But ... I didn't want my friends to know any of that.

THE NEXT MORNING, I put on a brave face and forced myself to follow my usual routine, including my mint green tea before class. Instead of waiting to stalk my neighbor and his dog, I took a seat three rows from the front and kept my attention on the professor, not once looking back to see if Slade and Jericho were there.

It wasn't that I wasn't curious. I was. I just felt out of sorts about not only the incident the previous week, but about Jericho watching over me.

Slade called the police on me for trespassing. He threatened to do bodily harm to me for offering his dog a piece of pear.

Guys like that didn't risk life in prison for girls like me.

After class, I made my way to my tree. Slipping in one ear-bud, I rested on my back, using my backpack as a pillow and closing my eyes. I felt safer in the light of day, surrounded by other students, than I did in my bed at night. And I was so very tired.

Nearly sleeping past my next class, I opened my eyes and glanced at my watch. "Shit!" I had two minutes to make the ten-minute trek to class. Thankfully, no one gave me a second glance when I slipped into the room a few minutes late. As I pulled my computer from my bag, a folded sheet of paper fell out with it. I picked it up and grinned. It was the note I gave to Slade.

Have you ever torn a person's arm off? No.
Ripped their tongue from their mouth? No.
Do you surf? Yes.
How old is Jerry? Five.
Would you happen to have a stick of gum on you?

Taped to the bottom of the paper was a stick of gum.

"Wylder ..." I whispered, unwrapping the gum and sliding it into my mouth. Peppermint.

Not spearmint.

Not wintermint.

Not cinnamon.

My favorite ... peppermint.

Later that afternoon, I parked my Jeep in the street and strode down to the firehouse, stopping at the end of the driveway with the black Volvo. Risking another trespassing warning, I meandered toward the garage, slowly turning the handle. It opened, giving way to a slightly offensive burning smell and Slade in a long-sleeved shirt, welding gloves, and a welder's mask.

He didn't stop or even give a glance in my direction as I closed the door behind me, inspecting the workbench, gas tanks, pieces of metal, and the vent in the ceiling above him. After a few minutes, he shut off the torch and flipped up his mask.

Hugging my arms to my body, I smiled. "Hi."

He let his gaze work its way down my body and slowly back up to my eyes. But he said nothing.

"Where's Jerry?"

The muscles in his jaw flexed.

I cleared the frog from my throat. "Jericho."

He nodded toward the house.

I glanced behind me, even though I knew the door was shut and there was nothing to see. Maybe I just needed a few seconds away from the intensity of his gaze on me. "Did you ..." I forced my attention back to him. "Uh ... did you ..." I couldn't ask. What if it wasn't him? Then I'd be confessing my near rape. "Yesterday. I um ... I needed Jericho ... what I mean is I needed something, and he was it."

Slade relinquished three full blinks.

After nervously scraping my teeth along my lower lip for a few seconds, I lifted a shoulder. "So ... thanks for letting him hang out with me. I don't know why you did it, but I'm grateful to you for ... well ... whatever the reason."

Did you kill that man? Did you? Why did you? Tell me! Say something!

Slade nodded once, flipped his mask down over his face, and started his torch again. I wanted to ask what he was doing or making or fixing. I wanted to ask him so many things, but I decided to quit before the cops were called. He wasn't going to give me everything in one day. That much was clear.

So ... I decided to wait. After all, I knew he hadn't ripped anyone's arm from their body or tongue from their mouth. He surfed and had perfect taste in gum flavors. That was enough for one day.

Chapter Six

I F I WAS home alone, Jericho was perched at the door. How did he know—either Jericho or Slade—that I was alone? It was both incredibly comforting and oddly frightening. The man who had spoken less than twenty words to me seemed to know a lot about my whereabouts and that of my roommates.

More than that … he knew I needed protection.

This went on for weeks. Every day I tried to get the nerve to ask that unanswered question. Did he kill that man?

Slade went from vigilante to total enigma in a matter of a month.

"Coffee?" I stepped over his legs to sit next to him in class, something I hadn't done since the day he threatened my tongue. "Or tea?" I eased into the chair, trying to not spill either hot drink. "I'm good with either. You just come across as a coffee person. I'll set it by your feet. So don't knock it over." I placed the cup by his black-booted foot.

"No worries, Jerry. I didn't forget about you." I retrieved a dehydrated duck neck from the Barkery bag in the side pocket of my backpack and leaned my torso over Slade's lap to hand it to Jericho.

His lethal glare hadn't eased up much since our first encounter, but he managed to hold his tongue and the disturbing threats I knew sat on the end of it, waiting to intimidate me. After Jericho took the treat, I slowly lifted my chest from

Slade's legs, resting my hand on his thigh to steady myself as his gaze ensnared me in a bubble of something so intoxicating my lips had to part to find my next breath.

"You smell good," I whispered, *not* meaning to say the words aloud. When his gaze shifted to my hand on his leg, I lifted it slowly in a silent "oops" as if I didn't mean to touch him. Our eyes remained locked in place for several moments like an unbreakable trance.

And ... I said it.

The words tumbled softly from my lips, yet desperately from the pit of my stomach. "Did you save me from that man?"

Slade's lack of any sort of reaction did nothing to answer my question. And before I could press him more for an answer, the professor started to speak. Ten minutes before the end of the class, Slade made his usual early departure, but not before leaning down and snatching the coffee to take with him. It put a huge smile on my face.

Twenty minutes later, I arrived at my tree for my morning nap, but a dark, sexy guy and his dog were in my spot.

"I realize you've been off campus for a few years." I dropped my bag on the opposite side of the tree. "But during that time, I made claim to this tree. It's common knowledge, like the house you're living in is haunted. However, since I kinda love Jerry, I'll share the shade with you two."

If Slade's chest hadn't been rising and falling, I would have thought he was dead. Eyes closed. Hands resting at his sides. Jericho smiled at me, and I winked at him, digging a pear out of my bag. I started to take a seat on the opposite side of the tree but feeling a little more confident than I did during our last tree encounter, I took a seat right next to Jericho and shared my pear with him.

"We're not friends," Slade said without so much as peeking open one eye.

I bit off a piece of my pear and fed it to Jericho, leaning over and kissing his soft, erect ear. "That's fine. Jerry's my friend. And he's infinitely more awesome than any man I have ever been *friends* with."

"Jericho."

Ignoring his correction, I took several more bites from the pear and offered the rest to Jericho. "I'm from San Francisco. Where are you from? Here?"

When he ignored me—not at all surprising—I continued the conversation as though he was partaking in it. "Oh, wow! You're from Montana. I wouldn't have taken you for a Montana guy. You have more of a Carolinas vibe to you. I went to Asheville last summer with my friends. It's beautiful. Siblings? Yes, I have an older sister, but she moved to France five years ago. Oh ... really? You're an only child? I can see that about you. I think it's your poor social and conversational skills that give it away."

The humor died quickly with his total indifference to engage in any sort of personal interaction. Even with my morbid curiosity about him living in the firehouse or staying out until the wee hours of the morning, I could have given up on Slade the asshole. However, the tiny possibility that he saved me that night or even if he just heard about it and chose to protect me through Jericho ... well, it made it impossible to walk away— even if he didn't acknowledge me.

I crawled around Jericho, nestling myself on my back between him and Slade. Staring up at the trees, I let the back of my hand brush his. "Wylder ..." I whispered. "Was it you?"

He jackknifed to sitting and grabbed his bag. With the slightest of nods, he gestured for Jericho. I didn't sit up or say another word. I didn't try to make him stay. I closed my eyes and imagined him taking a life for me.

The problem? I had no idea why he would do that or *if* he did it.

LATER THAT DAY, I knew I should stay away, but my feet automatically took me there. I couldn't resist peeking in on Slade in his garage.

Sculptures.

He welded sculptures. That was what I'd deduced from the configurations on the floor, like a puzzle waiting to be put together. Like everything I thought I knew about Slade Wylder, it was just speculation.

He had nothing to say.

In what had become our routines since the convenience store incident, I slipped into the garage. He ignored me.

I checked my social media pages and responded to messages.

He ignored me.

Occasionally, I'd touch some of the pieces on the floor, trying to figure out what they would make. That always got his attention.

Nothing life changing. Just a pause. On a good day, he'd flip up his welder's mask and give me a look. I'm pretty sure it said, "You're crossing a line." Since he didn't say the actual words, I kept doing my thing—getting a little braver ... a little more curious each time.

"It's hot in here. And I'm going surfing with the girls.

Wanna come?"

He flipped up his face shield and inspected the piece in his hands, sweat trickling down his forehead, snagging on his long eyelashes.

"Well, we'll be leaving around four. So ..." I opened the door. "You know where to find me."

Nothing.

After closing the door, I heard Jericho bark from the house. A rare thing. I'm not sure I'd ever heard him bark. I followed my instinct—in spite of it failing me fifty percent of the time—and opened the back door to the house.

A holy-shit moment. I was going into the infamous fire-house. Not even the eighty-five-degree day could stop the goose bumps from popping up along my arms.

"Hey, Jerry. What's up? You okay?" I squatted just inside the door and scratched behind his ears as he licked my face. It was just a kitchen. No big deal. Except it was *the* kitchen. The place Professor Dickerson prepared meals for his wife and the young college girl he kept in the dungeon.

Then my mind wandered to the other mystery ... did Slade have drugs in here? The granite countertops and tile floor were tidy. What I could see of the living room seemed just as clean. No white residue or haphazardly discarded bongs.

"I should leave," I whispered to Jericho as I slowly stood. *Should* always had the best intentions. I really *should* have listened. Instead, I did nothing to stop my feet from moving toward the fridge.

I did nothing to stop my hand from opening it. For some unknown reason, I felt like a map of his daily diet would let me into his head.

No such luck.

Inside were just the basics: eggs, condiments, a bag of lettuce, carrots, bottled water, beer, white butcher-paper wrapped meat, string cheese.

After closing the door, I peeked out the back window and glanced at my watch. I needed to get home, but my insatiable curiosity pulled me farther into the house to the living room with a small, modern gray sofa, a dark blue recliner, a dog bed, and a TV on a console in the corner.

"Go home, Livy …" I whispered to myself, unsure which was more disturbing—the need to talk to myself or the fact that I was seriously contemplating going upstairs.

"You're taking trespassing to a whole new level."

"Shit!" I whipped around at the eerily calm but stern voice behind me.

Jericho stood from his bed and took his place at Slade's side as if he needed to pick a team.

"You let her in. Why?" He kept his intense gaze on me, but the question was for Jericho.

"He was b-barking. I-I hadn't heard him bark before. So … I just wanted to check on him." My voice shook like the rest of my body. With the front door a few feet to my left, I knew I could probably make a mad dash if necessary, but the chances of my sweaty hand unlocking it in time were slim at best.

He pushed the long sleeves of his shirt up to his elbows, showing me those veins. I curled my lips together to hide their uncontrolled trembling. How could one man make me feel so protected and utterly terrified at the same time?

"Are you going to cry?"

My eyes widened as I shook my head a half dozen times.

"Are you cold?"

My wide eyes narrowed at him. "What? No."

"You're shivering."

We were having a conversation. Sort of. I was uninvited and shaking like the San Andres Fault waking up. He moved his lips and actual sounds came out. Good words that didn't feel threatening. I didn't know what to do with his curious way of communicating or showing concern.

"You make me ..." I hugged my arms to my torso.

He took three steps forward, keeping two small steps between us. I could feel the heat of his sweaty body.

"I make you what?"

My gaze stopped mid-chest, unable to withstand the weight of his stare. "Nervous," I murmured.

"You're in my house without permission. You *should* be scared."

"No." I forced my gaze to his face. "Not scared." My head inched side to side. "Nervous. Like ..." I risked a step closer to him. "Butterflies."

"You're delusional."

I lifted a shoulder and dropped it on a slow exhale. "Feelings are real, not delusional. I think pretending you don't have feelings is what's truly delusional."

He studied me with an unreadable expression—not that I could ever really read him, but that particular expression was new.

Contemplative.

Distant.

Subdued.

"You need to go."

My gaze flitted along the sculpted lines of his stubble-covered jaw and the prominent angle of his cheekbones while I fisted my hands, holding back the need to touch him. "Yeah." I smiled before hunching down to massage Jericho behind his ears and cupping my hands to smooth them up to the pointy tips. "Love you, Jerry." Stretching forward, I kissed the top of his head and stood up again. "I'm sorry. I overstepped."

Before he could respond—not that I think he had anything left to say—I unlocked the front door and opened it, pausing for a second with my back to him. "A month ago ... something bad happened to me. It could have been worse, but someone saved me. I know you either heard about it or you were there. If you heard about it, and that's why you've been letting Jericho watch over me ... then I want to say thank you. If you were the one who saved me, then ..." Tears filled my eyes.

I still hadn't told my family.

I still had trouble sleeping.

I still felt a constant fear when I went someplace alone.

"Well ..." I swallowed the emotion building in my throat. "Then there are no words for what that means to me. Bye, Wylder."

Chapter Seven

A WET SUIT, my board, and good friends awaited me when I walked up the street.

"Seriously … what have you been doing? You went in his house?" Missy eyed me with suspicion. "Voluntarily?"

I grinned. "Yes. Voluntarily. And probably illegally." My nose scrunched, remembering how my heart nearly exploded when he caught me.

"Dude, you broke into his house?" Kara's jaw dropped as she tossed a bag into the back of the SUV.

"I entered his house uninvited. Nothing was *broken*. Let me go change. Give me five minutes."

We spent three hours fighting the choppy waves, bailing, paddling *forever,* and waiting in the Friday line. There was a reason I preferred dawn patrol.

"That was not fun." Missy sighed when we piled into the vehicle to make the trip home—windows down, heater on, music blaring.

"It was brutal." I tried to run my fingers through my hair, but it was not happening.

"This song is everything." Missy played her list that was only a third country.

"It is." I leaned my head back in the passenger seat and closed my eyes as James Arthur serenaded us with "Falling Like The Stars." My aspirations to climb the political ladder straight to the top didn't deter me from wanting *everything*.

Kids and an adoring husband—the kind that never let me forget why I fell in love with him.

One of the things I would never forget about my parents is the way my dad loved my mom so completely, and he never hid it. He worshiped her with every look and every touch. At the time, I thought their PDA was a little gross.

When she died and I watched him mourn her to the point of wondering if he would survive, I realized it wasn't gross. Their love was the most beautiful thing I had ever witnessed. If I could find a love that felt even remotely close to what they had, I knew I would be the luckiest woman in the world.

My mom was the luckiest woman in the world.

"Gah!" Missy turned up the music on the chorus. "I need to find a man who loves me with the same passion as James Arthur sings this song. You think he's married? I'd marry him in a heartbeat. And he'd sing to me every night."

We laughed.

We sang the words.

We replayed the song the whole way home.

"Whoa … does he think you're home alone?" Kara nodded to the German shepherd barking at our front door.

I hopped out and rushed toward Jericho. Something wasn't right. I felt it in the pit of my stomach.

"Hey, baby. What's wrong?" I hunched down, my wet suit half off and a sweatshirt covering my swim top.

He took off toward the firehouse. When I didn't follow, he turned and barked at me.

"I think he wants you to follow him." Missy brushed past me and opened the front door. "I'd stay here. He's probably luring you to the murder dungeon."

Jericho barked again.

"I don't think so. I'm going to see what the deal is."

"Want us to come?" Kara asked.

"No. It's fine. I'll call if something is off when I get there," I called as I followed Jericho.

He led me to the back door that was ajar about three inches. I paused. Something was definitely off. I pulled my phone out of the front pocket of my sweatshirt, contemplating calling someone like I said I would do.

"Hello?" I said with a jittery voice as I slowly opened the door.

Jericho rushed inside and up the stairs.

"Oh god …" I whispered, halting halfway through the kitchen when I saw the trail of blood.

The tiny part of my conscience that spoke complete reason told me to get the hell out of there and call the police. Not too shockingly, I ignored that tiny, but very smart voice of reason. Instead, I followed Jericho and the trail of blood to the last bedroom at the top of the stairs.

A small lamp on the bedside table dimly lit the bedroom. When my eyes adjusted to the light, a bloodied Slade came into focus.

Jericho hopped onto the bed next to him, licking his face and neck.

"Oh god … what happened?" I took quick steps to the bed. "I'll call an ambulance."

"N-no …" Slade's hand grabbed my wrist as I started to dial 9-1-1. "Go home."

Shirt off.

Blood on the bedsheets and pillowcase.

Crimson-saturated gauze bandages on his shoulder.

I jerked my hand away as panic sank its claws into my murky conscience. "You're bleeding. A lot. Slade ..." The torn open suture kit and empty bottle of vodka on his nightstand snagged my attention. "Did you stitch yourself up?" My head inched side to side as I backed away, eyes unblinking at his bloodied hand. "Are you in danger? Did you do something? Is this about the drugs?" The fear flowed freely.

"Livy ..."

My name.

He said my name for the first time.

Stopping at the threshold to his bedroom, I swallowed hard. "Am *I* in danger?"

"Livy ..."

"Y-you need a doctor, something I can't—"

"I stitched it. Go home." His words slurred as he surrendered to his heavy eyelids.

"Are you drunk? Did someone stab you? Is that a gunshot wound?"

"Go ... the ... fuck ... home." Exasperation mixed with pain and exhaustion punctuated each word.

"You've lost a lot of blood. I should—"

"Fucking hell!" He reached over, grabbed the empty vodka bottle, and threw it at the wall beside me.

I jumped, my hand flying to my mouth to contain my gasp as I gawked at the shattered pieces on the floor. Was he aiming for me or the wall?

Jericho whined a few times, perched next to Slade. He hadn't asked his dog to come get me. It broke my heart.

Not for Slade. For Jericho. He was genuinely worried about his owner.

From hundreds of miles away, my dad whispered in my ear

to get the hell out of there. Per my usual, I didn't listen.

Instead, I cleaned up the glass in spite of Slade's weak mumbling telling me to go. Eventually, he fell silent—passed out or asleep—and I peeled off the soaked gauze, taking a closer inspection of his half-assed stitched wound. It looked pretty mangled. More like a gunshot wound than a stab wound. Did he have a bullet inside his shoulder? If so ... he would likely not survive long.

Who shot him and why?

"I should go," I whispered to myself ... to that overly curious part in my head that overstepped a boundary with Slade Wylder that felt like real danger.

Jericho turned in a circle on the bed before collapsing beside Slade again, resting his snout on Slade's neck while giving me a look like he thought I could fix everything.

I couldn't.

"He'll be fine. I hope." I gave Jericho a sad smile. Tearing open a new packet of gauze, I exchanged it for the bloodied ones and secured it with the tape he hadn't used the first time. "I'll check in on him tomorrow. Okay, buddy?" As soon as I started to leave, he followed, overtaking me on the stairs. By the time I got to the back door, Jericho had perched himself in front of it. "Scooch, Jerry. I'm leaving, and you have to stay here. He needs you, not me." My nose wrinkled, and I lowered my voice. "He drank too much to numb the pain, and I don't know what happened. So I don't feel safe staying here."

He cocked his head to the side, stirring up a new round of guilt. Of course ... he would protect me. Jericho was my fiercest protector—after my dad.

"Please, scooch." I nudged him with the toe of my shoe. He growled.

My eyes opened wider and unblinking while my jaw dropped. It wasn't threatening like he'd planned on harming me; it was a stern warning that it was *not* okay for me to leave.

"Did I mention he doesn't want me here? That he wants me to go home?"

After he refused to budge, I leaned forward and locked the door. "Fine. But you'd better not think of sleeping for one second. If I die, people will miss me, and I won't become president. Got it?"

Still, he didn't budge, not until I retreated to the stairs, committing to staying the night ... In. The. Haunted. Firehouse!

Slipping off my shoes and my wet suit—leaving me in Lycra boy shorts and a sweatshirt—I jerked my head at Jericho. "Scooch."

He remained sprawled out on the opposite side of the bed. "You're sleeping in the middle."

No scooch. No budge. Total stubbornness.

"Shit ..." I frowned, shutting off the lamp then turning it right back on. Nope. No way was I sleeping in the haunted firehouse with Slade oozing blood from a gunshot wound *and* with the light turned off. So I crawled up the middle of the bed and wedged myself under the covers, trapped by an eighty-pound dog on one side and a probably close to one hundred and eighty-pound man on the other side.

After a good ten minutes of resting on my side and inspecting shirtless Slade close up—his defined torso, his beautiful face, and those full lips—I had to turn toward Jericho. Perfect pooch made me smile, unlike his owner who made me think inappropriate thoughts.

My brain wouldn't shut down for the longest time.

Thoughts of who shot Slade and why he didn't go to the hospital danced with the memories of detailed stories about Professor Dickerson and the haunted firehouse. To make things exponentially worse ... Jericho decided he no longer wanted to sleep in bed with us.

Traitor ...

He hopped out of bed and took off downstairs.

"Jerry!" I whisper-yelled when he disappeared around the corner.

After I cursed him under my breath, I decided that him being on the frontline of defense downstairs was the best idea. Putting more than two inches between us seemed like another fantastic idea, so I moved into the spot Jericho abandoned.

I didn't anticipate the noises. *So* many strange noises that kept me from falling asleep. Ghosts ... it had to be ghosts. That girl. It was her ghost. Maybe she was trying to warn me. I was next. If I fell asleep, it seemed like a real possibility that I could wake up in the dungeon or not wake up at all.

I couldn't sleep.

I couldn't breathe.

I tossed and turned.

And it was cold as fuck in the house. He must have had the thermostat set to sixty or cooler.

Eventually ... I'm not even sure when it happened ... I fell asleep.

Chapter Eight

Wylder

*T*HE. *FUCK?*

Arms. Legs. Hair. Heat.

I woke in the early morning hours to intense pain on one side from the unexpected altercation the previous evening and *her* attached to my other side.

Her bare leg tangled in the sheets and draped over my jean-clad leg. Her hand splayed out on my bare chest. Her warm breath in the crook of my neck. Her wavy, golden blond hair ... everywhere.

She was everywhere.

Grimacing, I attempted to move, hoping to slide out of bed and get a safe distance from *her*.

"Five minutes ..." she mumbled, rolling off me and curling onto her other side. "Just ... five more—" The rest of her words blended into a fading mumble.

Then.

She jerked.

Her body went ridged and completely still for several seconds before she slowly glanced over her shoulder at me. "Oh my god ..." she whispered, eyes making a slow inspection of me before she flew out of the bed, tripping a bit as she untangled herself from the sheets and straightened her sweatshirt.

I gave her nothing. Not a blink or tiny twitch of my lips.

"You … he …" She pointed toward the door. "Jerry came to—"

"Jericho," I corrected her with a slight narrowing of my eyes. His name was Jericho not Jerry.

With her own tiny squint, she rubbed her lips together and dipped her chin into a tiny nod. "*Jericho* was barking at my door last night when I arrived home. Clearly concerned about you and your…" her head nodded toward my shoulder "…gunshot wound. I tried to leave, but he wouldn't let me, so I stayed, but then he—"

"Go home."

Her mouth paused mid-sentence. As her jaw eased shut, she turned, slipped on her sneakers, grabbed her wet suit, and drifted to the door. "Do you need help?"

As my groggy brain worked to interpret her question, she glanced over her shoulder—hair falling in her deep brown eyes, cheeks painted bronze from hours in the sun.

"If it's drugs. If it's not. If you don't want to tell me, but there's something I can do. Something you need …"

"I need you to go home." My gaze drifted to the window and the hint of light from the rising sun pushing its way through the gaps in the blinds.

"I stayed because—"

"You stayed for Jericho." My attention shifted back to her.

Slowly running a hand through her long, blond hair, her gaze dropped to the floor between us. "I stayed for you," she murmured just before continuing out the door and down the stairs.

I eased to sitting, letting my feet dangle off the bed, wincing from the pain and too much alcohol—which I needed for the pain. After popping a few pills to make the day bearable, I showered, changed the bandages, and made my way downstairs.

"Traitor." I eyed Jericho as he hopped up from his bed and followed me into the kitchen where a large cup of coffee and two bags sat on the kitchen counter. The cup had "Wylder" in black marker along with one of the bags. The other bag said "Jerry." I shouldn't have touched any of it. I didn't want her doing shit for me. But I *needed* the coffee. And once I opened the bag with my name on it and found a fresh bagel, I decided I needed it too.

Easing into a chair, feeling every single bend pulling at my stitches, I watched the concern on Jericho's face, the twitch of his right eyebrow and the tilt of his head accompanied by a little whine. "She didn't leave you anything, buddy. Something for some dude named Jerry. Maybe next time she'll think of you too."

Next time.

I internally reprimanded myself for thinking that. There wouldn't be a next time. Livy was trouble, but her timing wasn't awful. I drained every drop of coffee while eating the bagel and sending off a message.

It's done.

"Done ..." I tossed my phone on the table and rubbed my temples. "A bullet to my shoulder ... but fucking done."

Chapter Nine

Livy

"**Y**OU SLEPT WITH *him?*"

After I delivered breakfast to the boys, I attempted to sneak into the house before my friends awakened. I should have known Mom Aubrey would be up making her green smoothie and updating the chore list for the week.

"Slept?" I yawned before sipping the rest of my tea. "Yes. Literally slept in his bed next to him. He got injured yesterday. That's why Jericho came to get me. How sweet is that?"

Aubrey eyed me with suspicion. "Sweet. Yeah … um … what kind of injury?"

I shrugged, opening the fridge to look for nothing in particular. It's possible I sucked at acting casual and natural. "He didn't actually say. Something with his shoulder. Arm. That area."

"Out with it."

I continued to absorb the cool air from the fridge as the heat of her questions licked my back like hot flames. "Out with what?"

"That's the biggest line of crap. He's not injured. You had sex with him. Just say it. Who cares? Why are you acting so weird about it?"

Shutting the door, I leaned my back against it. "I didn't

have sex with him." Narrowing my eyes a bit, I scraped my teeth along my lower lip. "He got shot."

"Wait ... what?" Her hand paused, mid-cut through the celery. Eyes wide.

"I know nothing about it. He was drunk and basically passed out on his bed when I got there." I stopped short of mentioning he sutured himself up.

"Who? Why? Livy! What happened?" Aubrey dropped the knife and dried her hands, going into full concern mode.

"I don't know." That wasn't a lie. I had *no* idea what happened, and I felt pretty certain I would never know.

I felt pretty certain I should stay far away from Slade Wylder.

I also felt pretty certain that would never happen.

"Probably a deal gone wrong. I don't know. Legit." I offered another shrug because it was the truth.

"Please tell me you're done with him. The curiosity. The hanging out with his dog. I actually think I should say something to my parents and have them report suspicious activity at his house. This is supposed to be a safe street, not a street where someone comes home with a gunshot wound."

"Uh ..." I lifted an eyebrow. "Sure. Safe. Except for the professor who kidnapped a student and kept her in his creepy dungeon."

Aubrey rolled her eyes. "Okay, yes. Except for that."

"I'm going to shower."

"He's sexy ..." Aubrey said like a question or maybe a warning.

I stopped midway up the stairs. "I've seen my fair share of sexy guys ... I've even dated a few. What's your point?"

"No point. Just an observation."

Before she could make any more observations, or anyone else had the chance to wake up and ask me too many questions, I showered and headed to the library to do some research for one of my classes and escape the dizzying events of the previous twenty-four hours.

As I made my way to the far corner of the library with my computer and a few books recommended by my professor for my paper, I halted my steps when Jericho came into view at the feet of my mercurial neighbor. If someone had shot me, I wouldn't have been at the library the next day. Before I could resume my steps toward the back table by the window, Jericho eyed me and hopped up.

"Down," Slade said with his back to me, not knowing why his dog wanted to abandon him for someone with a much brighter personality and the best treats in her bag.

Yeah, I quickly learned to always have Jericho treats in my backpack.

When Jericho didn't respond instantly to his owner's command, Slade glanced over his shoulder.

I smiled, forcing my feet to continue onward, even with his unreadable gaze tracking my every move making each step feel like trekking through treacherous terrain—a battlefield of nerves. "You should be home, resting," I said with a shaky vibrato.

That gaze ... gah! It shot a million jolts of adrenaline and anticipation racing through my veins.

"Why?" Rather impertinent eyes continued to strip me bare.

At least, it felt intrusive, bold, and intentional.

I swallowed again and again. So much for nervous dry mouth. Nope ... everything felt wet in his presence. "I guess we're pretending last night didn't happen. Huh?" I deposited my books on the table across from him and rested my bag on the ground as I took a seat.

"Last night?" He squinted.

I could tell from his curious inspection that he wasn't planning on me inviting myself to sit next to him.

"I don't know what happened last night..." he tipped his chin to focus on his notepad, left hand scribbling away "...but this morning you were in my bed, half-naked, and wrapped around me."

Liar.

I wasn't wrapped around him. I wasn't touching him.

"Sorry. You must be remembering a dream. I'm flattered. Really. But you're not my type, Wylder." I opened my laptop.

"What's your type? Women?" Haughty, arched lips challenged me without looking up from the table.

"Guys that don't come home with gunshot wounds."

"So ... boring?" he continued, chin to his chest.

Bringing up my Word document, I shrugged. "If virile, sober men is your idea of boring, then ... yeah. I guess my type is boring."

Glancing up slowly, he rubbed his full lips together for a few seconds. I tried really hard not to stare at them, but I failed fantastically. My mouth moved on instinct—telling him how unmanly and not my type he was while my eyes fucked him every way imaginable.

"You don't think I'm masculine?" His wolfish grin led me into a trap.

Ripping my gaze from his mouth, I forced my lips closed and refocused on my computer screen. "I'm just saying ... last night you were not energetic or vigorous. My *type* would have been able to …"

"Able to what?" He angled his head.

Lifting a shoulder in a partial shrug, I mumbled.

"Sorry … I didn't catch that."

Clearing my throat, I said it a little louder and slower. "Copulate."

His eyebrows slid up his forehead, eyes dancing with mischief. I didn't recognize the man across from me. "You wanted me to fuck you last night, and because I was dealing with a gunshot wound, that made me inadequate in your eyes?"

My head sprang up, eyes wide, breath choking on a quick gasp. "I didn't want you to *fuck* me. Your dog came to get me. Poor thing probably thought you were dying. I was simply meaning that I prefer guys who don't do shit that involves guns or the need for urgent medical attention. Not being a criminal is sexy. That's …" I typed a bunch of gibberish into my document like I had some serious stuff to do. And I did. But there was no way I could focus after the conversation shifted to sex. "That's all that I meant. Way to have your head in the gutter."

He leaned forward, resting his arms on the table and invading my space with his soapy scent and his pheromones. "You said copulate. I responded with fuck. Pretty synonymous if you looked it up in a thesaurus."

It didn't matter what I said. My cheeks filled with fire, yet goose bumps exploded along my arms, and my nipples dissolved all concealing efforts made by my shirt and bra. Every part of me screamed, "Fuck me, Wylder!" Except my words.

I had words. Words mattered.

"Again …" I pulled my mouth into a tight smile. "Your fantasy, not mine."

He shook his head, the hint of playfulness in his expression vanishing as he shoved his notepad and computer into his bag before pushing his chair back and standing with Jericho. "It's not my job to fuck you, Livy."

I coughed, mangling the word "what" as he turned. By the time I cleared the knot of disbelief from my throat, he and Jericho were at the stairs, disappearing in a blink.

Job?

"I LOVE THIS life." I grinned the next morning, peering over at Kara as we paddled out a little after six in the morning.

She reciprocated the grin and shot past me a few feet. "You know ... there's no surfing in D.C. If you love this life, I'd shoot for Governor of California and call it good."

I laughed. "You might be right. Or maybe I should marry rich, buy an island, and just surf the rest of my life. President is a pretty crappy job."

She giggled. "So crappy. Governor is good. Marry a surfer. Raise several grommets to be wave hogs like their mom."

"I'm not a wave hog," I countered just before stealing the next one.

After four hours, Kara insisted we leave. Missy had set them up on a double-blind, double date, and Kara thought she needed the whole day to get ready.

"GSW is home." She jerked her chin up as we passed the firehouse just as Slade was climbing out of his car.

Biting my bottom lip, I nodded. "I forgot to mention ... he was at the library yesterday. And particularly ..."

"Hot as fuck?"

"That. Of course. But arrogant as fuck would be more accurate. Our conversation took a weird turn. The next thing I knew, he was telling me it's not his *job* to fuck me. A direct quote." I pulled into the driveway.

"He what?"

"Yep. Like I asked him or made a move on him or flirted with him … which I. Did. Not." I hopped out and grabbed my bag from the back.

Kara climbed out and shut her door, staring at the firehouse and Slade standing at the back of his car while Jericho took a piss in the yard. "Is it his *job* to fuck someone else? I mean … maybe he's not into drugs. Maybe he's a male escort. Maybe the bullet was from a disgruntled husband."

"That's …" I started to say ridiculous, but in reality, I knew nothing about him. "An interesting theory."

She shrugged while turning to retrieve her bag from the back of the Jeep. "I guess the obvious next question is … how much does he charge?"

I grinned. "You'll have to ask him. I'm not touching that one. Since he's renting that place all by himself, I'd guess it's more than we can afford. Maybe Aubrey could afford him."

We giggled and strode toward the house. I made one last glance down the street at the exact moment Slade turned his gaze in my direction. It was too far to make out his expression. Probably part of the scowl family.

Later that night, after Kara and Missy left on their double date and Aubrey went to dinner with her parents, I decided to take a walk—just down the street. It was the extent of my comfort zone after the near rape incident. On the third time down and back, I slowed my stride as the black Volvo passed me and pulled into the driveway. He was home a little early for his late-night routine. Before I could cross the street to avoid walking directly in front of his house, a gray Lexus SUV pulled in behind him.

Slade climbed out of his car first. His motions were slow … like he had a gunshot wound. A woman with straight brunette hair to her shoulders and sophisticated black-framed glasses slid out of the SUV, bent down, and gave Jericho some love before standing straight again and giving Slade a gentle hug and kiss on his cheek.

A wickedly irrational emotion shot up my spine. An unexpected possessiveness toward both Slade and Jericho. Who was Miss Sophisticated and why was she showing so much affection to …

To what?

It was a sane question.

I'd known Slade for approximately six weeks. Maybe he had a girlfriend. Maybe it was his job to fuck *her*.

After their kissy-huggy greeting ended, they walked toward the house with Jericho in tow. I waited for him to glance back at me. He saw me. There was no way he passed me a few seconds earlier on the street and didn't see me. Yet, he made no attempt to acknowledge me.

Until …

My boy Jerry stopped abruptly and turned like he caught whiff of my scent. All the warm fuzzies filled my chest. A *dog* gave me more feels than any man had given me in a long time. Maybe ever.

Jericho liked me. Hell, maybe he loved me.

He protected me.

He smiled when he saw me—tongue out, tail in a low wag. I continued my way up the sidewalk, feigning surprise when he trotted toward me in spite of Slade barking his own command.

"Hey, Jerry." I squatted down to give him double the love Miss Sophisticated gave him … and I had a treat in my pocket because part of me anticipated—hoped for—a chance encounter. "Oh, buddy … I love you too." I closed my eyes and turned my face side to side while he showered me with kisses.

Slade cleared his throat.

I opened my eyes—noticing his friend must have gone inside. "Sorry." I stood, sliding a treat into Jericho's mouth along the way. "I know it's hard for you to know he likes me more." On a shrug, I bit my lips together to keep my shit-eating grin under control.

"Inside," he said to Jericho while looking at me.

Jericho turned and headed to the back door.

"If you have a *job* to do … Jerry can hang with me tonight. I'm alone this evening."

"Jericho. And he doesn't need a babysitter."

"Maybe I do."

His brow tensed a fraction, contemplation settling into a slight frown for a few seconds, before he whistled and Jericho came running. "Send him home when your friends get back."

Why was the only word that sat on the tip of my idle tongue? Why protect me?

"What are you going to do?" Okay, apparently "why" wasn't the only word on the tip of my tongue after all. Six other words were in line first.

"Does it matter?"

Letting my gaze settle over his shoulder to the firehouse and images of Miss Sophisticated waiting for him, I lifted a single shoulder. "No. Just curious. Is she your girlfriend?"

"Does it matter?"

"I hate you." I rolled my eyes. "Worst communication

skills ever."

"Good. Hate me. I prefer it."

I recoiled. I didn't really hate anyone. It wasn't my personality to be hateful, vengeful, or hold grudges. Why did Slade Wylder want me to hate him? It was a joke. I hated his lack of sharing information.

"If you're selling her some shit that will ruin her life, may I suggest you rethink that? Not cool, Wylder."

"Noted."

Tipping my chin up, I gave him several tiny nods. "Okay then. I'll take Jerry to my house and spoil him. Maybe he comes back to you … maybe he doesn't."

Slade let his gaze slide down my body, a slow and easy trip. He didn't do that when we met. Somewhere along the way, he decided it was okay. I wasn't sure what reaction he desired from me.

Maybe nothing.

Maybe he did it out of pure selfish desire.

"I'm only allowing this because I love Jerry."

Curious eyes met mine, slightly squinted.

I smirked. "Stripping me with those eyes of yours."

Moments …

I collected moments in my mind, my heart, my soul, like Aubrey collected rare coins—my mom dying, my dad spending a few years thoroughly drunk. Mostly bad moments—permanent scars.

That moment I tucked into my memory forever as one of the first truly great moments.

Wylder …

The corners of his mouth quirked into pure sin. If Satan was hot as fuck, his name would have been Slade Wylder, and I would have been in a whole helluva lot of trouble.

"He'll come home."

"We'll see." I turned making a few kissy noises for Jericho to follow me.

"I know where to find him."

A grin filled my face as I continued up the sidewalk. "I'm counting on it."

I made it to the house with my shoulders back and some extra sway to my gait, but as soon as I shut the door behind us, I deflated. Who was that woman? He had no business doing anything physically straining with a wound that hadn't healed. I should have reminded him of that.

Jericho and I watched a movie, ate popcorn, stared out the window at the firehouse, and played hide-and-seek.

"How do you feel about slumber parties?" I asked him.

He tilted his head to one side and then the other side. I took it as a solid maybe.

"It's a full bed. But I hug the side, so we'll make it work. Come on."

I spied out my window at the firehouse. The Lexus SUV was still there. A knot formed in my stomach. It was almost midnight. How long does it take to screw someone?

Then again … Kara and Missy were still not home from their double date. Lots of sex happened that night … except at my house. Jericho was the best companion. He didn't care if I shaved my legs. I didn't care if he had questionable breath.

After brushing my teeth and letting him out for a final round of pissing his name in the tiny yard, we settled into bed. Ten seconds tops … that was all it took for me to fall asleep. The early morning waves wiped me out completely that day.

I woke from a dead sleep. Minutes? Hours later? I had no

idea. All I knew was my warm, fuzzy friend climbed out of bed.

"Jesus!" I sat up and scooted to the back of my bed, hugging my legs to my chest as a dark figure towered over me at the edge of the bed.

"I told you to send him home."

The flirty joke about keeping his dog and him knowing where to find me ... well, it went too far. Could he not go one night without his pooch?

When my breathing settled down, I swallowed to lubricate my dry throat. "It was almost midnight. My friends weren't home and your *friend* was still there doing whatever the two of you were doing—drugs, sex ... whatever. You really should take it easy until your wound heals."

"Thanks for your concern." He turned and headed toward my bedroom door.

"Have you changed the bandage?" I slid to the side of my bed and stood.

"Don't worry about it." He opened the door completely.

"Well, I do." I took several steps toward him.

He turned. "Why?" he asked just above a whisper.

Because I think you saved my life.

"I don't want your arm to fall off. How would you hug Jerry?" I turned around and flicked on the lamp by my nightstand, squinting against the ocular intrusion. As soon as my eyes adjusted to the light, I focused on Slade, but his focus remained glued to my nighttime attire—pink bikini panties and a matching pink tank top slid up past my belly button and the piercing in it.

"It's been changed." He blinked, wetting his lips.

"I don't believe you. I'm sure it's hard for you to do with one hand. Just give me a sec to grab the first aid kit." I broke through the confines of his intense gaze permanently parked on my body and brushed past him to the bathroom. When I returned, he was sitting on the end of my bed, and Jericho had collapsed onto the cold air vent by the window.

I set the supplies on the bed beside him. "It's three in the morning," I said in a soft voice. "How did you get in here? If Kara and Missy are home, they would have locked the door."

He refrained from answering.

"Is this payback for you thinking I broke into your house?"

No answer.

Standing in front of him, waiting for answers I knew he would never give me, I nodded to his shirt. "Can you remove it?"

After a hard swallow, he used his good arm to grab the hem of his shirt and pull it up his torso, over his head, and gently down his injured arm. I made every effort not to look at his bared chest, his rigid abs, his full lips. My gaze locked to the injury as I focused on my breathing.

Three seconds in.

Three seconds out.

As I eased the gauze and tape from his skin, my legs straddled one of his legs so I could see the wound better.

It had been recently changed. He wasn't lying. Yet, he let me change the bandage again.

Why?

With damp cotton balls I cleaned around the stitched area. His head turned away from me. I applied an ointment to the wounds and covered them with fresh bandaging.

"Does it hurt?" I asked, applying the last strip of tape.

His head turned back toward me, putting his face so close to mine I could feel his breath—almost taste the peppermint from toothpaste or his last stick of gum. I felt the warm intensity of his gaze on my face, making my hands shake a little as I pressed the tape to his skin.

He never flinched; it must not have hurt too much in that moment. However, *I* flinched … jumped … froze in place. My heart remained the only muscle in my body that continued to move because his hands slid up the back of my naked legs— barely touching them—like he wasn't really trying to make contact with my skin.

But he did, and I felt it *everywhere.*

Not the hands of a greedy lover.

Not the hands of a drunk one-night stand.

Not the hands of the man who tried to hurt me.

No. These hands were different. The kind of different that didn't have words or emotions. It was just this … *feeling.*

The feeling paralyzed me with fear.

Fear that if I moved, the moment would vanish.

Fear that if I moved, he would give me a look.

Fear that if I moved, he would cut me with his tongue.

My eyes drifted shut as I drew in the tiniest of shaky breaths, letting my hands ease to my sides.

Don't move. Don't open your eyes. Don't breathe.

His hands ghosted higher along my legs, over the curve of my ass, easing to my hips. As he slowly stood, I took a step back, taking a huge swallow while trying to open my eyes.

I couldn't.

I couldn't let him see my need. My fear. My pain.

Then … he was gone.

His touch.

His scent.

His warmth.

Chapter Ten

MONDAY MORNING JITTERS couldn't be soothed with all the caffeine in the world. I picked up my mint green tea and a coffee for Slade on my way to class. By the time I made it to the lecture hall, I'd drank both, which meant I needed to use the restroom before class.

A few minutes late to class, I eased the door shut softly behind me. The professor showed me a bit of mercy by not drawing everyone's attention to me. I spotted my neighbor and my favorite dog, but there were no empty seats around them, so I took a seat on the opposite side of the auditorium.

When he made his ten-minute-early exit, I snatched my bag and chased after him. "Hey! Wait up!"

He didn't. Not that shocking.

When I caught up to his speed-walker pace, he gave me a quick side glance without slowing down. "What?"

What? Really? That was his one-word good morning after leaving me a puddle of nothingness on my bedroom floor the previous night.

"How's your arm?"

"Fine. It was fine yesterday. It's fine today. It will be fine tomorrow. Speaking of tomorrow…" he stopped abruptly and turned to face me with a flicker of hesitation on his face "…can you watch Jericho?"

I chuckled. "Funny. I thought he watched me."

"Is that a yes?"

"It's a maybe. Where are you going?"

"Doesn't matter."

Crossing my arms over my chest, I flipped out my hip. "It does to me. Will you come home with a bullet wound again? Will you come home at all? Is this drug-related? Should you give me his vet records in case you don't come home? Are you screwing the Lexus lady from last night?"

Oops.

I got on a roll and just couldn't stop.

"Scratch that last question. I don't care."

I cared.

A LOT!

"I'll drop him off around eight."

"If you don't die, when will you be back?"

"Saturday."

"*Saturday ...*" My jaw dropped. "That's ... that's not watching him tomorrow. That's watching him for four nights. And days ... what am I supposed to do with him during the day?"

Slade's forehead wrinkled. "What do you mean? Wherever you are ... that's where he'll be. You shit. He watches. You surf. He sits on the beach. You—"

"Yeah, yeah ... I get it. What if one of my professors asks me about him?"

"Tell them he's none of their fucking business."

"Yeaaah ..." I quirked an eyebrow. "I'm not sure that will work for me like it works for you."

"Don't stress." On a pivot, he continued walking away from me.

I STRESSED.

I stressed for the next day and a half, until there was a knock at the door.

"Got it!" I ran down the stairs just as Aubrey was getting ready to turn the handle.

"How do you know it's for you?" She rolled her eyes and opened the door, giving me a shove to the side. "It's for you," she said breathlessly. "Hey. Slade, right?" She held out her hand.

He ignored it, glancing past her to me.

"Slade. Aubrey. Aubrey. Slade." I nudged her out of the way more gently than she did to me.

"Nice to meet you," she said like an afterthought when I stepped outside and shut the door for some privacy.

"You weren't in class this morning. And you're missing the rest of the week? It's hard to recover from that."

He handed me a bag. "His food. His health records. A number to call if I don't come home."

My heart stopped beating and cracked into little pieces. "Um ..."

"Questions?"

"Where—"

"About him, not me." He returned a stern expression.

I cleared the emotion from my throat. "Shouldn't I have your number? If something happened here, wouldn't you want to know?"

"You have him. Nothing should happen unless you do something stupid and reckless."

I coughed on a laugh. "That's rich coming from the drug

dealer who's nursing a bullet wound while getting ready to put himself in harm's way again. You're going to get caught. And if you happen to live to tell about it, it will be from a prison cell. That makes you a terrible dog dad. Jericho will not come visit you."

"Are you done?"

Curling my hair behind my ear on one side, I nodded.

"Thank god. Bye."

"Is it her?" I said to his back when he turned away from me. "Are you going someplace with her?"

"Let it go."

I didn't want to let *it* go. I didn't want to let *him* go. Even if he wasn't mine, I felt like he … like *we* were something.

When his taillights disappeared, I stepped into the house with Jericho, shut the door, and leaned my back against it. "Don't be stupid and fall for the drug dealer, Livy," I whispered.

"Whoa … what did you just say?"

I glanced up as Missy came down the stairs with her bag over her shoulder. "Hi, puppy." She hunched down to pet Jericho.

Drawing in a slow, deep breath, I released it while responding with a drawn out, "Yeah …"

"He's trouble. Sexy trouble. But big, huge, hard-time-in-his-future trouble."

Pushing off the door, I focused on Jericho. "I know. Hence the reminder to not fall for him. But…" I made a kissy noise and Jericho followed me to the kitchen with Missy right behind him "…in spite of his gigantic efforts to be a total asshole ninety-nine percent of the time, that one percent is *killing* me." I grabbed a LaCroix from the fridge and popped

81

the top.

"And you're sure you haven't had sex with him?"

I giggled, almost spewing sparkling water out of my nose. "Yes. I realize I can get distracted and forget stuff, like when it's my turn to clean the bathroom, but I'm very certain I have not had sex with Wylder."

"Wylder?" Missy leaned against the archway into the kitchen, hands gripping her backpack straps.

Grinning behind my tin can, I shrugged. "It's his name."

"Yes. I'm just wondering if you're using it as a proper noun or an adjective."

"So who's your study date?"

"Smooth subject change. And it's Ryan."

"Double date Ryan?"

Biting her lip, she nodded.

"What are you studying? Anatomy?"

Missy giggled. "Only if I'm lucky. If not … we're studying cross-culture communications."

"Well, I hope for your sake it's a lucky night. Have an orgasm for me too."

Laughing, she pushed off the wall and shook her head. "Maybe what you need is mind-blowing sex to get your mind off the criminal down the street. Maybe Elias."

"I'm not letting him conquer me." I sipped my drink.

"Then conquer him. Booty call. No spooning. No snuggling. Let him in then let yourself out before he has a chance to discard the condom. Make him feel like it was adequate … like he served the purpose and you no longer need him."

"Is that what you're doing with Ryan."

"Fuck yeah. I have my computer and a box of condoms in my bag. Not a change of clothes or a toothbrush. In. Out.

Home. Bye, bae."

With a slight chuckle as I focused on Jericho watching me with his usual smile, Missy headed out for cross-cultural communications and sex.

Was I jealous? Yes.

———

MY NERVOUS ANTICIPATION of professors asking me why I had a dog in class was met with nothing. Not one single professor said a word. Maybe rumors about my assault had gotten around and they assumed I needed an emotional support dog.

By Friday, I was a wreck. Slade and I hadn't exchanged numbers, and the disconnect and fear of the unknown—of the worst—weighed heavily on my mind.

What if he was with *her*?

What if I was a dog sitter while he had lots of sex with someone else?

So many what ifs …

A half day of classes meant an afternoon surfing with my buddy Jerry perched on a towel under a beach umbrella.

"You adopt a dog?" Elias asked, paddling up next to me.

"Dog sitting for a neighbor."

"Cool. But too bad. I thought we could hang out later."

Smirking, I paddled ahead of him with every intention of catching the next good ride. "No time to hang out … but if you want to give me a quick orgasm, I could spare fifteen minutes."

As I glanced over my shoulder, Elias met me with a wide, white grin. "Sounds a little one-sided."

"If you get off too, I'm fine with it. But you won't be a priority."

His throaty chuckle faded as I found my wave.

I needed something to prevent me from totally losing my shit when—if—Slade returned. It was impossible to think about anything else but him touching *her* the way he touched me. I'd made it twenty-one years without being that girl … the jealous, needy, clingy kind. I wasn't about to start with Slade Wylder.

It wasn't his job to fuck me.

It wasn't my job to be anything more than a dog sitter to him.

"Not gonna lie … I'm a little surprised by your change of heart," Elias said as he unlocked the door to his condo.

"Don't be." I gestured for Jericho to go in first as Elias held open the door. "I'm not here to sleep with you. Not here for some big seduction. Just here for the orgasm."

He shook his head, wearing a grin that turned into a cough as he shut the door behind us. "Surely you can give yourself one. Do you need me?"

I turned and slipped off my sweatshirt, revealing a bikini top. "For the kind of orgasm I want … yes."

Jericho sniffed around the condo as I shimmied out of my jean shorts, leaving me in only a bikini.

"You want to go to the bedroom?" Elias shrugged off his tee, revealing his perfect bronze body.

"Nope. I'm not staying. Floor. Sofa. Kitchen counter. Your choice, but we don't need a bed."

"Damn …" His grin doubled.

I drank up his expression, his body, and the look in his eyes.

"What happened to me being your favorite fantasy?"

I shrugged, untying the top of my bikini. "Fantasies are

overrated."

Before my top fell from my breasts, there was a knock at the door.

"Company?" I frowned.

"I'll get rid of them. Keep stripping. If I'm going to pleasure you, the least you can do is show me what I've been dying to see *for … ever.*" Elias opened the door. "Hey."

I started to retie my bikini top in case the unexpected guest needed to step into the house.

"Jericho."

My head snapped up, breath caught in my throat at the gritty voice saying Jerry's name.

"Oh …" Elias took a step back. "Is he your dog? Livy said you weren't coming home until tomorrow. Come in."

"No need." Slade pinned me with a look that made me internally cower as Jericho took his spot next to his master. "I'm just here for my dog … and the girl."

"Livy?" Elias's face wrinkled with confusion as his gaze shifted to me.

I was surprised. Elated. And pissed off. Where had he been? Why couldn't he have left me his phone number? Was he a drug dealer? Did he screw that woman? "I have plans with Elias. And my car is here. Thanks anyway."

"Livy … get your ass in your car. Now."

To say I was flabbergasted and appalled would've been an understatement. Never had a man talked to me that way—except my father. And I wasn't a fan of it. The bones in my body weren't submissive. Not a single one.

Once I picked my jaw up from the floor, I narrowed my eyes. "I'm not your pet. He might do as you ask…" I nodded to Jericho "…but I won't." I tipped my chin up as Elias held the door open, wearing an uneasy expression.

"Are you going to give yourself willingly to him … or is he going to take something that's not his to take like he did with Bella Blackwell?"

Elias started to shut the door. "Good talk, whoever the fuck you are, but it's time for you to leave."

Slade pressed one hand to the door, shoving it back open, while his other hand gripped Elias's throat, ramming him into the wall.

"Slade!" I winced.

"Livy, Go. Get. In. Your. Car."

"What are you talking about? Let him go!" I tugged at his arm as Elias's face turned a reddish-blue.

"In Florida … your surfer friend raped a seventeen-year-old girl, but he got off on a technicality because the investigators fucked up the case. Then he moved here. And you were getting ready to let a rapist crawl between your legs." He tsked several times. "Not smart. Now … as soon as you're in your car, I'll let him breathe again. It's that simple."

"Elias …" I whispered, not wanting to believe Slade.

He wouldn't look at me. Maybe because he couldn't breathe. Maybe because he did it. I grabbed my sweatshirt from the floor and ran out the door, shaky on my legs, head spinning to the point of nausea. It had to be a bad dream. My fantasy for months wasn't a rapist. No.

No … no … no …

I collapsed into my car and inched the door shut, fastening my seat belt with unsteady hands.

A few seconds later, Slade slammed the front door to the house with Jericho at his side as he marched toward his SUV. He didn't look at me until they were in his car. With the slightest nudge upward of his chin, he gestured for me to go.

I did.

I drove straight home.

I flew out and stomped to my front door.

"No," I said to myself just before sliding the key into the lock. "You do not get to win." Angry steps took me down the street to his house. Rage fueled me with an unscripted speech waiting to be unleashed on Slade Wylder for whatever that was at Elias's house.

Ordering me around.

Spewing insane accusations at Elias.

And just ... gah! Everything!

Without invite or a single knock, I threw open his back door just as he set his keys on the counter and started to shrug off his denim jacket. He pinned me with a look that dared me to say one word. "Turn around and go home."

"*Stop* bossing me around," I said through gritted teeth. "Why did you do that? Why did you say that? Elias is not a rapist."

"Google it." He took several steps in my direction, trying to intimidate me.

I stood my ground. "*I* asked him for sex."

He narrowed his eyes for a few seconds like my words bothered him. "I'm sure it was going to be a nice break for him to get it without having to take it forcefully."

"Why do you care?"

His gaze intensified as his jaw set. "I don't."

I grimaced, waiting for my head and my heart to agree on a reaction. How could he be so *everything* and so awful at the same time? "Why?" I whispered, letting my heart speak first.

"It's not my job to care."

I refused to blink until the burning tears retreated. Then I swallowed back the ball of anger and hurt swelling in my throat. "Then what exactly *is* your job? And how does it involve me at all? Why do you *care* if someone rapes me?" Words I never imagined coming from my mouth.

"Go home."

"I'm not going home!" I shoved his chest.

His eyebrows shot up his forehead as he took a step back.

I stepped into him and shoved him again.

"Watch it ..." he warned.

"I don't want to watch it."

Shove.

"I don't want to be told what to do!"

Shove.

"I don't want to be touched unless you're going to fucking kiss me!"

Shove.

His back hit the fridge. Mint and soap assaulted my senses as the only sound in the room was the hum of the air conditioner and my labored breaths.

My lips parted as my chest violently rose and fell. "Put your hands on me, Wylder," I whispered.

Pity dripped from his expression.

I didn't want his pity. I wanted his hands on me. When did my seduction become so desperate?

When Slade Wylder infiltrated my world. That was when.

My gaze slipped to his chest. I couldn't endure those eyes without him giving me *something* back.

"Then stop. Stop saving me. Stop watching me. Stop sending Jericho to be with me. Stop existing in my world." I turned and drifted slowly toward the door. "Buy a girl flowers and reject her. Don't take the life of the man who threatened her life then expect her to not want you beyond reason." I opened the door and stared at my feet for several seconds. "It's not fair."

Chapter Eleven

THE NEXT MORNING, I let the girls go surfing without me with a warning about Elias. I wasn't in the mood to get out of bed. I wasn't in the mood to do life at all. After searching up Bella Blackwell and finding out that Slade was right about my fantasy guy, I just ... couldn't.

When a relentless knock at the door brought me out of my pout session, I grumbled a few expletives and dragged my ass downstairs. "What?" I threw open the door, my anger bleeding through every pore.

"Good morning to you too."

A grin broke through my grumpiness in record time as I threw my arms around my Aunt Jessica—my dad's twin. "What are you doing here?" I pulled back and gestured for her to step inside.

She slipped off her sneakers and flipped her long, dark hair over her shoulder. "I'm in LA on business this week, and I wanted to see my favorite niece."

"And my dad wanted you to check in on me." I shuffled my bare feet to the kitchen in need of caffeine.

"That's a given, Livy." She followed me.

"Tea?" I glanced over my shoulder as I filled my electric tea kettle.

"Please." She perched on a barstool, depositing her purse on the counter. "You look good."

I laughed, cranking open the window to let in questionably fresh air and the hum of the neighbor's lawn mower. "My friends say I'm too skinny."

"You surf twenty-four-seven. Of course, you're going to burn calories like mad. I did too. Tell your friends to go fuck themselves."

Aunt Jess was one of my favorite people in the whole world. She was the calm in the storm that was my dad after Mom died.

Grinning, I poured her a cup of hot water and handed her the jar of mixed teas. "Can't tell them that. I like them too much."

She shrugged. "Suit yourself."

I leaned into the counter across from her, resting on my forearms while dunking my tea bag up and down in the mug, fresh mint and citrus waking me up. "I wish I had half your strength."

She lifted her gaze from her tea, eyes narrowed a fraction. "What do you mean?"

Rubbing my lips together, I kept my attention on my tea, hoping to keep my emotions in check. "If I tell you something, can you promise not to tell my dad. Like … ever?"

"Does it involve your dad?"

"No."

"Then yes. I won't say anything. Unless … you're pregnant. Livy, are you pregnant?"

Grunting a tiny laugh, I shook my head. Sex was required to get pregnant. I hadn't had that in many months. "No. However, I almost had sex shortly after school started. But …" I fished my tea bag out of my mug and set it on a saucer. "It wasn't going to be consensual."

There was just no way to ease into an I-was-almost-raped conversation.

"Liv …"

Total lost cause.

The tears flowed freely. I hadn't given myself permission to grieve the piece of my innocence he took without even raping me. Not with my dad. Not with my friends. Not even with Aubrey's therapist.

"Livy …" Jessica hopped off her stool and had me in her arms in seconds, her warm embrace a salve to my raw emotions. She didn't ask me what happened or a million other questions that my confession evoked. She just held me like my mom would have held me.

After my tears dried into streaks of salt settled on my cheeks, and my breathing faded to a hollow rhythm, she released me and pressed her soft palms to my cheeks. "There's nothing you can't tell me. There's also nothing you have to tell me."

God … I loved her so much.

Sniffling, I snagged a wad of paper towels and blew my nose, the unladylike sound buying time for me to muster enough courage to keep talking. "I stopped for gas. Went inside to grab a slice of pizza. Came out. And he was there. In a blink. Shoving me against the Jeep." I drew in a shaky breath and spewed out the rest. "My bag with the pepper spray was in the Jeep on the floor. And everything Dad ever told me about escaping an attacker …" I shrugged. "It just vanished in a cloud of fear. I felt so helpless and weak. He shoved the tip of his knife into me and forced me to the side of the building behind a dumpster. Shoved me to the ground."

I fisted my shaking hands and hugged my torso, hating the

way my whole body relived that night.

"He put the knife to my neck and got on top of me. All I could imagine was my mom seeing it happen from … somewhere. I closed my eyes. And in a blink … he was gone."

"Gone?" She tipped her head to the side.

"Yes. They found him not too far from the convenience store … dead. Someone slit his throat with the same knife he used while attempting to rape me."

"Who killed him?"

Another shrug. I didn't *know* for sure that it was Slade, so I didn't say it was him.

"So … someone saved the day, but you don't know who and they haven't caught him … or her?"

I nodded.

Her lips twisted to the side, eyes narrowing as I practically heard the whirl of thoughts spinning in her head. "Who was the guy … the one who tried to rape you?"

"Some guy named Stefan Hoover. Twenty-seven. Lived in Nevada. No prior record. He had a wife and a two-year-old son."

Rubbing her glossed lips together, Jessica nodded slowly while humming. "You need better skills."

"I don't think better skills will protect me. It's not like I tried anything I was taught, and it failed. I just didn't try. I froze up. You can't really prepare for something like that to happen through step-by-step role-playing."

"Then we don't role-play."

"I'm not following." The stiff breeze through the window picked up as if to breathe understanding into my scattered thoughts. I shut it a tad.

"Do you have some good coverup?"

"Coverup as in makeup?"

Jessica nodded, eyeing me like a puzzle with several missing pieces.

"Yeah. Why?"

"Because you're going to need it. I'll text you an address. Meet me in two hours, bring lots of water to rehydrate."

"What are we doing?"

She took another sip of her tea and grabbed her purse. "Making sure you never feel helpless again."

***

TWO HOURS LATER, I drove to the address. It was an abandoned building, barn-like, that I would normally not go into by myself, but Jessica's car was parked by the door, so I felt safe.

"What is this?" I asked, inspecting the empty building with the chirp of birds and ruffle of feathers in the rafters, an odd musty stench in the air, and nothing but a cold, dingy dirt floor beneath my feet. The only light was from the holes in the roof, which were numerous so we could see pretty well.

"It's where you will train."

"Train with what?"

She unzipped a black bag and pulled out some equipment that looked like something a boxer might use.

"For now, we'll train with these." She shoved headgear on me.

I took a step backward. Dirt and tiny rocks crunched beneath my shoes as I gained my footing. "I didn't know you boxed."

"I don't. I spar. Used to spar with your dad all the time."

"Really?"

"Yep."

"He never mentioned that."

She nodded. "Yeah, well … there's a lot parents don't mention to their children. We protect you with lack of knowledge until it starts to harm you. Then … we arm you with things you need to know."

"Do you have some sort of crash pads or something?"

Moments …

The next moment tipped my world completely on its side. It wasn't one I cared to remember or collect for my life scrapbook, but it made a mark. Many marks.

Whack!

Jessica punched my face so hard, it knocked me to the ground. The headgear protected my cheek, but my hands and knees and one elbow took a serious hit, like wiping out on a bike where little rocks made tiny cuts along the skin and embedded into my flesh.

"Wh … what the hell?" I wasn't sure if I should cry, run, or beg for her to never do that again.

"No crash pads, Livy. Men who force women behind dumpsters to rape them don't care about crash pads. Now … get up."

"I'm bleeding, Jess." My hands burned as I gingerly brushed away the tiny rocks from my bloodied hands and knees.

"It's a few scrapes, Livy. Get your ass up before I kick you while you're down. Because I guarantee … men like Stefan Hoover will kick you when you're down. Then they will rape you in any hole they can fit their dick into. They'll leave you ripped, raw, and drowning in their cum … then they'll kick you some more."

Stunned.

There was no other way to describe it. I didn't recognize the woman hovering over me. I was taller than Jessica. Yet, I couldn't bring myself to stand up because her confidence towered me by miles.

"Three … two …" She counted down.

My gaze homed in on her black combat boots that inched closer to me—two dogs ready to lurch toward me.

Something inside of me stirred to life just enough to send me scrambling to my feet.

"I don't want to do this …" I shook my head as tears filled my eyes and fear pulsated from my lungs to the pit of my stomach.

"Do what, Livy? Be abducted? Sodomized? Left for dead?"

"Jess …" I shuffled backward several steps.

"Then what are you going to do about it? Run? If you don't seriously wound me first, I will chase you down like the fucking animal I am. And I will make you pay."

I shrieked when she grabbed my shirt and shoved me back down to the ground.

"Fight, Livy."

I tried to crawl away, acid building in the back of my throat and the rotten stench of the ground just inches from my face feeding my need to vomit.

She kicked my leg. Hard. I clasped it and pulled it to my chest.

"If I would have aimed for your ribs, I would have broken them."

"Stop!" I barked with more force.

"Stop means *go* to sick fucks like Stefan Hoover. Try again, Livy." She struck my backside when I rolled into fetal position.

"Ouch! Please … stop!" Tears breached my eyes and ran hot down my cheeks.

"No *please*. No *stop*. GET. UP. LIVY!" she thundered like a drill sergeant.

I scrambled to my feet again, hobbling because my right glute and left thigh throbbed along with all the scrapes and bruises from being knocked to the ground twice.

"Jess …"

She shook her head. "Not Jess. Stefan." Her hand shot forward, and she fisted my shirt and ripped the neck. "Show me your tits, Livy. I want to fuck them."

Who. Was. She?

Her hand dove to my crotch, cupping me with an iron grip. I felt so broken, fearful, and violated by the one person I loved the most, second only to my dad.

"Do you have a tight cunt? I bet you do."

Her hand shifted to my inner thigh where she dug her fingers into my flesh until I saw stars. "Spread them for me, Livy."

I clawed at her hand.

She shoved me down again and tried to straddle me like Stefan did. And … something snapped. I saw *him*. The ugly, inhuman face that tried to take everything that wasn't his.

"GET OFF ME!" I kicked and scratched at her. All of her.

Her face.

Her hair.

Her torso.

My body flailed and wriggled as my hands and feet fought back with more strength and desperation—no longer caring if they landed somewhere on her that could cause injury.

And I did. My foot collided with her face, splitting her lower lip.

I stopped.

She stopped, her tongue darting out to swipe the blood.

"Oh my god! Jess … I'm—"

"Ready." She wiped her mouth with the back of her hand.

I blinked more tears, pushing myself to sitting then hugging my knees to my chest.

She kneeled in front of me and removed my headgear. After tossing it to the side, she pulled me into an embrace, stroking my hair. "You're ready to never be a victim again. I just needed to bring out your will to live. I will bend you so no man can ever break you. Then I will shape you into something stronger than you ever imagined."

Chapter Twelve

JESSICA TOLD ME the details of her past were still on a need-to-know basis, but she shared some details of the time she was raped. She trained under some elite people and learned to defend and kill if necessary.

I asked her if she'd ever had to kill anyone. She rolled her eyes as if the question was ridiculous and said, "What do you think?"

"You can't role-play true fear." She put in her mouth guard as I slipped in mine.

We were a month into my training. She hooked me up with a coach and came down once a week to one-on-one spar with me and evaluate my progress.

I'd made her bleed three times; she drew blood from me too many times to count. She said I needed to crave the blood, welcome the pain, and harness the fear. After four weeks, I did none of those things.

At best, I ignored the blood, took over-the-counter meds for the pain, and hid the fear from her. I also hid the bruises with makeup and wore a full wet suit to cover other bruises while surfing.

During that month, I also saw very little of Slade Wylder. I didn't look for him in class or go to my favorite tree to nap. I allowed myself no more than a two-second glance when passing his house.

Truth?

I missed Jericho. And I missed Wylder.

But clearly ... he didn't miss me.

For Halloween, Aubrey did the unthinkable—she had a party at her house. Well, her parents' house. I think it had something to do with the news that her parents were getting a divorce. She didn't take it so well, said she hated both of them.

I'd come to learn that there were two kinds of people in the world: those who lived for Halloween and those who didn't even set out a bowl of candy if they weren't home. I fell into the love Halloween category.

"Whoa ..." Kara's jaw dropped as I strutted down the stairs in my sexy SWAT costume—black onesie with a built-in pushup bra that gave the impression that I had a lot more cleavage than I actually did, garters, fishnet stockings, black combat boots, and a black hat with SWAT in white. My hair was pulled back in a ponytail, and I felt pretty badass.

It was my silent statement that I could be both sexy and tough.

"Let's just hope a few available options from the opposite sex show up to the party." I rubbed my glossed lips together and wrinkled my nose at the pumpkin spice overkill. Aubrey didn't want any candles lit, but she wanted the smell, so she bought a gazillion bowls of pumpkin spice potpourri and air spray.

"Still haven't had sex?" Kara adjusted her seductive skeleton leotard.

"No." I frowned. "I may never have sex again."

"I think you stand a really good chance of it tonight."

I laughed. "If this doesn't work, I'll know I'm simply broken."

An hour later, the party was in full swing with body odor, perfume, and possibly some pot competing with the pumpkin spice. And it was *hot* in the house.

Sticky, gross hot.

There were easily just as many men as women. My chances of having sex seemed good. Sadly … the pool of viable options dwindled as the party dipped into the early morning hours. Everyone seemed to be coupling, except me. Missy suggested I have a drink. She thought guys were intimidated by my costume and my sobriety.

I didn't drink. Not for special occasions and not to get laid. When I discovered my room and bed were taken, I escaped the house for some fresh two-in-the-morning air. Plunking my ass into the hammock Aubrey put in the front yard for her spiderweb display, I closed my eyes, and it swayed gently side to side. At some point, I fell asleep.

A cold, wet nose woke me up. It was dark, and I felt certain from the hum of the music, my bedroom was still being used for a bone fest.

"Jerry …" I sat up, nearly falling out of the hammock onto my ass as I rubbed my eyes. "What are you doing?" Then it happened, I fell onto my ass. "Oof!" I laughed a little as he licked me. "I've missed you. Where is he? Is he injured again? Is that why you're here?"

Climbing to my feet, I straightened my hat and messy ponytail. "Let's take you home and see what's up."

I followed him to the back door of the firehouse, not expecting to have *those eyes* render me motionless and speechless the second I stepped into the kitchen. Slade glanced up from the table and his laptop.

"Hi," I whispered, suddenly overwhelmed with nervousness

and vulnerability. My costume might have had something to do with the vulnerability part.

His tongue swept across his bottom lip as his weary gaze managed to find enough strength to check out my entire getup. "Hey," he responded softly when our eyes met again. "Nice costume."

I gave him a shy smile, adjusting the top of my onesie, but it wouldn't cover another inch of my breasts. That seemed to be the point when I picked out the costume. However, with fully dressed Slade's intense gaze all over me, I wished it gave me a little more coverage. "Thanks."

I folded my hands near my chest, using my arms to cover some bare skin. The AC and lack of bodies made his kitchen feel twenty degrees cooler. The lack of pumpkin spice and sweat delivered a nice breath to my senses.

"I uh … just wanted to make sure you were okay since Jericho showed up at my house."

He studied me a bit more. "He was making sure nothing happened to you while you were sleeping alone in your front yard wearing…" he gave a slight nod toward me "…that."

"I see. So … you're protecting me again? A month and no word from you, but tonight Jericho comes to watch over me?"

"What makes you think he ever stopped looking out for you?"

What the hell?

After I let that hit my heart and bounce off it—but not without making a little dent—I untied my tongue and said the only thing that made any sense. "I don't need you to watch after me. I've been learning self-defense. I'm not the weak girl you saved behind the dumpster."

His eyes narrowed a hint. "That's always been an interesting assumption on your part."

"Because it's not true or because admitting it would be admitting that you killed a man?"

He retuned nothing for close to a minute before nodding to the door. "Go home. Sleep in your bed, not the front yard."

"Someone else is in my bed. Sleeping or ... something."

For a girl who truly hated very few things or people, I *hated* how much I missed him. It wasn't until that moment that the true impact of his absence in my life settled into my conscience with the grace of a bulldozer.

He shut his computer and sighed, staring down at it with a contemplative expression. "You can sleep on my sofa."

I scuffed my boots along his floor until I was standing beside him. After a few moments of silence, he scooted his chair away from the table, allowing me to stand between his spread legs. I rested my ass on the edge of the table.

His gaze raked along my legs to my breasts, finally finding my face. "You're not seducing me, Livy."

Gah! I loved my name sliding from his full lips with that manly badass timbre to his voice. The kitchen fell silent again with the exception of the refrigerator humming. He smelled like a fresh shower and the most tempting prey.

I lifted one boot to his jean-clad leg, putting more weight on the table as I lifted my other boot to his other leg, the table beneath me creaking a bit. "You're right. I'm not going to seduce you." I slowly unlaced my boots and slipped them off, dropping them to the floor with one thud and then another. Unhooking my garters, I eased off my fishnet stockings one at a time.

He swallowed hard, jaw muscles tensing, eyes flared.

Sliding off the table, nestled between his legs, I bent down, brushing my lips along his ear, my hands folded behind my back so I wouldn't touch him with anything *but* my mouth when I whispered, "Sweet dreams, Wylder."

As I moved to stand straight again, his hand snaked up my back, fisting my ponytail, slowing my ascent as he lifted his back from the chair and followed my body—followed my exposed cleavage.

For the longest pause, he didn't move a muscle, not one twitch—his breath hot on my chest, his hand still clenching my hair. "There's a pillow and blanket in the trunk behind the sofa," he murmured, releasing my hair.

I. Couldn't. Fucking. Breathe.

It was like he lit me on fire and pointed to the extinguisher ten yards away.

I grunted a painful laugh through a long exhale, bent down, and gathered my boots and stockings. "You're such a head case," I mumbled. Shoving my way out between the caged area of his legs and the table, I headed to the door instead of his sofa. "I'm going to go fuck the first guy I find with a condom in his wallet. Night, Wylder."

The second I got the door open six inches, his hand landed on it above my head, slamming it shut. I remained unblinking at it while he hovered so close to my backside, heat radiating from his body. My eyes closed when his forehead rested on the top of my head, rolling slowly side to side like he was in some sort of agony.

I didn't move. I wasn't lying … I would not seduce him. *He* would seduce me.

He would touch me.

He would kiss me.

He would surrender to me after months of holding his

shield of emotionless bullshit.

His hands gripped the material to my onesie, his breaths quickening as he lifted his forehead pressed to the top of my SWAT hat. I stood stone-still, letting him peel the stretchy material down my body to my hips, leaving my breasts completely exposed. I sucked in a sharp breath when his hands covered them, my back arching to press my body into his touch.

It was torture. So slow. His grip firm, touching me with a need that felt like it was teetering on the edge of losing control.

My heart tried to have a full-on heart attack. My breaths chased each other so fast my lungs nearly exploded. When his head dipped, lips grazing my ear, my neck, my bare shoulder, I dropped my boots and stockings, pressing my hands flat to the door to keep from surrendering to my weak knees.

When his tongue flicked my skin, my breath hitched and released on a low moan. One hand slid from my breast to my neck, forcing my head back for him to plant his face in the crook of my neck as his other hand slid down my stomach— under my onesie and into my panties, stopping just shy of my clit.

He sucked and bit the skin along my neck, and my hat fell to the floor with my boots and my stockings. If he didn't hurry up and put those lips on mine, I was going to self-combust. After months of dreaming about that mouth on me, those veiny arms and hands possessing me ... I *needed* to know if he tasted like the drug I imagined him to be.

Turning my neck as far as I could, his gaze locked with mine. Those intense eyes drowning in agony. Why did he always look at me like I was bad for him?

I didn't stop long enough to ask. I lifted onto my toes and

forced him to let me turn around. My fingers thrust into his hair as I took those lips.

When his tongue slid into my mouth, giving me a taste of perfection, like mint and beer and months of longing, I closed my eyes and lassoed that *moment*.

The moment I realized I'd kissed a million wrong people in my journey to him.

The moment I realized Slade Wylder would take me so completely I would never be the same.

The moment I *knew* he killed another human to save me.

Not a million bouquets of roses.

Not a ten-carat diamond.

Not a mansion in Malibu.

Nothing would ever mean more than that night behind the dumpster when he literally slayed the beast.

Lifting me up, he guided my legs around his waist and pressed my back to the door. Deepening the kiss, he found my hands and pressed them above my head, interlacing our fingers.

I devoured every inch of his minty-flavored mouth, humming my pleasure while breathing heavily through my nose as we twisted and turned our heads to explore each possible angle of the kiss.

My fingers went numb, squeezing his hands so hard, desperate to have him … *all* of him. As if he read my mind, he guided my arms around his neck and planted his hands on my ass before peeling my back from the door.

Our kiss broke and we paused—him holding me with my arms and legs wrapped around his body. A whisper of fear slithered up my spine. Would he overthink it and release me to the floor with a hard "go home?" I didn't want that to happen. My heart wouldn't survive the rejection at that point, so I ducked my head and kissed his neck, working my way up to suck and bite along his earlobe.

He gripped my ass harder and carried me upstairs, but just barely. When we reached the top, he laid me down, kneeling on the stairs while sliding my onesie and panties completely off.

"Wylder ..." I clenched his hair when he kissed his way up my naked body. Arching my back, I writhed beneath him while clawing and yanking at the hem of his tee. He lifted his mouth from my breast long enough to shrug it off with one arm before sucking my nipple into his mouth and trapping it with his teeth until I hissed.

Who needed alcohol? Months without sex ... months with Slade Wylder crawling under my skin ... had me out of my mind.

Need.

Want.

Need.

Want.

I yanked his head from my chest to my mouth. The feast wasn't over for me. As he hummed into the kiss, I wrapped my legs around his waist. He rested his body weight on a forearm while his other hand grabbed my ass and worked me over the bulge in his jeans.

My brain begged for his bed, but I couldn't say it.

My other thoughts involved begging him to remove his pants and find a condom, but I couldn't articulate those thoughts either.

With his tongue in my mouth, his chest brushing my nipples, and his erection stroking between my legs, all I could do was take what I *wanted*.

What I *needed.*

"Wylder ..." My back bowed again as his mouth traveled along my jaw and down my neck. "I ... I can't wait," I stammered through labored breaths.

His tongue retreated back up to my ear, flicking it before biting it. "Then don't," he whispered, gripping my ass tighter while stilling his pelvis as mine rocked slower but harder, my need spiraling past the point of no return.

As my eyes drifted shut, my jaw fell open, and the pleasure he gave claimed every inch of my body. Had it not felt *so* damn good, I might have been a bit embarrassed. With little effort, he hugged my body to his and carried me to the bedroom.

I relished the hunger in his mouth on my neck, my cheeks, my lips, as I clung to him—the man that not only gave me pleasure, but the man who protected me. No one's arms would ever feel the way Wylder's felt.

He sat on the bed. I stayed wrapped around him.

We kissed without urgency.

We kissed like it was our language.

We kissed like our mouths were made to meld together forever.

His hands feathered up my back to my neck and my jaw, framing my face to angle my head to kiss me deeper. Such a simple gesture ... but it felt different with him. My fingers curled into his back like they needed a constant reminder that it wasn't a dream that might vanish if I tried to grasp it.

Our kiss ended as sirens screeched nearby. I knew they had to be on our street. As people did with sirens, we waited for the sound to fade ... to go beyond us. But they didn't fade, they intensified and multiplied. He remained expressionless, like a dog listening for something.

I couldn't wait, so I jumped off his lap and ran to the window in his room that faced the street. "Oh my god! Our house!"

Flames engulfed Aubrey's house and panic ripped straight to my heart. So many people were still in the house when I left. The second I turned, Slade was there, shoving one of his tees over my head like a child.

"Pants ..." he held up a pair of his sweatpants.

I didn't need pants. I needed to know if my friends were okay. In only his tee, I ran down the stairs, out the door, and up the street—bare feet slapping against the sidewalk, the cool breeze engulfing my skin as the burn of smoke crept up my nostrils.

"Miss, please stay back." A policeman stopped me as firefighters scrambled to put out the fire and help people out of the house.

More sirens in the distance sounded as dogs barked and rescue workers barked instructions.

"It's my house! Those are my friends!" I wriggled as his grip tightened to keep me from running closer to the house. Endless tears spilled down my cheeks.

Missy ... Aubrey ... Kara ...

When I stopped fighting the officer, I surveyed the area and I found Missy at the back of an ambulance with paramedics checking her over.

"Missy!" I ran straight to her.

The paramedic stepped aside to let me hug her, so I assumed she must not have been seriously injured.

"Oh my god! Livy! We thought you were still in there. She's here!" Missy coughed several times as she yelled to one of the firemen.

"Where's Aubrey and Kara?"

She nodded to another ambulance. "Kara's over there. Aubrey had some minor burns. Another ambulance just left with her."

"I'm going to check on her."

"Go." Missy nodded.

"Where were you?" Kara batted the paramedic's hand away as I approached her.

I grunted as her hug knocked the wind from me. "I was out front. Then I went to Slade's house. What happened?"

She shook her head. "We don't know. I was asleep and so was Missy. I think Aubrey was cleaning the kitchen when smoke detectors went off. Everything escalated, going from zero to the …" She choked on a sob as she watched the firemen work to put out the fire with little luck. It was gone. "The wh-whole house was up in flames and … and e-everyone was trying to get out."

I hugged her again. "Are you okay? Have they gotten everyone out?"

"I'm … f-fine." She shrugged as I released her. "But we don't know for sure who was in the house. You …" She wiped her eyes. "We thought you were in there."

I winced. "I'm sorry. I should have told someone where I was going but …"

Of course, I didn't think the house would go up in flames, causing a big search for me.

"We need to call Aubrey's parents. I …" Reality sank in one drop at a time. I didn't have my phone. It was in the house. "Do you have your phone?"

Kara shook her head. "Neither does Missy."

I blinked at the flames. Shocked. Mesmerized. Barely coherent at the moment. "We should get to the hospital."

"Yes. But unless you have your Jeep key on you, we don't have wheels."

Tearing my gaze from the house in ruins, I scanned the area. Partygoers in costumes, some half-clothed, some wrapped in a sheet or a blanket. I'm pretty sure I recognized the blanket from my bed wrapped around a couple heading across the street to their car. Did they have their key on them? When they stopped at the door that was locked, their heads dropped.

Nope. No key.

My gaze continued to sort through the crowd and chaos until it landed on Slade and Jericho hanging out on the sidewalk about a yard up from their house. Most of the area was blocked off. "Let's go. I found our ride."

Kara sobbed softly as she followed me, and we grabbed Missy just as the paramedics deemed it fit to leave on her own without a trip to the ER.

"You guys grabbed shoes." I eyed their flip-flops. "I'm not sure I would have had the sense to do that."

They didn't respond. Their heads remained canted over their shoulders toward the burning house.

"Can you take us to the hospital? We don't have keys to our vehicles, and Aubrey was taken there."

Slade nodded once. "Inside," he said, and Jericho headed to the back door. He unlocked his Volvo, and Kara and Missy climbed into the back seat as I made my way around to the passenger's side.

"Pants and shoes." He rested his hands on my shoulders and steered me toward the house.

"I don't need—"

"You do." He opened the back door, and I followed him

into the kitchen and just … stood there. Everything smelled like smoke. I wasn't sure if it was his house too or just the stench embedded permanently in my nose.

Coherent thoughts were nowhere to be found.

"Leg." He squatted in front of me and put his sweatpants on me like he put the tee on me. Then he pulled them up my naked lower body and tied the drawstring before rolling the waistband over several times. I was little help as he guided my feet into my black combat boots and stood in front of me.

My blank gaze affixed to his T-shirt clad chest. "I think … everything I owned except my Jeep was in that house. But nobody died … that's what matters. Right?" I lifted my gaze to his.

He never gave me much to read on his face, and that moment was no different. After a few heartbeats, he nodded once.

When we pulled into the hospital parking lot, Kara and Missy thanked Slade and plodded inside, the weight of the night evident with each slow step. I started to open my door. Then I twisted my torso to face Slade. It wasn't that I expected endless warm embraces and soothing hushes while stroking my hair and promising me everything would be okay, but I thought there would be something more. At least a touch that acknowledged how close we had been just seconds before we heard the sirens. But maybe that was sex, and I needed to explain to my heart that the physical and emotional elements of life didn't always coincide.

"Thanks for the ride. And …" And what? The orgasm? "I'm going to call Aubrey's parents if someone hasn't already done that. Then I'm going to call my dad. I'm sure he'll be here in a flash. Not sure where I'm going to stay for now or when I'll get someplace to get a new phone. So …"

The skin between his eyes wrinkled a bit. "Okay."

Okay.

That was his response to the tragedy, our displacement, and my recent status change to homeless.

Okay.

"O-kay … I'll make sure to get your clothes back to you as soon as I buy new ones."

He answered with another infuriating nod. That stupid nod felt like a boot to my already bruised heart, an eviction notice to my already lost emotions.

I climbed out and drew in a shaky breath to calm those emotions as I scuffed my boots along the sidewalk to the hospital entrance. Without the fire, it had been an emotional, life-changing night for me. The fire and the fact that it was almost six in the morning … that just added to my fragile state.

Chapter Thirteen

AUBREY'S BURNS WERE treated, and she was discharged later that afternoon. Her parents put on a united front in spite of the recent divorce announcement. Kara and Missy left with their boyfriends, and both of their parents were booking flights to LA.

My dad was on his way, but he had been in New York for a work conference. He was having trouble finding a flight, which meant he wouldn't be there until the next day. He was going to have Jessica come to me, but I told him I'd be fine. I told him I had a place to stay.

I lied.

Overprotective dads didn't like to hear that their daughters were homeless.

I also lied to Aubrey's parents about having a place to go and a ride or money to get there. When they left the hospital, I stood by the entrance, pretending to wait for my "friend" until their car disappeared into traffic. Then I turned to go back inside to find a waiting room to sleep in until my dad made it there the next day.

"Forget something?"

I stopped. Emotions raced to my eyes, but I did not give in and cry like the fucking mess I was at that moment. Instead, I swallowed what little pride I had left and gave myself a mini pep talk before turning toward Wylder and Jericho.

"No. Yes." I frowned and cleared my throat. "What are you doing here?"

"Waiting for you."

I died inside but kept something resembling composure on the outside. "Welp ..." I shrugged. "Here I am."

His scruff-covered face softened as his boots closed the distance between us. "Need a ride?"

My gaze parked at a piece of smashed gum by the toe of his boot. "I'm ..."

"When's your dad coming?"

"Tomorrow."

"Where are you going?"

I scraped my teeth over my bottom lip several times. "Not sure yet." My arms crossed over my stomach as I hugged myself to soothe my insecurities.

"My place?"

"Are you inviting me to stay with you tonight?" I glanced up at him, squinting against the sun.

"Sofa offer still stands." He delivered everything with zero sarcasm.

"K ..." I lifted a shoulder in a half-shrug.

He jerked his head toward the parking garage, and I followed him, shocked that the numbness in my body allowed my feet to move. No conversation took place on the way to his place. I cringed when we pulled onto the street.

The charred house.

Two vehicles from the fire department were parked on the street. Maybe they were inspecting something.

Once we pulled in the driveway, I climbed out and stared at the house again. Of course, Slade said nothing. He and Jericho sauntered inside. After several minutes, I made my way into the house too. Slade retrieved several dishes from the fridge while I slipped off my boots and tugged up the sweatpants that were way too big for me.

Jericho trotted to his bed and collapsed onto it, and I followed him into the living room. On the sofa were department store bags. Women's department stores. I peeked inside a few of the paper bags.

"Hope something fits."

I glanced over my shoulder. "You did this for me?"

He twisted his lips. Had I not known better, I would have said he was trying to hide a grin. "Too much pink for me. And Jericho looks hideous in skinny jeans."

A joke? Did Slade Wylder deliver a joke?

I poked around in a few of the bags, glancing at labels and sizes. He did good. Really good. Then I pulled out a bra and pair of panties. A thong and a very sexy lace bra. With them dangling from my finger, I eyed Wylder.

"I know for a fact you're not wearing a bra or panties at the moment."

I chuckled, inspecting the undergarments. "These will definitely keep me warm on breezy days."

"Hungry?"

I nodded, depositing the sexy goods back into the bag. He opened a container with salad in it and set a jar of dressing next to it on the table. Then he pulled another container from the microwave with penne pasta in it, sprinkled it with parmesan cheese, and dished some out onto two plates.

Sitting at the table, I tucked one knee to my chest and rested my chin on it as he put some lettuce next to my pasta and drizzled dressing. The garlic and herb aroma offered a nice alternative to the smoke.

Our gazes met for a few seconds, and he let those lips of his turn upward into a barely detectable smile.

I saw it.

More than that ... I felt it. And it felt incredible in spite of the events of the previous twenty-four hours.

Nobody died.

That was my new motto. The incessant chant of gratitude circling in my brain,

Midway through eating dinner with nothing but the clinking of forks, I wiped my mouth and cleared my throat. "Thank you for everything ... the chauffeuring, the clothes, the food, the sofa."

He nodded.

Another nod.

"If you talk to me ... I won't tell anyone. It can be our little secret that you know how to say actual words ... not just nods and scowls."

He slowed his chewing, giving me a milder version of said scowl.

"There it is." I grinned, standing and circling the table to his side and straddling his lap, forcing him to sit back in his chair. His hands rested on my legs.

Leaning forward, I brushed my lips along his jaw, his cheek, and his mouth ... without actually kissing him. His hands slid up my shirt—his shirt—stopping just below my breasts, fingertips ghosting over my ribs.

"Can I use your shower, Wylder?" I whispered over his lips instead of kissing him.

He edged forward, trying to take my mouth.

I pulled back and grinned. "I need to brush my teeth ... and shower. Did you buy me a toothbrush? Deodorant? A hairbrush?" Teasing him brought intense satisfaction to me.

Withholding actual words seemed to bring him an equal amount of satisfaction. His mouth reached for mine again.

Again, I dodged his attempt to kiss me. In hindsight ... that was a mistake. His plate and mine crashed to the floor with one swipe of his arm. In the next second, my back hit the top of the kitchen table. His right hand cuffed my wrists above my head while his left hand slid down the front of my—his— sweatpants where he slid two fingers into me. Our mouths collided and his tongue and fingers fucked me to the same rhythm. A minute or so later, I hiked my feet onto the edge of the table to thrust my pelvis into his touch. He released my hands and they flew into his chaotic hair.

Off with his top.

Deep kisses.

Off with my top.

Deep kisses.

My pants.

"Where do you want me?" He tore his lips from mine and slowed his fingers.

"Wylder ..." I lifted my pelvis, chasing his hand.

"Here?" He added a third finger. "Do you want me here, Livy?"

Words melted on my tongue into puddles of lust, so I nodded as heavy breaths pushed past my lips. Need multiplied in the bottom of my stomach and was heavy between my legs.

He withdrew his fingers and retrieved a condom from his wallet, setting it on the table beside me while unbuttoning his jeans. I sat up, keeping my feet on the edge of the table, spreading my knees a little wider.

Intense eyes moved, focusing on my breasts and my blond

hair covering part of them. As he rolled on the condom, his gaze dropped to my fingers sliding between my legs.

Our eyes met, like he needed to verify I was pleasuring myself for his pleasure. I bit my lower lip and closed my eyes on a soft moan.

"Fuuuck ..." he said in a throaty groan two seconds before attacking my mouth again.

His fingers joined mine, but only briefly before he moved both of our hands and pressed the head of his erection against my entrance. He leaned me back on the table again, sinking into me one slow inch at a time while my fingers curled, clawing the flesh covering the tight muscles along his back.

We screwed on the table for a while before relocating to the fridge door, bent over the back of the sofa, and finishing at our original spot ... the top of the stairs.

Sweaty and searching for oxygen, he rolled off me and onto his back. We stared at the water stain on the ceiling for several minutes. I had a million questions. The first one being ... who was the woman in the Lexus and where did he go for those three nights that I watched Jericho? Did he have sex with her? Did he have it with her the way he had it with me? Did he kiss her like he was trying to consume her entire body with one never-ending kiss?

I turned onto my side, admiring the sweep of his long lashes as his eyes rested shut and the splay of idle hands on his chest. After I ate up the vein porn, I straddled his abs and planted my palms on the floor beside his head. My long hair tented our faces. He blinked open his eyes, searching mine.

"Wylder ..." I whispered as his hands parked on my hips.

"Hmm ..." he responded, blinking heavily.

I took a few seconds to bask in the warmth of our bodies so

close and him surrendering to me.

"Was it you?" My face lowered to his. I kissed along his cheekbones, across his forehead, and down his nose to his lips where I whispered over them again, "Was it you? Did you take that man's life? Did you save me?" My lips ghosted back and forth over his.

"You know the answer." He gripped my hips and lifted me from his torso as he climbed to his feet. His sexy-as-fuck, sculpted nakedness moseyed to the bedroom while I stayed on my knees at the top of the stairs.

I knew the answer. I just didn't know the why. Of course he would think it was obvious, but it wasn't. A normal person might have tried to pull my attacker from me. Throw a few punches. Call the police.

The man who tried to rape me just ... disappeared in complete silence with precision ... flawless execution.

On a defeated sigh, I stood and followed his path to the bathroom and the buzzing of his beard trimmer. The shower was on, room filling with steam, as tiny whisker trimmings fell to the sink. A navy towel hung low on his waist.

I imagined sidling up to his back, pressing my lips to his spine as my hands snaked around to his waist, tracing the lines of his abs.

I imagined asking him if I could shower with him.

I imagined all the ways I could come across as needy or insecure. And while I *did* know in my gut that he was the one who saved me, I didn't want to be that girl. The one who needed saving. The *needy* girl.

He offered me the sofa, so I grabbed a new T-shirt he bought me and the only pair of panties that weren't a thong. During my more thorough search, I stumbled across a bag of toiletries. A jackpot of shampoo, conditioner, a comb and a brush, deodorant, and the greatest of all … a toothbrush and peppermint toothpaste. Scurrying back up the stairs—naked— I locked myself in the hall bathroom for the next thirty minutes.

Easing the door open, I listened for him, but the house was silent. Light filtered through his partially open door. I shut off the bathroom light, tiptoed down the stairs, cleared the bags off the sofa, retrieved a pillow and blanket from the metal trunk, and snuggled onto the sofa while blowing Jericho a kiss good-night.

The top stair creaked, and I snapped my eyes shut for several seconds. Peeking one open, I tracked Slade sauntering into the kitchen in nothing but boxer briefs. He filled a glass with water and drank it down. After flipping off the lights, he started back up the stairs.

"If I have to come back down and carry your ass up here, it's not going to be gentle."

Gulp …

I counted to ten to see if he by any chance was talking to Jericho, but the pooch didn't budge, so I took a guess that he meant me. Ascending the stairs with patience and stealth, I peeked into his room, standing in the doorway. With his back against his solid wood headboard, he kept his gaze on his computer opened on his lap.

"You said I could sleep on the sofa."

"And you can." His fingers continued to move over the keyboard as his brow wrinkled a bit at the screen.

"But you just ordered me to sleep in your bed."

"I didn't. I ordered you up here … but there will be no sleeping anytime soon." He closed his laptop and set it on the floor under his nightstand.

"What are you wearing?" He cocked his head to the side.

I glanced down at my tight, white tee and bikini cut panties. "Um ... the closest thing I could find to pajamas."

"I didn't buy you pajamas."

I returned my gaze to him. "Yeah, I saw that."

"Then take that shit off." He did it again. That barely detectable grin hiding just beneath the surface.

"I think your attitude is taking up too much space in the room. I'm going to sleep downstairs with Jerry." I turned and headed toward the stairs.

"I missed you," he said.

It wasn't loud.

It wasn't desperate.

It was ... life.

I paused at the top of the stairs.

"Jericho missed you too. But ... not as much as I did."

My brain hit pause, but my feet followed my heart's lead and carried me back to his bedroom. As I took slow steps toward his bed, I shrugged off the tee and shimmied out of my panties before crawling up his body. His hands claimed my face, his lips claimed my mouth.

Our kiss ended slowly, but our mouths lingered a breath away from each other.

"Wylder ... if you want this to be a one-night stand, you're saying all the wrong things."

He kissed me again ... and again.

We spent the better part of the night becoming thoroughly acquainted with each other's bodies. When the first rays of sun broke through, the pad of his finger traced my forearm. "How did you get this scar?"

Keeping my tired eyes closed, I hummed and smiled. "Surfing. Seven stitches. The morning of my high school graduation. My dad was livid. I wasn't supposed to go out that morning. But ...*everyone* was going."

Wylder ran his lips along the scar. "Rebel."

I giggled, peeling open my eyes as he moved down my body, grabbing my leg and bending it toward him.

"And this one?" His tongue traced the scar along my knee.

"Jellyfish. Ended up with a rash and I scratched the hell out of it. The scar is from the scratching more than the sting."

His whiskers tickled my skin, and I wiggled away from his touch.

"This ..." I ghosted my finger over his shoulder and the red scar still in its stages of healing. "Who shot you?"

He kissed up the inside of my thigh, well on his way to the perfect distraction, the perfect change in subject. "You don't want to know."

"I do. I want to know if I'm in danger. If you're a bad person. A drug dealer. A serial killer. A collector of human body parts." My fingers claimed his hair, and I steered him away from his destination, forcing him to look at me. "Wylder ..." I murmured, scared to be with him, scared to be without him. Not every truth made sense, but it didn't make it less true.

My truth—he saved my life.

He dropped his gaze to my stomach. "You're not in danger."

My fingers released his hair, and I closed my eyes as his mouth navigated up my body and his hand reached for another condom on the nightstand.

Chapter Fourteen

"I'M NOT GOING to be here when your dad arrives." Wylder set a key on the table and kissed the top of my head before whistling to Jericho.

"Oh thank god ..." I covered my mouth, but it was too late.

He raised an eyebrow as he slid his wallet into his pocket and snatched his keys from the counter.

"I mean ..." I sipped my tea to buy some time to formulate a better explanation. "I'm just not ready for you to meet him. He's ..." My nose scrunched. "Complicated."

"He will hate me."

Pressing my lips together, I nodded several times. "That too. Not because there's anything wrong with you ... or at least there's not *a lot* that's wrong with you. I mean ..." I cringed. "I have no idea, and *that's* why I'm not ready for you to meet him."

"It's fine." He opened the back door. "I don't want to meet him yet either."

"Why not?" I took immediate offense to his comment, like when my high school friends accused my dad of being a psycho.

"It's complicated." He shut the door.

I ran after him. "Where are you going anyway?"

"To take care of some business." He opened the back door

for Jericho then closed it after he hopped in the back seat.

"Business?" I folded my arms over my chest while he opened his door.

"Yep." He slid into the seat.

"Does it have anything to do with that woman who drives the Lexus?"

He grabbed the inside handle to the door. "Jealousy is an ugly color on you, Liv ... find something that's a little more flattering."

"I'm not jealous." I stood in the way of him shutting the door.

"Then go inside and stop worrying about my business."

"A simple 'I'm not fucking that woman' would suffice. But since you can't say that, don't plan on me still being here when you return later ... or next week ... or whenever your *business* is complete." I stomped back into the house and slammed the door shut behind me. If he wanted to have my body in the most intimate way, he needed to give me more emotionally too.

Still ... he was right. Jealousy was an itchy, teal bridesmaid dress.

The door flew open on my heels. The second I turned, he grabbed my face and kissed me, backing me into the wall, my head barely missing the clock. Everything about it felt brutal. His passion and anger tangled into an unforgiving attack on my body. I moaned from the intensity but also because I couldn't breathe. He released me, though his hands didn't budge from my face.

"Are we clear now, Liv?"

I gingerly pressed my bruised lips together and nodded slowly.

"Good. I don't want to have this discussion again," he muttered as he exited the kitchen with nearly as much intimidation in which he entered it.

———— ∿ ————

"DAD!" I RAN out the door to the rental SUV as soon as it pulled into the driveway.

My solid rock of a father caught me without a blink when I threw myself into his arms. A few seconds later, he set me on my feet again and brushed my hair away from my face with his gentle but strong hands.

"You okay?"

I nodded.

"Everyone else okay?"

"I think so. It was a party with lots of people, but as far as I know and have heard, everyone escaped with no more than minor injuries or a little smoke inhalation.

"Did you get burned? Are you having any breathing issues?"

"No. I'm good. I wasn't ..." I scrunched my nose. "I wasn't home at the time of the fire."

He frowned.

"Don't." I hooked my arm around his and led him to the back door. "You're not allowed to be anything but relieved and grateful that your daughter is okay." I opened the door and waited for him to step into the kitchen.

"Who's your friend?"

I shrugged, fetching him a cup of coffee left over from the pot Wylder made earlier that morning. The rich nutty aroma still lingered in the air. "Well, clearly a neighbor ... and someone I know from school."

"And how long has he been screwing my daughter?" Dad sipped his coffee and took a seat at the table.

I sat across from him and smirked. He could no longer ground me or chase my boyfriends down the street. "Less than forty-eight hours ... if you really must know."

"Livy ..."

"Daaad ..." I rolled my eyes. "Before I left for college, wanna know what Jess told me?"

"No." He scowled at me from behind the coffee mug.

"She told me you were the most loving brother and husband. She told me the two of you had been through so much that no one would ever be able to fully understand. She said you, in so many ways, have been and always will be the greatest love of her life."

His expression softened into the admiration I had seen so many times before on his handsome face—when people talked to him about me, when he talked about Mom, and at the mention of Jessica's name.

"She also said in spite of your flaws, no father has ever loved his daughter the way you love me."

He relinquished an actual smile and a guilty shrug.

"But then she told me ... until you met Mom, you were a total manwhore, and that I should never feel ashamed for sowing my wild oats."

Curling his lips together and lowering his mug to the table, he inspected me through narrowed eyes. "That's a terrible exaggeration and dangerous misinformation. Not settling into a long-term relationship before reaching my thirties didn't make me a manwhore. It simply meant I had scrutinizing taste in women."

"Before you met Mom, how many women did you have sex

with? Just trying to gauge my own sex life to see if I'm on track to live up to the legacy."

"Livy ..." he warned with a look.

That look made me think of Slade, and that gave me chills.

No. No. No.

I did not fall for a guy like my dad.

Fall? Had I fallen for Slade Wylder?

"Where's your friend? Too scared to meet me? That's not a good sign. If you're going to let some guy screw you, at least show some of your own scrutinizing taste and make sure he owns a pair of balls."

"I love this." My lips pulled into a smirk just before taking another sip of my tea. "I love that we can talk so openly about sex and the balls of the men I'm dating. Mom would be so proud of us."

Another well-earned frown. "So this guy ... you're dating him?"

Good question.

"I'm not sure. Maybe. Maybe not. We haven't been on an actual date."

"For God's sake, Livy ..." He leaned back in his chair and ran his hands through his short, dark hair.

"He's different." I let sincerity seep into my words. "We haven't labeled our relationship, but it's different than any relationship I've had with a guy. You'd like him. He's very protective of your daughter."

"If your idea of protective is just some asshole being posses-sive, then I promise you ... I won't like him."

I drummed my fingers on the table. "Would you want me to date twenty-something Jackson Knight?"

He grunted a laugh, focusing on his drink, tracing the handle with his finger. "That's not a fair question."

"It is. Everyone has said I'm destined to find a man just like you. I'm just curious how that makes you feel."

"Terrified."

On a giggle, I pulled my knees to my chest and rested my chin on them, gazing adoringly at my father. After a few seconds, my smile faded. "I lost everything. I know they're just *things*, but ... they were my things. And some of them were Mom's things."

"What do you need?"

I shrugged. "Slade bought me some clothes, but I need more. My computer is gone. My—"

"Slade?"

I nodded. "That's his name."

"It's a terrible name."

"It's a cool name, *Jack*."

"Watch it ..." He relinquished a grin. "So is this Slade guy a political science major too?"

"He is."

"Rich family? Or is he working to pay for this place? Roommates?"

"I don't know anything about his family. We just started screwing ... I mean dating."

Dad's nostrils flared.

"No roommates. He has a dog, Jericho. A German shepherd. Totally makes me think of Gunner. As for a job ... rumor has it, he's a drug dealer." My mouth pulled into a toothy grin.

"Not funny, Livy."

It was quite funny because it was true, at least it was true about the rumors.

"He's a bodyguard."

"A bodyguard?"

I nodded. Mine ... but that detail wasn't necessary at the moment.

"Like a bouncer at some club?"

"I don't know all the details. Again ... we've only been screwing for a day or so."

"Go to your room."

I erupted into more giggles. "Sorry. You set yourself up for that one."

"Where are you planning on staying now? I've looked at some options." He pulled out his phone and opened the screen. "There's an elderly couple a half mile from campus who have a room for rent. Two hundred a month. Or a single woman who works nights ... she's in her forties and has a room for rent. She has a pool and security cameras. Or—"

"I'm waiting to see what my friends are doing, but thanks, Dad. That elderly couple option is really tempting."

He scowled at me, setting his phone on the table. "And in the interim ... where are you staying? If you say you're planning on staying here, I'm going to take your ass home right this minute."

"Dad ..."

"I have a hotel room for the week, and I'll stay longer if need be. So you'll stay with me until we find you something."

"Dad ..."

"Don't give me that look and don't *Dad* me. Let's go get you what you need, grab some lunch, and get checked into the hotel."

"I'm twenty-one."

"And homeless. Get anything that's yours and let's go." He

stood, sliding his phone into his pocket.

For years, Dad was Daddy, and I was his little girl. My friends loved my daddy. They thought he was handsome. Then, as teenagers, they thought things about him that were very inappropriate and made me nauseous because ... he was my dad. When family said I'd marry a man just like my dad, I didn't like that either.

Seeing my dad, after meeting Slade Wylder, changed the way I looked at him. My dad was ripped. I didn't care to acknowledge it.

Again ... *my dad.*

He had elaborate tattoos and very countable abs. Rugged scruff covered his face most of the time—like Wylder's face. And his eyes were just as intense, but I never felt threatened.

Again ... *my dad.*

"Were you crazy about Mom? Did you feel protective of her?"

I knew her first husband abused her, but she never shared the details, just that I should find a man like my dad who would burn down the world to keep me safe. At the time, her advice fell on deaf ears.

He rubbed the back of his neck, exhibiting palpable discomfort from my questions. Aside from Jessica, I was the only one he would talk to about her—not that he did it willingly. I was pretty sure he felt I was genetically entitled to the information.

"Yes. I was crazy about her. And protective ... well ..." He shook his head. "That's an understatement."

I gathered the bags of clothes from the living room while Dad stood in the entrance with his hands casually in his back pockets. "Did you ever punch anyone to defend her honor ...

like a true *Knight?*"

"I did whatever it took to defend her honor and protect her." He grabbed a few of the bags when he realized I wasn't going to be able to carry all of them.

"And what did it take?" I led him to the back door, leaving the key on the table that Slade left for me. Clearly, I wasn't going to need it anytime soon. Not with protective Papa in town.

"Why are you so curious all of a sudden?" He opened the back to his rental vehicle.

"I don't know … I guess the fire has made me a little sentimental and a walk down memory lane is what I need."

That … and I wanted to know if he would have killed a man to save her. Like Slade did for me.

We loaded the bags and climbed into the SUV.

"Do you think you have what it takes to kill another person? I mean … I know you teach self-defense classes, but you know what they say. Those who can, do. Those who can't, teach."

Before he backed out of the driveway, he gave me a side glance with the most unreadable yet disturbing expression I had ever seen on his face. "If what you're really asking is … will I kill this guy Slade to keep you safe and out of harm's way? The answer is yes. I have what it takes."

I snorted a laugh. "I'm not sure you could take on Slade. He's younger and very strong."

"You realize … I'm not exactly weak, Livy. And strength is only one factor and not the most important one. Skill and mindset are the most dangerous weapons."

"Wow … Jessica said the same thing."

His forehead wrinkled. "She did?"

"Yeah ... uh ... I think it was when she gave me the rest of her good advice before I left for college."

It wasn't then ... it was weeks earlier when we were sparring, and she was kicking my ass with one hand tied behind her back.

"Where to first?" he asked.

"Phone. I need a phone. Then I need a new computer, and I sure as hell hope I can figure out how to retrieve my important files and school stuff from the magical cloud. Oh! And I need keys made for my Jeep. They were in the house."

Dad took care of everything, including finding all my computer files on the cloud and downloading them to my new computer. We enjoyed dinner at a great Ethiopian restaurant. Then we settled into our hotel room for the night.

I focused on my new phone, searching social media sites for Slade Wylder. No luck.

No phone number.

No way to contact him without going to his house—I didn't foresee my dad being cool with that.

I should have left him a note. After threatening to leave because of his mysterious female friend, then up and leaving with all of the things he bought me looked like that's exactly what I decided to do. I thought about his secrecy—his leaving without saying where he was going, what he was doing, or when he'd be home. And ... well ... I thought he could come home to a place without me and just deal with it.

Chapter Fifteen

AS IT HAPPENED, I didn't see Slade until Monday morning in the lecture hall where he strategically planted himself and Jericho where there were no empty seats around him ... and the asshole didn't save me a seat.

Apparently sucking dick didn't earn reserved seating.

Noted ...

He didn't leave class early. Maybe he felt trapped in the sea of students. Maybe he fell asleep. I'd noticed him drifting off several times. The downside to not making the early exit was the throng of students made it really hard to find him after class.

Staying true to the I-don't-owe-you-anything attitude, I didn't spend more than ten seconds looking for him before heading to my tree. I approached it with my head down, reading a text from Aubrey.

> **Her:** *They salvaged a handful of things from the fire that are yours. Possibly too damaged by smoke??? Go by the house after class and look through things.*
>
> **Me:** *K. Thx*

When I glanced up from my phone, Jericho trotted toward me with that irresistible smile as the light breeze caught my hair ... blowing in my face. The sexy man behind him ... not smiling so much. He sat with his back against the tree trunk, jean-clad legs stretched out and crossed ankles. His brief glance returned to the computer on his lap.

"Hi, baby." I bent over and kissed Jericho's head, giving his pointy ears the attention they deserved from me.

I strutted in my Wylder-purchased skinny jeans toward him, long-sleeved white tee with the arms pushed up to my elbows like he wore his long-sleeved shirts, and black boots. Straddling his crossed legs, I squatted while grabbing his laptop and setting it aside.

"Miss me?"

He rested his hands on the toes of my boots. "No."

Pressing my hands to his chest, I lowered my mouth to his, grinning while I hovered a breath away. "Liar." My mouth moved over his.

He didn't surrender so easily. I would have been disappointed if he had. My tongue traced the seam of his lips as my right hand moved to the nape of his neck, gently caressing his hair.

His fuse ran out, shifting his hands from my boots to my face. Our one-sided teasing kiss turned into him lashing me with his tongue—almost punishingly. When his left hand threaded through my hair, pulling it hard, my lips ripped away from his, and his mouth sucked and bit its way down my neck. I knew my life would be hell if he left any marks on me. My father wouldn't miss that.

"Where the fuck were you?" he whispered, his words coarse and chilling.

"To use some of your favorite words ... *it's none of your business.* However, I don't keep secrets from you. I'm awesome like that. So ... I'm staying at a hotel with my dad for the week. Longer if I don't find a place to stay."

He gripped my ass with his other hand and scooted me closer so his erection pressed between my legs. "You're staying with me." He nipped rather firmly on my exposed shoulder.

"I'm not sure my dad will go for that."

"Then he can go fuck himself."

I chuckled, closing my eyes because his mouth on me did really embarrassing things to my body. And I needed to focus on remembering where we were so I wouldn't go to town dry humping him. "I'm not sure my dad is the kind who willingly sulks off to fuck himself. If I relay your message, I think he'll be at your door, laser focused on fucking you up."

His mouth bent into a tiny smile against my skin. I did it. I fell for a guy with an ego as big, if not bigger, than my dad's. "I'm not worried about some elderly guy."

I pulled away, reaching back to remove his hand from my hair. "Um ... that's my dad you're talking about. He's in his fifties. That's not elderly. And he's in really good shape. I wouldn't take threats from him lightly."

"You think your dad's going to beat me up?" Slade's head canted to the side.

"Going to? No. I won't allow it. Capable?" I shrugged. "I'm not sure. I was thinking about that yesterday. Your age gives you the clear advantage, but my dad's really smart, and you might be more impulsive, which could put *you* at a disadvantage if you underestimate him."

"Fine. I won't underestimate him. But ... you're staying with me." His lips dragged along my neck.

"I can't."

"How old are you?"

"Twenty-one."

"Wrong," he murmured over my skin. "You're too old to

do what Daddy tells you to do."

"But I'm officially mature enough to make decisions based on common sense and kindness, not just strong-willed knee-jerk reactions." My fingers slid into his hair. "I love my dad. We're each other's rocks. We have been since my mom died. And I haven't seen him in months. He's done a lot for me since he's been here. And while he makes it seem like he's here just to make sure I get things settled, I know he's staying because he misses me. He misses my mom. I'm her. In his eyes, I'm the best of her. So ... I'm going to let him have that part of her for a week. It's a blink in time."

Wylder lifted his head as I caressed my fingers over his scruffy jawline. "You'll need my help studying ... a few hours ... every night."

I laughed. "I was valedictorian of my high school class. I'm here on a partial academic scholarship. I've never received anything but an A in a class ... ever. I'm pretty sure you need my help more than I need yours."

Lips parted, he drew his eyebrows together. "Studying is code for sex. Clearly, you're not as smart as you claim to be."

Tipping my chin, I gave him an unblinking expression. "I know what you meant. I just didn't appreciate being the one who needed pretend help in your little scenario."

"What if I graduated top of my class too? What if I'm a straight-A student too?"

My eyes widened. "Are you?"

"Fuck no. I'm just asking *what if.*"

More giggles ensued. I loved fun Wylder. "Well ... then our studying together excuse wouldn't be believable, so good thing I'm smarter."

"Book smart. Or maybe you just have a gifted memory. It

won't get you far in life if you're not street smart."

"I'm street smart." My head jerked back.

"A man tried to rape you."

"But he—" My words died on the spot.

And I knew ... I had always known. He never confirmed or denied it.

I just ... knew.

Yet his unintentional admission knocked my emotions on their ass. I wasn't prepared to deal with one hundred percent certainty.

"Wylder ..."

He shook his head. "Stop with your theories of my heroism."

"Wylder ..." I whispered as a couple tears escaped.

"Don't." His head continued to ease side to side. "You said it yourself ... I heard about it on campus. The rumors."

"Wylder ..."

"Liv—"

"There was a knife. He demanded my wallet. I never told you he tried to rape me. And I know my friends never said anything. *That* wasn't the rumor."

He took a hard swallow while letting his gaze drift off in the distance just over my shoulder.

I wiped my face. "He could have killed me."

"He didn't." His tone sounded as distant and unemotional as his blank, unfocused eyes.

"And why is that?" I let myself believe my gut feeling—that voice in the recesses of my mind—was enough; I didn't need to hear him say the actual words.

I was wrong.

I needed the words.

His focus returned to me. Steadfast, steely-eyed Slade returned. "Because your life wasn't his to take."

His words echoed in my head as I tried to figure out what to do with them. "Was *his* life *yours* to take?"

"Yes." His immediate absolution gave me pause.

If I killed someone, I would have second-guessed *everything ... forever.*

Slade answered me with the ease of confirming he took out the trash or brushed his teeth before bed.

With his honesty exposed, I took my chance on a few other pressing questions. "Are you a drug dealer?"

"What do you think?"

"I think I deserve a straight answer."

"So ... yes. You think I'm a drug dealer."

I shook my head. "I didn't say that."

"No. You asked it; so in your mind, it's a possibility."

"That's not fair." I stood. Taking a few steps back, both physically and emotionally.

"I haven't asked you if you're a whore or an escort. I haven't asked if you torture animals."

"Wh-what are you talking about?" My fingers combed through my hair as I closed my eyes and tried to make sense of our conversation.

"I know there's no way you'd sell your body for money or torture animals, so I don't need proof and I don't need to ask you."

Parking a hand on my side, I used my other hand to pinch my lower lip for a few seconds as I watched Jericho shift on the grass, resting his head on the ground. "Where were you the week I watched Jericho for you? Where were you the day my dad arrived?"

"I can't tell you."

"Why?"

"Because I'd lose my job if I told you."

"That's ridiculous." My arms crossed over my chest.

"I deliver things."

"Drugs?"

"No." He leaned his head back against the tree trunk and closed his eyes.

"Underage girls?"

"No."

My outrageous question didn't make him flinch. That fed the toxic lump in the bottom of my stomach. If *underage girls* didn't make him flinch, even a little bit, then he wasn't working part-time for UPS, accommodating the Amazon addictions of the masses.

"Is it legal? Your job?"

Dropping his chin, he opened his eyes and studied me for several seconds. "It's a gray area."

Forcing out a long, exasperated breath, I pivoted. "I have class."

"Are we studying tonight?"

Before I had the chance to turn toward him, he was at my back, his hands sliding around my waist, his face burrowing into my neck.

"Why should I?" I bristled.

His lips ghosted along my ear. "Because it was me."

Because it was me ...

Because it was me ...

Because it was me ...

It took me a few seconds to blink, swallow, or breathe for that matter. "Wylder ..." I interlaced my fingers with his at my waist. "I have a feeling you're not going to like this ... but I'm not going to be able to stop myself from doing it anyway."

"What's that?"

"Loving you."

His grip on me loosened. I let my hands drop from his, giving him space. When I no longer felt any part of him touching me, I forced my feet forward.

Right. Left. Right. Left.

No glances back.

No making my case.

No more words.

I wasn't asking for permission to love him.

I wasn't asking him to love me back.

I wasn't asking for anything.

Chapter Sixteen

Wylder

"I'M NOT A babysitter." I slid into the booth at the back of the dark, third-rate cafe, just before the dinner rush. The clattering of plates and blend of conversations provided its own privacy. The stench of overcooked grease hung heavily in the air.

Abe flicked his lighter several times, knowing damn well he wasn't allowed to smoke in the restaurant. It gave him something to do with his fidgety hands. "Last I checked, you're whatever I need you to be."

The waitress brought me ice water. "Ready to order?"

I shook my head. "Not eating."

"Okay." She took my menu.

He dunked several fries into ketchup and shoved them into his mouth, licking his sausage fingers. "What's the most important thing I've taught you?"

"Patience," I answered without emotion, keeping my gaze trained to the patrons coming and going instead of the bitter man opposite me.

"Yes. Patience. I've thrown you a few bones."

"Amateur shit. You didn't need me to do it."

"True. I knew you needed it to stay focused."

"Focused on what?" My attention returned to him.

"The girl."

"When are you going to tell me about her?"

He wiped his mouth and slurped his soda. "Since when am I required to give you detailed information? We've gone over this a million times. The less you know, the better."

"Better for who?" I tossed the straw out of my water glass and gulped down half of it.

"Everyone involved. Are you keeping her safe?"

I chewed on a piece of ice for several seconds before shrugging one shoulder. "She's alive."

"Thanks to you." He smirked.

I didn't share his odd amusement. Instead, I blew out an exasperated breath. "Why did you need to see me?"

"Her dad's in town."

"I know."

"Have you met him?"

"No."

"Good. Let's keep it that way."

"Why?"

He gave me a look. I hated that fucking look. It wasn't simply that he kept me in the dark. It was the way he made it seem like doing so was protecting me. I found knowledge to be empowering. Maybe he liked having all the power.

"Things could get uncomfortable if you meet him."

I bit my tongue for a few seconds, knowing he wasn't going to answer my question if it was too broad like, "Why?" So I tried to figure it out on my own and present it to him in a way that I could at least read his reaction enough to see if I was at least warm. "Her dad hired you, didn't he? To watch over her? Is she in danger?"

"Cast away, boy ... I'm not going to bite. Just do as you're told. Keep her safe but keep your distance from her father. We'll be in touch when the status quo needs to change again."

"I'm sick of this."

He tossed the napkin down along with thirty dollars cash and scooted out of the booth. "Poor boy … must be exhausting having that sweet piece of ass suck your dick all night."

I stiffened.

As he started to dawdle past me to the restrooms, he rested a hand on my shoulder. "It's fine. You've earned it."

That rubbed me all the wrong fucking ways but acknowledging it would have only proven his point that I wasn't emotionally ready to deal with knowing everything.

～～

As SOON AS we got home, Jericho ran to the back door like he knew something I didn't. Of course, he did.

"Did you already eat?" Livy sat on the back step looking like the life I would never have, hot as fuck in a low-cut tank top, cut-off denim shorts, and partially dried hair—long, blond, and so fucking gorgeous.

"Been playing in the waves?" I lifted a brow, sidestepping her and the pizza box on her lap to unlock the back door.

"Duh …" She stood.

"I gave you a key. Why did you leave it on the table?"

"Didn't think I'd need it since I knew I wasn't staying, but I'm rethinking that." She followed me into the kitchen, bringing fennel and cheese aroma with her.

"Too late. It was a one-time offer." I tossed my keys onto the counter.

She ignored my verbal jab, which made her exponentially more attractive. While I didn't mind keeping an eye on her, I didn't want to deal with a twenty-four-seven damsel in distress.

"Beer?" I held out a bottle with the fridge door open.

"No. I don't drink."

"No?" I closed the door and opened my bottle of beer.

"After my mom died, my dad drank. A lot. I had a shitty relationship with alcohol before I ever graduated from high school."

"I see."

She blew out a long breath. "So ... what class are you struggling with the most? That's where we should start tonight." She set the pizza box on the counter and hopped up beside it instead of sitting at the table.

I wedged myself between her legs and grabbed her wrist, redirecting the slice from her mouth to mine. She frowned as I took an overly indulgent bite. Her thumb wiped the side of my mouth.

"I think we should do something different. I think I should teach you some self-defense skills."

She snorted. "I'm good. I could probably teach you a few things."

As if there weren't seven other pieces of pizza in the box, I stole the rest of her slice after she managed one tiny bite. "Because your dad teaches people how to use pepper spray?" Folding it in half, I stuffed the rest of the slice into my mouth.

She scowled at my thievery. "No. My Aunt Jessica has taught me a few things. In fact, she'll be back next week, after my dad leaves, to train me."

"*Train* you?" I failed at hiding the amusement in my tone. "Is your aunt close to your dad's age?"

Livy nodded. "Really close. They're twins."

"Is she a martial arts instructor or something?"

"No. She's an actuary."

"An actuary? For the mafia or something?"

She chuckled. "No. But she was … *attacked* many years ago and learned to defend herself. She's a total badass."

I took another slice of pizza, and she grabbed my wrist, like I did to her, and took the first bite, grinning at the same time.

"So are you going to show me your moves?" I asked.

"I don't want to hurt you."

"I'm not too concerned."

"It's not like I'm ready to snap anyone's neck or anything like that. Jess said that's a ways down the road. I need to work on my strength before I can do that."

I released something between a cough and a laugh. "Wow … she's going to teach you to snap someone's neck? That's … interesting." I stepped back. "Hop down. Show me your moves."

"Why?"

"Because I want to know that she's not giving you false confidence."

On an eye roll, she hopped off the counter. "Okay. Attack me."

I grinned. Slowly and gently, I grabbed her arm to jerk her toward me. In a flash I ended up with a bloodied nose. She didn't break it, but fuck … it stung a bit as my eyes watered. I wasn't expecting it. In fact, I went out of my way to not hurt *her.*

"Oh shit! I'm sorry. I … I didn't know how to show you without actually doing that to you. Wylder … I'm so sorry." She grabbed the towel from the counter and ran to the freezer to get ice.

I pushed her hand away when she tried to blot the blood

and hand me the ice. "I'm fine." Taking the towel from her, I dumped the ice into the sink and blotted my nose. It wasn't a lot of blood, but I couldn't hide my shock that she drew blood. And really fucking quickly. If I were fighting a bear, I'd come prepared for a bear. This was like going to pet a kitten and a goddamn mountain lion appeared out of nowhere.

"Wylder …" Her nose scrunched.

I held the towel to my left nostril. "Good girl."

Her concern slowly morphed into a tiny smile. "Yeah?"

I nodded, tossing the towel aside, no longer feeling blood trickling out of my nose. "An actuary, huh?"

"Yes." She lifted onto her toes and wrapped her arms around my neck. "Forgive me? Can I kiss it? Lick your wound?"

My hands slid around her back, finding their favorite place on her ass. "You can lick something, but it's not my nose."

White teeth peeked out from her red lips as she ran her tongue along the bottom one in anticipation of my mouth on hers. "I have a curfew. If you need something licked, we'd better get to it."

"A curfew?" I lifted her like a monkey hugging my body and headed toward the stairs.

"Yeah. Dad said since we're sharing a hotel room he expects a little courtesy."

"What time?" I bit her lower lip and sucked it into my mouth as we reached the top of the stairs.

"Ten."

Depositing her on my bed, I grabbed her wrist and read the time on her watch. "It's eight thirty." Her nose wrinkled like it did whenever she assumed I was upset.

"Sorry. It's my life for the week. He retrieved my schoolwork from that mystical cloud. I owe him ten o'clock."

"Fine." I unbuttoned my pants.

"Will you tie me to your bed?" She shrugged off her shirt.

I paused my hands, certain I didn't hear her correctly.

She shimmied out of her shorts and panties then reached around to unhook her bra. "Jessica said that after her incident she had some serious issues with being restrained, and it fed her need for control, which ended up making her emotionally fucked-up. So … she said if I'm ever in a healthy, trusting sexual relationship, it might be a good idea to practice staying calm while being restrained." Walking on her knees to the edge of the bed, she pushed my shirt up, kissing my chest while I pulled it the rest of the way off with a bit of hesitation.

"Yeah …" My hands pressed to her cheeks, forcing her to look up at me before they disappeared into her hair. "If you find a healthy, trusting sexual relationship … you should definitely practice staying calm while being restrained."

"Wylder …" Her fingers eased down my abs, one bump at a time.

"I'm not him, Livy."

Her gaze dropped as she deflated.

"I'll tie you up, but you shouldn't trust me in that way."

"Why?" she whispered as the weight of her disappointment kept her chin tipped toward her chest—along with me … the anchor that threatened to pull her to the bottom of the ocean.

Drowning her dreams.

Obliterating her hope.

Suffocating her existence.

"I'm not a trusting-relationship guy."

She shook her head. "You saved me."

"I killed a man to do it."

"Because you love me." The gold flecks in her deep brown eyes shined when she lifted her gaze to mine.

"Because it's ..." I stopped short of the truth.

I could protect her.

I could fuck her.

I could be her illusion.

But I couldn't tell her the truth. It wasn't my job to tell her the truth.

"It's what?" Her fingers teased the palms of my hands hanging limp at my sides.

With a smile that felt sad but completely real, I interlaced our fingers and guided our hands behind her back. Her chest pressed into my stomach as her head fell back. "It's fucked-up, Liv," I whispered, my mouth descending upon hers. "It's my job to make sure no one ever ties you up," I murmured a breath away before kissing her.

Chapter Seventeen

Livy

"SAY SOMETHING ROMANTIC." I grinned, shimmying back into my shorts as Wylder stared at me from the bed—white sheet tangled around his legs and midsection, head propped up on his arm.

"Wrong guy." He shook his head like I should have known better.

No tying up.

No whispered words to make my heart swoon.

I twisted my lips to hide my frown. "Fine. What are you thinking right now?"

"Nothing romantic."

With a slight roll of my eyes, I grumbled, "Just tell me."

"I don't know. A couple things are playing around in my head at the moment."

"And they are?" I finished hooking my bra and pulled my tank top over my head.

Scratching his chin, he smirked. Wylder with a mischievous grin and naked in bed … it had to be a dream. I'd had many dreams about him long before he offered me the slightest act of kindness.

"I'm thinking about the rest of the pizza downstairs."

I laughed. "And?"

"And I think after you get settled and your dad goes home, we should see if you're really as good at surfing as you say you are."

There was no way I could have predicted that. I shoved my shoulders back and plastered a confident, maybe even a little cheesy, grin on my face. "Oh, Wylder ... the only thing I'm better at than sex is surfing."

On a throaty chuckle, he sat up and pulled on his jeans sans underwear. "Interesting comparison."

"Sex and surf are life." I checked my watch and hustled my ass down the stairs with twenty minutes to get back to the hotel. "When are you going to tell me what you're building in the garage? Or where your family lives? Or your favorite dessert? Basically *anything*?" I slipped on my shoes and grabbed my phone and keys from the counter.

He flipped open the pizza box and folded a piece in half before taking a monstrous bite while offering me nothing but a shrug.

"I'm going to start charging you for sex. You tell me something personal about yourself, and I'll give you some of this." I waved a hand up and down my body as I backed up toward the door. "And here you thought I wasn't a whore who charged for sex." I winked.

"Where're you going?" He wiped his mouth with the back of his hand.

"I told you. Ten o'clock curfew."

"I hate that your dad has that kind of power over you."

"He'd say the same thing about you." I grinned.

"Stay." He scratched his bare skin below his navel, drawing my attention to his happy trail.

Not fair.

"Nope." I shook my head but failed to keep my gaze away from his hand.

"Oatmeal chocolate chip."

Tearing my attention from his partially fastened jeans back to his face, I squinted. "What?"

"My favorite dessert is oatmeal chocolate chip cookies."

"Really? Huh ... wouldn't have guessed that. Thanks. See you in the morning."

"Livy ..." He drew out my name like a warning.

"I have to go." I wrinkled my nose.

"I just paid for *something*."

"Noted. The bank is closed. But you can make a withdrawal tomorrow." Turning, I opened the door.

"Orange zest." Wylder's voice closed in behind me. Just his nearness made me shiver ... made my pulse pound harder and faster. "My mom used to make oatmeal chocolate chip cookies. And I didn't know why I loved them more than anything I'd ever had at a bakery or friend's house. Then she told me her secret ingredient—orange zest." He pressed his naked chest to my back.

I reacted by leaning forward, the door closing under my weight. "Wylder ..."

"That's two things about me. You made the rules. I expect you to follow them. Clothes off, Liv ..." His hands pressed to the door above my head. I turned in the cage of his body towering over mine. His stance did all kinds of perfect things to his torso, including forcing his loose jeans down another inch.

I wasn't sure who had the most formidable expression—Jackson Knight or Slade Wylder. All I knew for certain was both men were playing me. Dad and his guilt trip. Slade and his ... *everything*.

My hands pulled at the button to my shorts as I held his gaze, a slight bend at the corners of his mouth signaling his pleasure at winning.

In his dreams ...

"On your knees, Wylder."

One of his thick, perfectly shaped brows lifted at my demand.

"Knees. Wylder." I kept a poker face.

Being ... *him* ... he drew out the standoff for nearly a minute before taking one knee and then a second knee. My hands parked at my sides, refusing to do anything else. He slid down my shorts and panties, lifting my foot to free them from one leg. Instead of releasing my leg, he lifted it over his shoulder. My hands pressed flat to the door at my back to steady myself.

He wasn't gentle or teasing.

"Fuuuck!" I sucked in a sharp breath and held it as his mouth attacked me. My fingers drove into his hair with the same force his tongue speared into me.

He bit my clit. I yelled.

I dug my nails into his scalp. He growled.

One of his hands kept my left leg spread open on his shoulder while his other hand gripped my ass.

He denied me again and again, brutally taking me to the edge then pulling back until I wanted to cry *and* kill him.

Oh the stars ...

He may have been physically on his knees, but there was little question as to who surrendered ... who had control.

My head fell back onto the door, jaw slack, eyes closed. He eased my leg from his shoulder, holding my hips for a few seconds until I found my balance. Then he worked my panties and shorts back up my legs. I could have helped him, but I didn't. Wylder seemed to know what he was doing. And I ... well, I was still drunk on the way he made me feel.

"Oops ..." He grabbed my wrist to look at my watch as he stood. "Ten-oh-five. My bad. Please tell your dad it was my fault."

I remembered Jessica's words. *"Sometimes our greatest strength is to know when to surrender."* Snarky, arrogant, sass-filled comebacks flooded my thoughts. He had one goal ... to prove he had more influence over my actions than my dad.

Maybe that night he did, but I didn't let him make it about my dad. Wylder told me something personal. Cookies? Yes. But sometimes the simple things defined us more than tangled webs of scars and bruises.

Instead of taking the bait, I slid my hands into the back pockets of his jeans and pressed my lips to his chest over his heart. "I like peanut butter cookies. Rolled in *lots* of sugar. And someday I'm going to be president. Unless I meet a nice, rich guy who buys me an island and lets me surf every day for the rest of my life. Night, Wylder."

"HE'S MAKING IT hard for me to like him," Dad said from his bed when I eased open the hotel room door. The TV screen illuminated his tattooed chest from his propped-up position on his bed, and the residual aroma of microwave popcorn lingered in the air—the frigid hotel room air.

I didn't need to see his face well to know displeasure marred it.

"Because I'm twenty-minutes late? Because you haven't met him? Because I think he's you in your twenties?" I plugged my phone in to charge and plopped down onto my bed. "Only less slutty, I hope."

"Watch it."

I giggled. "I like him. A lot."

"He'll break your heart."

Scooting onto my side and bunching up the pillow to rest my head, I gazed at him while he swiveled his head toward me.

"Did you ever break Mom's heart?"

Drawing in a slow breath, he released it in a deep whoosh of air.

"And for the record ... I already know that you did. So don't lie." I didn't know any more than just the fact that he did break her heart on more than one occasion.

"I kept some things from her. Told her half-truths. Stupid on my part."

"But she forgave you. She found something good and redeemable in you."

He grunted, shaking his head. "I'm not sure what. But ... yes. She did."

"So if she wouldn't have put her heart out there for you to break, you wouldn't have ended up together. I wouldn't exist. And ..." I bit my lips together.

And you wouldn't be a lonely widower.

Sitting up, I moved over to his bed. Lifting his arm, I wedged myself under it. The safest place in the world. "I know you don't regret it, but do you ever wonder why? Why did you fight so hard for something only to have it taken from you? Does the fragility of life ever scare you?"

"Only one thing scares me."

I rested my cheek on his chest, snaking my arms around his torso as far as they would reach. "What's that?"

"You."

"Dad ..." I whispered, feeling melancholy from our conversation.

He kissed my head. "I know you think I'm overprotective, but there is *nothing* I wouldn't do to protect you."

"I know. And I love you for it."

Chapter Eighteen

"IT'S FINE." I shrugged as we walked around the house Aubrey's parents bought to replace the one destroyed in the fire. "And it's cheap rent."

Aubrey's jaw dropped. "*Fine*? Uh ... it's bigger than the last house and it has an infinity pool. What's not to love?" She unpacked the new dishes. New everything.

And yes, there was a beautiful infinity pool.

My bedroom was twice the size, and I didn't have to share a bathroom.

And it was so close to campus, I wouldn't need to take a scooter or worry about parking my Jeep.

It just wasn't on the same street as Wylder and Jericho. They were in walking distance if I wanted to walk five miles each way.

"It's fine. Nice. Totally acceptable." I loaded the new bowls she handed to me and arranged them in the dishwasher.

"Slade's dick won't reach quite so easily." Missy snickered, lugging the last box into the kitchen.

"A guy? You don't like the house because of a guy?" Aubrey's scolding tone rose a notch.

"Dude ..." I shook my head while frowning at Missy. Not because she was wrong—because she called me out on it. "I said it's fine. That doesn't mean I don't like it. And for the record ... his dick is pretty fucking amazing. It just might reach."

We fell into a giggling fit. The girls drank wine. And I kept checking my phone for a message from Mr. Five-Mile-Long Dick. He'd been out of town on "business" again. Dad left earlier that morning, content with our new place and rather gleeful about the five-mile distance to the firehouse.

"You have to just ask him," Kara grabbed my phone and started typing.

"No!" I reached for it, but she turned in circles twice before running out the back door and around the pool like a race-track.

"Give. It. I'm not chasing you." With my hands planted on my hips, I waited for her to do whatever destruction she felt she needed to do.

"What are you doing?" I huffed as she taunted me from the opposite side of the pool, eyes glued to my phone screen. "I don't care if he's home or not."

"You do. And I want him to reply before I give it back, so you don't send off a take-back message."

"What did you type?"

"Wait ..." She held up a finger. "He's typing."

"You're a terrible person. You know that, right?"

"Oh my god! Total asshole!" She covered her mouth with her hand. Wide, blue eyes pinned me with a look of complete horror.

"WHAT. Did. You. Say?" I stomped my bare feet toward her.

"I ... uh ... said he needed to disclose his location so I ... uh ... *you* ... could decide if he would be dicking you tonight or if someone else needed to fill in until he returned."

Snatching the phone from her, I rolled my eyes. "Nice. Really nice." My brow furrowed as I read his reply.

Do what you need to do.

"Wow. Okay. That's …"

Kara cringed, lips pressed together. "Does that mean he's doing what he needs to do? Are you two not exclusive?"

"I don't know what we are."

"Maybe you need to have that talk."

"Talk," I murmured, contemplating whether or not I should respond, let him know I didn't send the original message. What if I had been the one to send it? "Yeah, Wylder isn't exactly the best talker."

"It was just a joke. Clearly. But that response …" Kara crossed her arms over her chest. "Not cool. Maybe you should find better company tonight. Show him you won't be treated that way."

Tucking my phone into my back pocket, I pivoted to return to the kitchen. "I'm not going to screw some other guy to make a point. Remember how well that worked for me last time? Besides … I do have better company." I smiled over my shoulder, and she hugged me from behind.

"Girl time!"

After we finished unpacking, I forced myself to put on my best face while we grabbed dinner and stocked up on groceries. One sober and three moderately drunk college girls.

Let's just say we bought way too much junk food. I knew green smoothie Aubrey would not be happy that I didn't make everyone stick to our list. We put the groceries away with music blaring, wine flowing, and me missing Wylder and Jerry so bad it angered me.

Why? Why did I let him or the *lack* of him affect me so

much?

"One glass …" Missy giggled, singing all the wrong lyrics to Blake Shelton as she held out a nearly empty bottle of wine while twirling in a circle next to the pool. Thankfully, it had a cover. I might have been able to save one drunk girl, but not three. The other two sipped more wine and stared at their phone screens from lounge chairs under strings of white and blue lights, blankets draped over their legs to keep the nip of the cool evening at bay.

"I'm good." I grabbed the bottle from Missy before she dropped it. Then I proceeded to pick up some trash from our late-night snack attack.

"Is he a drunk? Your dad. You've never elaborated," Kara murmured from her chair, chin tipped into her phone.

"No," I returned while shoving the empty licorice bag into the empty salt and pepper potato chip bag. "He just—"

"Corbin's coming over!" Aubrey jumped out of her chair. "Oh my god. I need to sober up. Shit …" She ran her fingers through her hair. "How do I look?" She giggled, swaying a bit. "Why? Why on my wine night? Do I smell like wine?" Lifting her arm, she sniffed her pit.

I laughed, the only one to see her odd behavior.

"Do we have to go to our rooms, Mom?" Kara snorted something like a giggle and a cough.

"Water, bae. Lots of water." I grabbed Aubrey's hand and led her into the kitchen.

"I'll have a full bladder." She reluctantly took a few sips. "Then I'll have to pee right after we … you know. Then he'll sneak out. He always sneaks out."

"You won't have to pee." Missy swayed, making her way into the kitchen with her empty wine glass and Aubrey's empty

Pinot bottle. "Not if he gives you an orgasm."

"Why? I'm going to pee if I orgasm?" Aubrey's nose wrinkled, showing her lack of sexual experience and apparently her lack of orgasms.

"I hope not." Missy chuckled. "When you climax, your body releases vasopressin, an antidiuretic hormone, which makes it hard to pee."

"Huh ..." Aubrey's head cocked to the side. "I've never had that issue."

"Poor baby." I guided the water bottle toward her mouth. "Drink up, and if he doesn't give you an orgasm ... pee on him."

Missy leaned against the counter, glazed-over eyes lifting to meet my gaze. I returned a tight grin, that sympathetic one for our friend who was orgasm deficient.

While Kara and Missy retired to their rooms, I made a peanut butter sandwich—knowing I'd be grateful for the extra energy when surfing early the next morning. Aubrey sobered up in the shower for Corbin, the surf shop owner whom Aubrey adored. Given the recent orgasm revelation, I couldn't figure out *why* she adored him. She didn't even surf. Maybe he was good at cuddling.

When the bell rang, I took a huge bite of my sandwich and set it on the counter to let Corbin in for his bootie call.

"Oh ..." I mumbled, covering my mouth, unable to say anything with peanut butter thoroughly coating every inch of my mouth.

"If you're done being *dicked*, I thought we could take a drive." Wylder gazed down at me.

Before I could finish chewing or even blink because I couldn't believe he was there, Corbin sauntered up the drive behind him. His overbearing cologne reached the doorway before he did.

"Hey, Livy."

I nodded at him, attempting to swallow. It was possible I overdid the peanut butter.

Wylder turned a fraction, eyeing stocky Corbin, a good five inches shorter than Slade. "This the guy who thinks he's going to *dick* you?"

Nearly choking, I slapped my hand on my chest as I swallowed repeatedly. There was something quite hilarious about Slade Wylder and his intimidating presence using the word "dicked."

"No ..." My tongue swiped around my mouth several times. "He's here to dick Aubrey."

Corbin's face wrinkled as his uneasy smile quivered. "Um ... I ... where is Aubrey?"

"Upstairs. She jumped into the shower because she had too much wine." I managed to get my normal speech back. "Go on up."

Without any introduction, Corbin squeezed past me and Slade. It had been five days since I'd seen my menacing lover. I had so many questions, like how did he expect to pass his classes if he missed them so often? Of course, I wanted to know where he'd been and if Miss Lexus was with him.

But ... mostly I just wanted to feel his arms wrapped around me, smell the cedar and spice in the crook of his neck, and taste the mint on his tongue.

"I didn't send you the text, dumbass." I smirked, grabbed a handful of his shirt, and tugged him inside the house.

"Dumbass?" He raised an eyebrow.

I lifted onto my toes, keeping my hand clenched to his

black tee. "Shut up and kiss me."

Something unreadable ghosted along his face for five seconds before he gave me his mouth. My arms wrapped around his neck as his hands slid to my ass, lifting me up to hug him like a bear in their favorite tree. He pressed my back to the entry wall, void of anything on it yet, and angled his head, deepening the kiss on a low groan.

When he tore his lips from mine, they moved down my neck. I drew in a harsh gasp from that kiss.

"You taste like peanut butter."

My fingers laid claim to his hair, slowly working up the back of his head, as his scruffy face tickled my skin, lips teasing my shoulder. "I love peanut butter."

"What if I don't?"

"Then you may never kiss me again."

His head snapped up, putting us nose to nose, but he didn't say anything. I rubbed my lips together, and if he couldn't see the sparkle in my eyes, then he had to be blind. Wylder lit up every inch of me. I wasn't sure which I feared more: him reading my clear feelings or him missing them.

"Where were you?" I whispered, hoping for something. Hoping he'd give me another inch into his life.

He shook his head slowly, gaze glued to mine.

A labyrinth.

An uncrackable code.

"Wylder …" I leaned my forehead against his, my palms pressed to his face. "Tell me something. *Anything.*"

"I missed you," he whispered before lifting his chin to brush his lips over mine.

It wasn't an explanation. It wasn't the inch I wanted.

But … it was something.

Being missed by Wylder made me feel pretty fucking special because he didn't seem like the kind of guy who missed anything or anyone.

My mouth curled into a grin against his. "Well ... *I* missed Jerry. Where is he? And where are you taking me? It's nearly midnight."

"Grab your wet suit. We'll be back in the morning."

"You stealing me for the night?"

He set me on my feet, rested his hands on my shoulders, and turned me toward the stairs. "Go," he said, giving me a gentle nudge.

Three steps up, I turned. "Don't you want to see my new room? My new bed?"

"You're wasting time." He leaned his shoulder against the wall and slipped his hands into the pockets of his dark jeans.

I didn't take time to protest or even offer a frown because I was too excited.

Knock. Knock.

I softly rapped my knuckles against Missy's door. "I'll be back tomorrow. Wylder is here."

"K ..." she mumbled in a groggy voice.

After throwing stuff into my backpack, I slung it over my shoulder and floated down the stairs, failing to contain a single ounce of my excitement. "Ready."

He remained in place, propped against the wall. Hands in pockets. All of Wylder's expressions involved an underlying concentration. Even when he made the rare move of smiling, his brow held onto a certain amount of tension. It felt like every decision he made was somehow life or death.

"What?" I tilted my head, slowing my last few steps to him. And just like that ... he let a flicker of happiness settle along his face.

For me.

"Nothing." He pushed off the wall and lifted my backpack from my shoulder, carrying it in one hand as I shut and locked the front door.

Then, in pure Slade Wylder-style, he showed his romantic side without saying a word by taking my hand and leading me down the driveway. It was the most intimate thing he had done to me, and that said a lot because his mouth had touched me everywhere.

"Where is your car?"

"Home."

"We're walking five miles?"

"No." He stopped at a sprinter van with surfboards on top, released my hand, and unlocked the doors.

"Whose is this?"

"A friend's."

"You have friends? Aside from me and Jericho?"

As he grabbed the handle to the sliding door, he gave me a look. The darkness prevented me from seeing it well, but I felt it. He wasn't amused by my comment.

"An acquaintance let me borrow it." As he slid open the door, Jericho popped his head up from his bed nestled under the raised bed in the back. A tiny sink, single burner, and a shelf with a few hooks occupied the middle of the van with a boho rug on the floor.

"Hey, Jerry. I missed you." I hopped in and kneeled by his bed, which was behind a secure gate for travel.

He poked his snout out at me and licked my cheek.

"Get up front and fasten in so we can go," Wylder said just before tossing my bag on the floor and shutting the door.

As he climbed into the driver's seat, I shimmied up the middle and hopped into the other seat, fastening my seat belt and slipping off my flip-flops before propping my feet up on the dash.

"Is this your thing?" I asked as he pulled away from the curb.

"My thing?"

"Taking your girlfriends camping in a van?"

"Girlfriends?"

"Yes, Wylder. How long was your longest relationship?"

"Relationships like that aren't part of my life."

I glanced over at him as he kept his eyes on the road. "Like what? Exclusive? Monogamous?"

His lips twisted a bit before he nodded slowly several times.

"What are we?"

He reached forward and adjusted the temperature on the dash. "We're two people who don't have to talk about what *we* are."

"So ..." I weighed my words. It wasn't that I wanted to have the relationship conversation with him, but I also didn't want to be the stupid girl being loyal to a man who was off screwing other people. *Doing what he needed to do ...* "Even though I wasn't the one to type or send the message to you, the reply you sent was honest. You don't care if I'm with other guys when you're not with me?"

"I don't have the time or luxury of caring."

So. Fucking. Vague.

"Do you have the time or luxury of sleeping with other women when you're not with me?"

He gave me the worst answer. No answer. Not one word.

So we drove in silence. Him being ... him. Unbothered by

166

frivolous things like relationships. I needed something more than blind trust. And that was just it … I didn't know if Slade expected me to trust him.

When we pulled off the road onto a small space nestled on a bluff overlooking the ocean, Slade jockeyed the van so the back faced the water. I unbuckled and climbed in back to assess the true sleeping situation in case I needed to sleep with Jericho instead of Wylder.

It wasn't that he'd said anything wrong. It was that he didn't say anything right. It was that he said nothing at all.

He climbed out and opened the back doors, letting Jericho free to do his business. Then he came around and opened the sliding door.

We stared in silence for a few seconds while I leaned against the cabinet and drew my knees to my chest. As if he read me like the most transparent human ever, he exhaled slowly. "What do you need?"

He wasn't alluding to something I forgot to pack. Us. He wanted to know what I needed out of us.

Truth? I didn't know.

I'd allowed myself to be with a man who tried to keep me at arm's length for the longest time. I wormed my way into his life without knowing exactly what I did need from him.

"Do you want another man sticking his dick in me?"

He rested his hands on the top of the van for a few seconds, glancing around to keep an eye on Jericho and maybe searching the dark or the moon's reflection on the water for an answer to my simple question.

I waited, a knot tightening in my stomach as each second passed. My gut waited for his answer, which I kind of knew would be "whatever you need."

Wylder faced me again, digging his teeth into his bottom lip while moving his head side to side.

A smile crept up my face as I leaned forward, lifting onto my knees and inching closer to him. As I slid his shirt up his chest, my lips pressed over his heart. "Then I want it on the record ..."

He grabbed the hem of his shirt and pulled it the rest of the way off, dropping it to the floor of the van before threading his hands through my hair as I looked up at him.

"... that I don't want you sticking your dick in some other woman without giving me advance notice. Deal?"

He dipped his head and kissed me just below my ear, holding my hair away from my neck. "Advance notice?"

My fingers worked the button to his jeans as my eyes drifted shut from the shiver his breath on my neck elicited. "A text. Voicemail. Postcard."

"Noted." He peeled my tee from my torso. Slowly. Like we had all the time in the world. And that night, atop the bluff overlooking my favorite place in the world, it felt like we could stop time and steal that idle moment forever.

As the cool, thick ocean air beckoned tiny bumps along my skin, he slid the straps of my bra off my shoulders, following the strap on my left with his lips. Patient Wylder.

I liked him.

Too much.

One hand cupped my breast, the rough pad of his thumb dipping under the fabric to brush against my nipple.

Slow.

So. Fucking. Slow.

"Jericho," he called lifting his mouth from my shoulder for a nanosecond.

Like the best dog ever, he hopped in the back, into his bed. Wylder continued to seduce me one kiss, one gentle touch at a time. When we were in nothing but panties and briefs, he whispered in my ear, "Get in bed."

I stole one more kiss from his perfect lips before pulling back, my breaths chasing one another. He shut the sliding door as I climbed into the bed. When he reached the back of the van, he closed the door to Jericho's area and climbed into the bed with me, carefully ducking his head since there wasn't much space above us. Then he pulled the magnetic screen over the entire opening, allowing us to see out without the bugs getting inside.

A perfect night. The perfect place.

When he rolled toward me, both of us on our sides, he did something so fucking glorious my heart stopped as my mind fought to recognize the man next to me.

He grinned from ear to ear. Seriously … who was that guy?

"Hi," he said.

There was nothing, and I mean *nothing*, I could have done to stop my heart from diving headfirst into everything Slade Wylder. It was like all the times I paddled out to catch a wave knowing there were sharks beneath me. The high made it worth the risk.

"Hi." I mirrored his grin a breath before he kissed me.

We kissed forever. He pulled me on top of him. And we kissed more. I felt him hard between my legs, the cotton of his briefs and my panties masking very little—serving only as a temporary barrier to build the moment, stoking the fire.

"Wylder …" I slid my hand down the front of his briefs, drawing a sharp breath from him followed by a long moan. "You suck at not being romantic."

His hands tangled in my long hair (where I loved them most) as I kissed down his chest.

"You suck at not being sexy." My mouth gave his abs some love as I stroked him.

He said nothing as I removed his briefs, but the second I slid my panties off, he flipped us over, settling between my legs, mouth working its way up my chest to my neck. We were cramped for space, but we made it work, pressing our bodies as close together as possible. He entered me so agonizingly slow I could barely take it.

The man hovering over me wasn't fucking me on the landing of his stairs or against his back door. This was different.

And I just ... couldn't ... take it.

"Wylder," I whispered as he started to move, each thrust slow and meaningful.

"Livy," he whispered back, drawing my bottom lip into his mouth.

I closed my eyes for a moment to decide if the words clawing at my chest really needed to be set free.

They did. Holding them inside would've caused too much pain.

"You suck at being unlovable."

He stilled, lifting his head just enough to see my eyes.

My right hand slid up between us to press against his face while my left hand feathered along his back. "So..." my voice shook "...just remember it's your fault. You made me love you."

He blinked slowly.

"But you don't have to love me back." Before he could respond, or worse, *not* respond, I stretched my head and captured his mouth as my feet dug into the mattress to lift my pelvis.

Urging him to move again, I snaked my tongue into his mouth while my hand grabbed his ass.

He moved.

We moved.

My heart? It leaped, free falling into Slade Wylder's world.

Vulnerable.

Frightened.

Suicidal.

Stupid, crazy, impulsive heart.

In the early morning, a good hour before sunrise, I opened my eyes, relishing the lulling sound of the waves below and the naked body at my back—legs and arms intertwined with the blankets and each other. Somewhere he began and I ended, but I had no clue where.

As if he sensed my open eyes, his hold on me tightened, and he buried his nose into my hair, pressing his lips to my ear. "I love you back."

Drawing in a shaky breath, I covered his hands with mine, squeezing them as a tear slipped down my cheek. One tear he would never see. I should have been elated, but I was too busy being scared out of my mind because I had this feeling … a terrible unexplainable feeling that he wasn't simply going to break my heart, he was going to shatter it beyond repair. And I would live my life as a jaded lover who would never trust another man again.

All in.

Smart women saved a part of their hearts—like if even a small part were left intact, it could grow a full heart again. One cell at a time.

Nope. I let the whole fucking organ dive off the cliff, which meant he would leave me heartless and broken.

Chapter Nineteen

Wylder

I NEVER ASKED questions.

I was trained not to ask.

I just did as I was told.

What I didn't do was look after young women like a bodyguard. It fell out of my area of specialty. But ... I *never* asked.

The less I knew, the better. A safeguard for everyone.

So there I was—protecting her, fucking her, *loving* her. I thought. Love wasn't part of my life in the way Livy gave it. I just felt something so foreign it scared me. And *nothing* scared me up until that moment. It had to be love.

Somewhere along the way, I think I was trained to not love that way. No one could have trained me for *her*.

"Fuck ... I've met my match," I mumbled to myself, straddling my board, feet numb in the cold water as Livy came down the barrel of the wave like a pro.

Long blond hair whipping to the side.

A grin fracturing her face in two.

And screaming, "Wylder!"

We spent the next three hours surfing. She would have kept going, but Jericho wasn't the best beach dog, and I had a paper to write if I wanted to graduate that year.

"You weren't too bad." She smirked, peeling off her wet

suit as I secured the boards to the top of the sprinter van.

"Thanks," I chuckled. "Jericho." I whistled for him to get into the van.

"You gonna feed me?" She sat on the floor of the van with her feet dangling out the side door in a pair of bikini bottoms and an off-the-shoulder faded sweatshirt.

Legs for days.

Sun-kissed skin.

The whole damn package.

I pushed down my wet suit past my hips and sat next to her to peel off the legs. She hopped out and grabbed it, releasing my legs quickly and tossing it in the back on top of hers.

"I'll feed you at my house. I have to get my paper done."

"Because you're behind ... from being gone so much." She inspected me through narrowed eyes, straddling my lap.

I waited for her to elaborate, asking me more about my absence, but she didn't.

"You on that board ..." I relinquished a slight grin and an easy head shake as I whistled.

Pride bloomed along her cheeks and curled her lips. "You like watching me surf?"

My hands slid up the back of her loose sweatshirt, quickly discovering she'd discarded her bikini top. "I like watching you *everything.*"

"Wylder ..." she whispered, just before kissing me and rubbing herself against my erection.

A gust of wind kicked up some dirt in the parking lot as some people got out of an SUV maybe twenty yards away. She broke our kiss and glanced over her shoulder at them. We could have climbed into the bed and shut the side door.

Not Livy.

She pushed down the front of my thin shorts and lifted onto her knees just enough to slide the crotch of her bottoms aside and sink onto me with a small gasp at her lips. I cupped her ass. Anyone looking at us from that distance wouldn't have seen any naked parts, but if they focused on our movement, they would've known exactly what we were doing.

We had no fucks to give to anyone but each other in that moment.

The problem?

I had this woman in my life, but I had no real room for her. No future to offer her. No promises. Nothing …

What were the chances of her not asking for anything beyond that moment?

WE FELL INTO an easy groove. If all "relationships" were like ours, I had no idea what so many guys complained about.

Livy spent a lot of time with her friends. She surfed a shit ton. Occasionally, she did some actual schoolwork that took her longer than thirty minutes. When I worked on my metal projects, she used my weights to work out. The way she attacked my punching bag stunned me on more than one occasion. Her aunt knew some solid shit.

Jericho loved her—nearly as much as he loved me. More … according to Livy. The sex … no words. She wanted it all the time and everywhere. Spontaneity was her specialty.

"What are you baking?" I asked, when Jericho and I came home after several days away. Several days of Livy not asking me one damn question about my whereabouts.

Again … the woman was perfect.

"Wylder …" Livy turned to face me, licking something

from her fingers. "I missed my boys." She wasted no time throwing herself into my arms and wrapping her legs around my waist.

After she kissed me, I grabbed her hand and sucked the fingers she licked just seconds earlier. "Mmm ... what is it?" I walked us to the island and set her on it.

"Cookies for you. They just went into the oven. Twelve minutes. Eleven now." Her hands worked the button and zipper to my pants.

Nobody had it better than I did.

We fucked on the island in eight minutes, dressed by nine, cookies out of the oven by the eleven-minute mark.

"I found a recipe that I think is similar to your mom's. They're hot, but I want to know what you think." She peeked her head into the bedroom, holding a plate with a cookie on it, while I unpacked.

"You made my favorite cookies?"

"Of course. And I got cow ears and dehydrated duck feet for Jerry." She lifted the cookie to my lips. Her blond hair was pulled into a ponytail but a bit mussed from my hands messing with it while we greeted each other on the kitchen island.

At first, everything tasted familiar. The oats, the spices, the hint of orange. Then my face contorted, and I stopped chewing. Worse than that, I grabbed the plate and spat out the half-chewed bite.

Livy gasped.

"What did you put in them?"

Her nose wrinkled in disgust as did mine when we stared at the plate.

"It's a raisin," she glanced up at me, eyes wide like "duh."

"Oatmeal chocolate chip cookies. Not oatmeal raisin." I

wiped my mouth with the back of my hand.

"I know, but I forgot to get chocolate chips at the store, and Kara was coming this way. We had raisins at our place, so I figured it would be fine. I mean … oatmeal raisin is kinda the original oatmeal cookie."

"Raisins are not even close to chocolate chips. You can't sneak those little fuckers in food without warning people."

She rolled her lips between her teeth.

"It's not funny." I turned and finished unpacking my bag.

A snort escaped her. "It's totally funny. They're just grapes. I've seen you eat grapes."

"Dead grapes. It's like digging up a corpse and trying to fuck it fifty years after burial."

Another snort followed as she bent over, resting her hands on her knees, laughing so hard she couldn't breathe. "Oh … oh my … god. I found your Achilles' heel." She wiped the tears from her eyes. Cheeks red. Body still vibrating with laughter. "Raisins."

Resting my hands on my hips, I let her work out her amusement for another minute or so. "Are you done?"

She swallowed hard, releasing her hair from her ponytail and pulling it back neatly as she nodded. "Yes. Sorry. That's just too funny."

"Last week, you were killing that bag in my garage. How would you feel about sparring me? Nothing too intense. I'm just curious how you are with an actual human."

She crossed her arms over her chest. "I made you bleed."

"Yes. But I wasn't expecting it."

"Jessica says to always expect it."

Without a second's warning, I grabbed her neck with both hands and started to push her backward. Not hard, but firm.

She instantly tipped her chin, took one arm across the top of my arms, latching onto my wrist while bringing her knee into me and cocking her opposite elbow to strike me in the face.

I released her just as quickly as I originally grabbed her, stepping back and holding my hands up in surrender.

"Why did you do that?" She breathed heavily like I scared her, eyes wide.

"I wanted to know if you're *always* expecting it."

She was. I didn't let on just how shocked I was that she responded so quickly and accurately.

Livy rubbed her neck, face tense like she still couldn't believe I did that to her.

I stepped forward and gently pulled her hand away from her neck, replacing it with my face, nuzzling into her and depositing kisses where my hands had been. "Good girl."

Chapter Twenty

Livy

"**N**O VISIBLE MARKS," Jessica warned as we taped our hands at an empty training facility near her house the day before Thanksgiving. "Your dad will know, and there will be hell to pay."

I nodded.

"How's Deb?"

I shrugged. "She's fine, but she's not you."

"I'm better?" Jessica lifted an eyebrow.

"Yeah." I grinned for a second before it fell from my face. "A week ago, Slade grabbed my neck."

"What?" Her gaze shot to mine, her voice hard with concern.

"He did it on purpose to see how I would react. He knows I'm working with you."

Jess nodded slowly. "And?"

"I did what you taught me to do, but before I could land my elbow in his face, he released me and stepped back. I think he thought I was going to kick his ass."

"No, Livy. Don't ever make the assumption that your opponent thinks you're better than them. That's a huge weakness on your part."

"You mean to tell me you don't think you're better than

me?"

"Of course, I'm better than you. I just don't want *you* to think I'm better than you. Nor do I want you to think you're better than me. We are only as good as our weakest day."

I took a step back and adjusted my headgear. "How am I supposed to save a life—*mine*—if I'm only as good as my weakest day?"

"We fight with the strongest parts of our bodies. We listen to the voice of reason in our heads. But on our weakest day, we fight with every single cell in our body. We fight out of a passion to live or to save another life. We feed off the pain. We give *everything* only when we feel like we have nothing left to lose."

"So fear is strength?" I dodged her first shot at me, and she nodded in approval of my move.

"No. Fear is crippling. Desperation will keep you alive. That moment you realize you will do absolutely anything to survive. Men have lost their penises to women who *desperately* did not want to be raped. Men have lost their lives to women who *desperately* did not want to be raped." She avoided my next swing, but then I landed one in her side.

Sadly, that landed me on my ass.

An hour later, all our bruises were contained to the torso area. Jessica called it "ribs and abs day." I didn't know what she meant until I eased into the vehicle hugging my midsection.

"So this Slade, is it serious?" She flipped down her sun visor and sped out of the parking lot.

"I think so. Not sure. It's hard to explain."

"Why didn't you invite him for Thanksgiving? If it's serious, you won't be able to hide him from your dad forever. And introducing him to the whole family at once would have been a great buffer."

"I did invite him, but he's spending the holiday with his uncle and mom in Florida, where his grandparents are in a nursing home." I checked my phone for messages, thrilled to see one from him with a turkey emoji and "missing you" after it.

I replied: Missing you more. x We'll be putting raisins in our stuffing. I'll refrain from spitting them out and equating it to fucking a fifty yr. old corpse. My family might not see the humor in it. Especially my dad. He will question if you've actually done it.

Wylder: You can tell him I'm exclusively fucking his only daughter. And the early Thanksgiving blowjob was exquisite.

I rolled my eyes.

"Is that him?" Jessica asked on a quick side glance.

"Yes. He's being obnoxious."

"And by obnoxious you mean inappropriate?"

"Maybe." My cheeks flushed as I typed my reply.

Livy: Did you tell your mom about the blowjob?

I wanted to know if he'd told his family about *me*. The blowjob disclosure was optional.

Wylder: Not yet. I'll mention it if I'm asked to give the blessing.

I didn't mean to giggle out loud, but I couldn't help it.

"Now you have to tell me what he's texting you," Jessica said.

"God, no. It'd be like telling my mom." I clicked off my phone screen.

"Did he invite you to spend Thanksgiving with him and

his family?"

I shrugged. "No. But I think he knew there was no way I'd leave my dad on Thanksgiving."

"Do you think he's as emotionally invested in your relationship?"

Emotions and relationships. Two things we didn't discuss.

"Well, he loves me."

"He said that?"

I nodded and grinned, staring out the window as we crossed over the Golden Gate Bridge. The whole truth sat on the tip of my tongue. The secrecy with his job. The fact that he killed a man for me. And the true depth of my emotions for him. I couldn't say it … not to Jessica. Out of everyone in the world, I wanted her, more than anyone else, to see my strength because she'd been working so hard to give it to me.

"My mom said my dad was a complicated man. She said you can't judge someone by the culmination of their actions. That *the* right person will see their soul in a way no one else can see it. She said she fell in love with his soul, and it branded her in a way that made it impossible for her to not love him with all her heart. I never thought much about it until I met Slade."

Jess nodded slowly, keeping her eyes on the road. "Is there something about Slade that I should know about?"

He killed a man for me.

"He's just mysterious. I feel like I know him. His soul of sorts. But he also has a mysterious side, and there are lots of rumors about him that I don't think are true. And sometimes I like that I don't know everything about him. You know? I like discovering him slowly. Like … he hates raisins."

"The rumors are things like him hating raisins?" She shot

me another quick sidelong glance.

I laughed. "No. Just the usual weird stuff that gets spread about anyone who keeps to themselves for the most part. Drug dealer. Male escort. Crazy stuff like that."

"So you may or may not be dating a drug dealer slash male escort. Maybe holding off the introduction to your dad isn't such a bad idea after all. Besides, if he hasn't already done it, he'll run a background check on him."

"What?" My mouth fell open. "You're not serious?"

She lifted a shoulder. "He's a computer geek. He can hack just about anything. If he knows where he lives, he's already saved everything from his birth certificate to any positive STD tests."

My brain snagged on that little piece of information, wondering if he knew who Slade's employer was. If he did and it was something sketchy, he would have told me. Hell, he would have physically kidnapped me and relocated me to my childhood bedroom. I let Jessica's revelation give me comfort. Slade must have come up clean in Dad's searches.

"So much for letting me find my own way in life."

Jessica grunted a laugh. "Your dad? Are we talking about the same person?"

I rolled my eyes. Come to think of it, I was pretty sure it was my mom who encouraged him to do that. When she died, all common-sense parenting died with her.

Chapter Twenty-One

I RETURNED SATURDAY night instead of Sunday morning as planned. Dad wasn't exactly in the best mood. No one knew why. I wondered if it was hardest during the holidays without Mom. She'd always done all the cooking.

When I realized my girls weren't at the house, I packed a few things and headed to the firehouse. Slade said he would be home late Sunday, but I just wanted to feel close to him. I wanted to bury my head in his pillow. In fact, that was what I did as soon as I got there. I tried to video chat with Slade for the first time, hoping to get a glimpse of his family or something more personal, but he didn't answer.

Livy: *Are you ignoring me on purpose?*

Then I sent a photo of me in his bed, wearing only his UCLA tee, my bare legs bent and spread—sexy but tasteful since the lighting didn't allow the full view between my legs.

I waited and waited for a response. Nothing.

Feeling thirsty and craving something sweet, I sauntered downstairs for a can of natural black cherry soda that he stocked in the fridge just for me. I slid my phone onto the table and took a seat while I popped the top to the soda.

"Shit!" The soda exploded like I'd shaken the hell out of it, but I hadn't. The dark liquid ran in a fizzy river from the table to the light-colored area rug under the table. "Nooo ..." I grabbed the roll of paper towels and threw a wad onto the table to stop the flow before blotting the ugly stain on his rug.

I couldn't imagine it being an expensive rug, but I didn't know because I didn't know much about his financial situation or the price tag on his possessions, which were sparse. When I tried to clean it with a product I found under the sink, the stain just got worse.

"Nooo ..." Plopping back onto my butt, I rested my elbows onto my knees and hung my head. Either I needed to buy a new rug, or I needed to send it off to be cleaned. Aubrey's parents had a company that picked up area rugs, cleaned them, and returned them to the house.

With lazy defeat settling into my bones, I climbed to my feet, finished cleaning the table, and moved the table and chairs to roll up the rug. A foot into rolling it up, I froze. A chill worked its way up my spine. There it was.

The access to Professor Dickerson's creepy dungeon. So much for the rumors that they filled it in when the house was restored. Ever so slowly, I continued rolling up the rug. With Slade, the house never felt haunted. Without him ... I swear I heard every tiny creak and crack. I smelled smoke from the original fire. And the temperature seemed to drop ten degrees.

The details of the kidnapping, the fire, the college girl being burned alive ... it all came to life in my head. The bigger question that haunted me was ... did Slade have anything stored in the dungeon? Surely not. At least that was my hope.

Potatoes. Dungeons were like cellars, right? Apples, potatoes, lots of fruits and veggies that liked it cool. Wine. It would have been the perfect wine cellar. If only I could have remembered Slade ever drinking a glass of wine.

Nothing.

That was what I was really hoping to find. It took me a good half hour of just staring at the wood plank trapdoor to get the nerve to lift it open. Had my girlfriends been home, I would have told them to come over and open it with me.

They weren't home.

So I had to brave it on my own. It didn't lift easily. The weight of it strained my shoulders as I used my whole body to pull it open. A musty smell wafted out of the black hole along with yet another drop in temperature. I couldn't see anything, so I grabbed my phone and turned on the flashlight, pointing it into the hole. The only thing that came into view was a ladder to climb into the dungeon and the dirty concrete floor below.

I blew out a long breath as my hand holding my phone shook a bit.

"I can't go down there," I whispered to myself and the ghosts watching over me. "But I have to." In nothing but his UCLA tee, I descended the ladder with my phone clenched in my mouth, the light pointed downward. My focus was on my feet, making sure I didn't miss one of the rungs and fall. Once I reached the floor, I grabbed my phone and aimed the light at the wall.

"Oh ... my ... god ..."

Fear came in waves. The first wave took my breath away. The second wave hit my heart, jolting it into a frantic rhythm. The third wave paralyzed me. I just ... stood there, trying to make sense of the display before me. Forcing myself to move, I turned in a slow circle, taking the light with me, trembling to the point I thought my teeth might start chattering. Every square foot of the wall was covered in hooks and shelves of weapons. An arsenal like I'd only seen in the movies.

Knives.

Guns.

Grenades.

Some missile-looking things that I couldn't imagine were legal for anyone to own except the military.

I no longer thought the rumors were wrong. They were understated. Slade Wylder wasn't just a drug dealer; he was bigger. Mafia? I didn't know. What I *did* know ... Slade wasn't a good person. He was dangerous. And I needed to tell someone. Call the police.

My breaths shortened into the beginning of hyperventilation. I couldn't get a full breath which made me want it—try for it—that much harder. Backing into the metal rung ladder, I tore my gaze away from the weapons and forced my shaky limbs to climb the ladder, my right hand trying to hold the rung and my phone. Just as I reached the top, my phone fell onto the ground below.

The staccato of my breathing intensified at the thought of climbing back down to get it. As I moved my right foot to start my decent again, the warmth of a firm hand around my wrist sent shock waves through my body. On a painful gasp, I jerked my chin up to the menacing face I thought I loved.

I was such a stupid woman.

"Livy ..." Slade pulled my arm to bring me out of the dungeon.

"NO!" I tried to jerk away. There was no escape, but just feet below me was a slew of weapons and ammunition. I could ...

Could what? My thoughts were flawed. I had no fucking clue how to load or use a gun. Maybe a knife. Jessica had taught me how to hold a knife and where to cut someone to make them bleed the most.

"Livy …" he repeated with more grit to his voice.

I let go of the ladder and wriggled to get out of his grip, even if it meant falling to the ground below. My struggle paled in comparison to his strength. He plucked me from the hole. I maneuvered out of his grip, falling back onto the kitchen floor, crab crawling backward toward the living room and Jericho, as Slade kicked the trapdoor shut.

"My phone," I whispered like he'd knocked the air out of my lungs.

"Whatcha doing down there?" He cocked his head, brow more tense than usual as he took calculated steps toward me.

"I … I didn't want to believe it." I eased to my feet so slowly—the prey all too aware of her predator.

He wet his lips and rubbed them together. "Believe what?"

"The rumors. The drugs." I shook my head. "I just didn't think you could—"

"Deal drugs?" He chuckled, scratching his stubble from his chin to his neck. "Any dumb fuck could deal drugs. I'm not dealing, Liv."

Not a drug dealer.

The weight of the only other logical explanation settled in my stomach like a grenade with the pin pulled. Weapons … he was a weapons dealer.

"You know … I liked us. Not that I have much to compare to. But us … I liked us. You're not needy and clingy anymore. You're smart. Jericho likes you. You're a badass on a surfboard. And don't even get me started on the sex. Sadly, you're a little too curious for your own good."

He was calm. Too calm.

Calculated. Too calculated.

I should have been throwing my arms around him. We

should have been ripping each other's clothes from our bodies.

Kisses mixed with whispers of love.

Hands exploring familiar territory.

Two desperate souls melding into one.

Emotions warred between my head and my heart.

Anger.

Fear.

Resentment.

Disbelief.

"I spilled soda on the rug, so I rolled it up to have it cleaned." I surprised myself with the monotone voice drifting from my lips.

"So what are your plans?" he asked, again cocking his head a fraction, closing in on me without taking actual steps. Slade had a way of controlling a situation with a single look.

"My plans?" I whispered.

"Yes. Your plans. Are you calling the police? Your friends? Your dad?"

"Why?" I shook my head. "Is it the money? Why sell weapons? You could go to prison for a long time. And … and how can you sleep at night? You're selling something made to take human lives. Are you arming terrorists? Do you sell guns that take innocent lives? Like children in schools?" My words escalated, fed by anger boiling in my veins.

"I don't sell anything."

Coughing on total disbelief, I ran my fingers through my hair. "So … you're what? A collector? All your unexplained absences are just you shopping gun shows?"

He shook his head. "Have a seat."

"No. I'm not staying." I fisted my hands.

Slade's gaze shifted to my hands before sweeping my entire

body and its change in stance—readying to fight. To escape.

"I'm not going to hurt you."

I laughed. "That's reassuring. So ..." I jabbed my thumb over my shoulder. "I can get dressed and leave. Right?"

His lips twisted, like he was biting the inside of his cheek. "I like you in my shirt."

"Yeah? Well, I like you unarmed."

He slowly raised his hands and arms, turning in a slow circle. "I'm unarmed. If you don't believe me, take off my clothes."

It hurt so badly. Him looking at me the way he looked at me in the sprinter van, on the beach, in his bed.

"I'm going to call the police."

His expression remained unchanging. It seemed like forever that he regarded me that way. I refused to move or speak. Finally, his eyes shifted, redirecting his focus to the floor between us as he offered a slight nod while retrieving his phone from his pocket and unlocking it before handing it to me.

It took me a bit to take it from him. There had to be a catch. I brought up the phone screen.

He did nothing.

I pressed nine.

He did nothing.

I pressed one.

He did nothing.

After the last one, my thumb hovered over the call button.

He. Did. Nothing.

Tears flooded my eyes, spilling over, and racing down my cheeks. "Just tell me why you have them." The 9-1-1 on the screen blurred behind my tears as my hands holding the phone shook.

No matter what my brain told me—and it screamed for me to call the police and run hard and fast—my heart loved him. It had the most irrational need to protect him. How could I feel the need to protect a man with an arsenal just feet below us?

As more hot tears burned my cheeks, I clenched my teeth with the same anger in which I squeezed the phone in my hands. "Why?" I said in something between a scream and a sob. "Why can you so fucking easily call the police because I was looking in your garage window, but I can't bring myself to push the goddamn send button when you have enough weapons to annihilate a small village? WHY?" I sent the phone flying across the room and covered my face with my hands as the sobs overtook me.

Gentle hands slid into my hair as his warm lips pressed to the top of my head. "Because you're infinitely a better person."

"Tell me ..." I cried. "You h-have to t-tell me ..."

"I protect people."

It took me several seconds to process his words. Slowly lifting my head, I aimed my teary-eyed gaze at him, wiping my cheeks. "Like a bodyguard?"

Taking my face in his hands, he rubbed his thumbs under my eyes. "If you think of *body* as something larger, like a population, then sure. I'm a bodyguard."

"I don't understand." I pushed out of his hold, taking a step backward. "You ... you have to just say it. Are you a bad person?" I pressed my lips together to hold in more impending sobs, and I shook my head over and over. "Please tell me I didn't fall in love with a terrible human," I whispered.

He narrowed his eyes, the muscles in his jaw ticking for several seconds before he swallowed. "I do bad things to terrible people."

"Why?" I muttered, wiping more tears before crossing my arms over my chest.

"So that defenseless college girls don't get raped behind dumpsters."

The vigilante card again.

"Is this a pastime? A calling like you're the only one who can lift the hammer from the ground?"

"It's a job."

"A paying job?"

He nodded.

"Who's your boss?"

"I can't say."

"So you ... you're ... what? An assassin?" I laughed a little because it was ridiculous.

"Yes."

My lips parted, muscles paralyzed as I waited for a "just kidding" or something more than a yes.

"No ..." My head began to twist side to side and it didn't stop. Turning, I fisted my hair, head still shaking as I paced several feet toward the sofa and back again. "No. No. No. This isn't ... no. Not my life. I'm going to run for president. I can't have 'slept with an assassin' on my record. No. And my dad ... oh god ..." My fingers curled, digging into my scalp, and yanking my hair harder as I closed my eyes and stilled my feet. "He's going to lock me in my room forever."

"I saved your life. He should feel pretty fucking indebted."

My eyes shot open, and my head resumed its shaking. "No. You don't know my dad. He's not going to feel indebted to you. He's going to suggest I send you a thank-you card and get the hell out of LA. I can't do this. I have to go." I ran up the stairs to get dressed.

"You're a liability now."

I paused my hands as they worked to hook my bra. Glancing over my shoulder at him, I squinted. "I'm not."

"I've revealed myself to you. That definitely makes you a liability."

Swallowing the thick sludge of unease in my throat, I finished hooking my bra and fumbled with my shirt to pull it over my head. "S-so ... what are you saying?" I pulled my hair out of the shirt's neck and grabbed my jeans, my hands working as fast as possible.

"I'm saying I'll be gone within the hour."

"Gone where? Why? I'm not turning you in, Wylder." I grabbed my bag while shoving my bare feet into my sneakers.

"Just gone. Because I let you live."

My frantic movements came to a crashing halt as my head snapped up to meet his gaze. "You *let* me live?"

"Protocol is to put you down."

"P-put me down? Like a rabid animal? The fuck!? I'm not a terrible human. You said you do bad things to terrible humans to save lives. Killing me isn't that."

"If I go to prison, it leaves a gap to be filled. While that gap waits to be filled, innocent people are in danger. It's a numbers thing, Liv. Sacrifice one to save a hundred."

Emotion contorted my face as I fought back the new round of tears. "Who are you?" I whispered in a thick voice. "Kill me? You can't love me and kill me, Wylder."

"I said I wouldn't hurt you. I'm just telling you ... this is it. You put me at risk, so I have to leave."

"You have to disappear because I know?"

"I have to disappear because you *don't know*. You don't

know what to do with this new information. And I can't wait around for you to figure it out."

My mouth opened as I shook my head. "I ... I'm ..."

"You're what? Not going to say anything? Not going to tell your friends? Not going to have a weak moment when your conscience gets the best of you? It's a lot, Liv." He brushed past me to his closet, pulling out a leather bag and shoving clothes into it. "I don't expect you to carry this in silence. We shouldn't have ..."

That reckless thing in my chest started to ache. "We shouldn't have what?"

"Any of it. All of it." He kept stuffing clothes into his bag. Regret poured out of every jerky move he made. He regretted us. He regretted me,

I didn't know how I felt. The intensity of the pain began to numb my body and my mind. "My phone."

He unzipped the side pocket to his duffle and pulled out a wad of hundreds, tossing them across the bed toward me. There must have been a thousand dollars waiting for me to take it.

"I don't need a new phone. I just—"

"New phones. New numbers."

Plural.

He was talking about both of us. New everything. *New* being defined as without Slade Wylder.

"Your school."

"Not your concern." He disappeared into the bathroom.

Minutes earlier I feared for my life, yet there he was letting me walk away.

He killed people for a living. His fate likely involved life in prison or execution, The bullet wound. He was on the receiving end of someone who refused to die so easily. I had no business being with him.

Not wanting to explain to my dad why I needed a new phone again, I scooped up the cash while more emotions bled from my eyes. My heavy feet took slow steps out of his bedroom and down the stairs.

"Jericho …" I kneeled by his bed and hugged him, swallowing my silent sobs. "Love you." Unable to take one more second of the firehouse and the terrible things that happened to people who spent time under its roof, I made a straight line to the back door and ran to my Jeep.

"NOOO!" I hammered my hands against the steering wheel as emotions wracked my body. The last time my chest hurt that badly, I was saying goodbye to my mom as she was being lowered into the ground. "Ouch …" I pressed my bruised hands to my chest as if I could keep my heart from crumbling into a pile of dust, complete wreckage from Wylder the earthquake.

I started the Jeep and put it in reverse, like backing off a cliff. If I left, there was no going back. No second chances. He would disappear forever. Nothing more than another ghost in the firehouse—a gaping hole in my chest. Months of memories that would haunt me forever.

For … ever.

I hit the brakes a few feet before the street and gripped the steering wheel until my knuckles blanched, closing my eyes. "Mom … tell me what to do."

"… you can't judge someone by the culmination of their actions. The right person will see your soul in a way no one else can see it. I fell in love with your dad's soul and it branded me in a way that made it impossible for me to not love him with all my *heart."*

Forever was too long. I'd been in the Jeep for less than ten minutes trying to leave, and my lungs couldn't breathe without him. Shoving it into *Park*, I picked up the pieces of my vulnerable ...

Frightened ...

Suicidal ...

Stupid, crazy, impulsive heart.

And I ran inside the firehouse just as he carried two bags down the stairs. He stopped on the bottom step, hands clenching the handles of the bags giving me ample vein porn. I panted, my heart outside of my chest on full display. Swallowing past the thick emotions choking me, bottom lip quivering as I tried to hold it together, I glanced at my watch and whispered, "Ten minutes." My gaze lifted to his. "It took me ten minutes to come back." On a slow blink, I lost the battle with my tears. "My brain told me to leave..." I batted at the tears "...but my heart never made it out the door. So if you need to save the world, I won't tell a soul. I just want to love you."

He gave me nothing when I needed everything.

I deflated. It was too late. He didn't trust me. I just needed one breath to realize that without him I would never take another one.

Did one breath break us? Did we end in ten minutes? Could I go back in time and un-spill my soda? Un-see the contents of the dungeon? Could I go back and not fear him, not start that call to the police?

"I broke us," I murmured in defeat as my posture deflated and my gaze fell to my feet, refilling with tears. After the silence between us began to tear at my soul, I drew in a shaky breath and turned, leaving because the choice to stay was no longer mine.

"You move in with me. If you're in … you're *all* in."

I stopped three steps from the back door, inching my head to glance over my shoulder.

He dropped his bags to the ground. "What's it going to be, Livy?"

My gaze shifted to the trapdoor for a few seconds before returning to his dark eyes unwavering with the gravity of his ultimatum.

"You …" I said so softly I wasn't sure he heard me because I don't remember meaning to say it. The word floated out on a breath, like every breath whispered his name. "It's always going to be you, Wylder."

"Then get over here so I can love you back."

In spite of the urge to run into his arms, I took each step with purpose, my heart making sure my brain understood we were all in. Even when I made it to him, toe-to-toe, hands itching to touch him, we took another breath before jumping off the cliff.

Fingers in hair.

Mouths colliding, reckless and passionate.

When we touched, it felt like he had a part of me ineradicably ingrained into him, and I frantically searched for that tiny part of myself to feel whole again.

So yeah … I jumped in … *all in.*

Chapter Twenty-Two

Wylder

W HAT DID I do?
　　　　I didn't need a college degree. It just looked good. Image mattered. The perception of normalcy mattered. Livy felt normal. Twenty-five-year-old men had girlfriends. Sex every night. They drank beer and surfed.

Normalcy meant nothing to me. Two parents, T-ball, and trips to Disney World weren't part of my childhood. Abe taught me to hunt small game by ten, and I hit the perfect lung shot for a prized elk by thirteen. After I mastered my bow hunting skills, Abe put a gun in my fourteen-year-old hands. He said I was a natural, just like my dad.

I hunted my first human on my eighteenth birthday. Abe called it a rite of passage. I didn't know his name or anything about him except he raped and killed the niece of a U.S. senator, but the DA lacked the evidence to convict him. So he walked … three days before I turned eighteen. Investigators said the assassination was clearly a hired job.

Clean.

Traceless.

Expertly executed.

I took pride in that, as did Abe.

Combat training followed, molding me into the perfect

killing machine. Abe said the people who really kept citizens safe were faceless. They didn't wear uniforms or badges. And they operated under a different chain of command.

Abe was it.

He was my chain of command.

The number one rule that I learned at a very early age, when he broke my middle finger for flipping off my mom, was don't *ever* question or disrespect authority. I didn't even know what "the bird" meant. I'd seen some other kid at school do it to a teacher when her back was to the class.

"Why is this knuckle bigger?" Livy held up my hand, tracing the lines along my palm, right up to that knuckle that never healed quite right.

I eyed the two guys taking seats in front of us that Monday morning. They eyed Livy like they had a fucking chance with her. I felt certain she got those looks a lot, but I hadn't noticed until then.

My instructions were to protect her, but my instinct to feel possessive of her didn't surface right away.

"Broke it when I was twelve."

She brought my hand to her lips, kissing my knuckle. "How?"

"Flipped off the wrong person."

Chuckling, she released my hand to pull her computer out of her bag. "Wish I would have known twelve-year-old Slade Wylder. I bet we could have stirred up a lot of trouble."

"You were a troublemaker?"

She smirked, giving me a quick side glance as she opened her laptop. "Oh, baby, you have no idea." Pulling a hairband off her wrist, she gathered her wavy hair and twisted it into a messy ball on her head, working the band around it in every direction. She did it at the beginning of each class, maybe waiting for her hair to dry from either the shower or early morning surfing.

Focusing on a woman felt foreign to me.

I kissed Jenny Pedersen in sixth grade because my friends said I should, not because I had that much interest in girls at the time. I screwed Erika Taylor in the back of her parents' Chevy Malibu when I was fifteen because Abe told me I needed to be a man. In hindsight, I think he was referencing taking out the trash and helping my mom around the house.

I'd never had an actual girlfriend. It was hard to focus on honing my knife and gun skills *and* girls. The internet provided all I needed to get off before falling asleep each night.

By the time I started college, I had no interest in or time for dating. When the situation presented itself, I found a meaningless one-night stand to scratch the occasional itch.

"Why the look?" she whispered, leaning toward me as the professor started to speak.

I shook my head slowly, not realizing that I'd been staring at her. "Nothing." I blinked a few times, trying to focus.

"Doesn't look like nothing."

My attention drifted from her eyes to her lips, down her neck and chest to her perky little breasts pressed to her tight tee.

"It's time to go."

Her eyes widened, lips parted. "Uh … it is?"

I grabbed her laptop and shoved it in her bag. Standing, I flipped my backpack over my shoulder. With one hand, I took her bag; with my other, I took her hand and dragged her out of the auditorium.

"Wylder …" She nearly tripped as I led her down the hallway to a string of offices. "Out," I said to the grad TA perched at his tiny desk.

"What are you—"

"How's the oxygen, Stu?"

He scooted back in his chair. "Good. W-why?"

"Get the fuck out. You can come back in thirty minutes." I only needed ten, but I didn't want to make Livy too nervous about his eminent return.

"O-okay." He grabbed his bag as I gave him a gentle shove out the door.

Jericho parked himself by the door as soon as I shut it and locked it.

"Wylder—"

I turned and crashed my mouth to hers, holding her face in my hands to reach as deep as my tongue would go. Her butt hit the metal-legged desk, her hands grabbing my arms to steady herself.

My mouth ripped from hers, and I devoured her neck, working my lips to her ear. "I need this so fucking bad."

She didn't question me. Her hands pulled my shirt up my torso. Mine pawed at her bra, yanking it down in the front to release her breasts.

"Ahhh!" Her head fell back as I pinched her nipple, possibly too hard.

I lifted her onto the desk, guiding her to lie back, pushing the computer monitor dangerously close to the edge, the keyboard crashing to the floor. Shoving her shirt up her chest, I sucked her breasts—biting and tugging her nipples as she arched her back off the desk.

"Wylder ..." She threaded her fingers into my hair, commanding me to move down her stomach.

I glanced up as my tongue dipped into her pierced navel. Her drunk eyes and parted lips fed my own intoxication. I unbuttoned her shorts and slid them down her legs with her panties. Staring at her spread before me like an offering from a god I felt certain didn't exist, I made quick moves to release my aching cock from the confines of my jeans.

The heels of her white canvas shoes planted on the edge of the desk as I pressed my hands to her knees, opening them and dipping my head to taste her.

"Wyyyllllderrr …" she shrieked my name for eternity, her pelvis jerking off the desk, chasing my tongue.

While I wanted to feel her come undone against my mouth, I *needed* to be inside of her.

A long "yesss" escaped her soft lips as I pushed in as far as I could fit, pausing for a brief moment until she opened her eyes. Then I moved.

Fast.

Hard.

Desperate.

I didn't know what it was … the dumb-ass guys checking her out in the classroom, the fit of her tee, the memories of my lifeless childhood, or that she knew my secret—and she stayed.

She. Fucking. Stayed.

All I knew was I couldn't get close enough.

I couldn't kiss her hard enough.

I couldn't make it last long enough.

Livy was the one part of my life I couldn't control. She disarmed the man who needed to feel the cold trigger at his finger to feel normal.

"Kiss … me … Wylder …" She grabbed my face, pulling me from her breast to her lips as I pistoled into her over and over, her legs around my waist, ankles locked together. "St-st-stop … stop …"

"Liv …" I pleaded, unable to imagine why she'd want me to stop something that felt unstoppable.

"Stop!" she said firmly. Not with anger, just very insistently.

I stopped. Panting. Confused. Worried.

She pressed her hands to my cheeks as our minty breaths mingled an inch apart. "Feel it?"

"What, Liv?" I said with impatience lacing my words and rolling off my body.

"Wanting something so much it hurts." Her breaths were just as labored as mine. "Wanting it beyond all reason. That moment when the rest of the world doesn't matter because you *need* something. The ache. The inability to breathe. Your heart beating out of your chest."

"Livy …" I grimaced, *needing* to move.

"It's why I came back. It's why I stayed. Feel it … and know that every cell in my body felt this way yesterday."

"I feel it," I whispered, taking her mouth with mine. Taking all of her as I found my release—a temporary moment of reprieve from the insane need. I didn't know what to do with the feelings.

All the fucking feelings piling up and no place to put them.

Chapter Twenty-Three

Livy

"IF HE FINDS out..." Kara helped me pack what few belongings I'd purchased after the fire into the back of my Jeep "...he'll be mad."

I closed the back door. "It's highly unlikely that he makes an unannounced visit. My bed is still here. And I'm an adult. I don't need Daddy's permission to move in with my boyfriend."

"Then just tell him."

"Hell no." I laughed. "I don't need his permission, but I do need him to just *not know* for a bit."

She rolled her eyes. "I still don't see why Slade didn't just ask you to live with him right after the fire."

I shrugged, opening the driver's door. "He kinda offered ... at least temporarily. But then my dad came. Aubrey's parents found this house, so I went with the flow since he didn't mention it again until two days ago."

"Do you hear ghosts?"

"No." I giggled.

"Do you wonder if there's still a hidden dungeon?"

"Nope. I don't wonder that at all." I shot her a toothy grin while starting the Jeep.

"Surfing in the morning?"

"Maybe. Depends on my night."

"You mean sex. It depends on how long he keeps his dick inside of you."

Sliding my sunglasses on, I repeated the same shit-eating grin. I didn't tell her or anyone about morning sex in the TA's office. Slade's only explanation after we pieced our clothes back together was that Stu "owed him one."

I picked up a pizza on my way to the firehouse, totally having a holy-shit-I'm-moving-into-the-firehouse moment. After I stopped my attempt to leave him and chose to be with him Sunday night, we had endless hours of sex without talking about the gravity of everything.

Monday morning school.

Insanely hot sex on a desk.

A kiss goodbye with a "see you later."

And that was it.

I pulled into the driveway next to the empty spot where Wylder's SUV was usually parked. He didn't mention going anywhere. When I headed toward the back door with the pizza, a noise from the garage stopped me before I got to the deck. I eased the side garage door open, freezing at the sight of a strange man smoking a cigar while inspecting the pieces of Slade's welding project.

"Livy Knight." The man who looked a little older than my dad—shaved head, leathered skin, tattoos along his right arm, and thick limbs—dragged his icky gaze down my body. He had the appearance of a nightclub bouncer with a side of extra creepy.

"Who are you?" I wrinkled my nose at his stench.

He took a few quick puffs of his cigar and smiled, teeth stained in nicotine. "Abe. A ... *friend* of Slade's."

"I doubt it." I kept the door open and my body in view of

anyone driving along the street.

His head slanted a fraction as he rolled the cigar between his fingers. "Why is that, sweetheart?"

"I don't think he has any friends."

Abe barked a hearty laugh, tipping his head back. "Touché. Good one. You're probably right. I've told him he needs to make friends, but he never listens."

"How do you know my name?" I highly doubted Slade talked about me with his "friend."

"He mentioned you'd be moving in. I told him it's a terrible idea. No offense."

I frowned.

"It's just that young girls are distractions. Messy. And I'd like to see him finish his last year of school without said messy distractions. If you two young things want to fuck like bunnies … I'm good with that." He took several more puffs of his cigar as my face morphed into disgust. "But I think you should crawl back to your own bed when you're done."

"Who are you?" I glanced out at the street, feeling uneasy.

"I told you … a friend."

"Well, *Friend* … as you can see, Slade isn't here, so why don't you call him next time before stopping by with your unsolicited advice."

His boots scuffed along the dirty garage floor, inching closer to me. I stumbled back a few steps, almost dropping the pizza box.

"Gotta hand it to him … you're a pretty little thing. You get those beach blond locks from your mom or dad?" He reached for my head, my shoulder, my hair … I didn't know. I just knew no man was ever going to take advantage of me again.

"Fuck!" he growled when I grabbed his arm, pulling him closer to me so I could land my knee in his groin while simultaneously planting my elbow in his face.

With the pizza box on the ground, I squared my body and readied for a fight, fists up to protect my head.

"Jesus ... I'm not fucking going to fight you, you scrawny little bitch." He took several steps away from me, pinching his bleeding nose. "Slade teach you that?" He pulled a hankie out of his back pocket to wipe the blood.

I shook my head.

"Your dad?"

I shook my head.

Then he got this look on his face, an eerie knowing kind of expression, and he smiled. "Nice meeting you, Livy Knight." He turned and walked to the white sedan parked across the street.

Once he drove away, I rubbed my elbow and pushed back the tears as my shaky hands retrieved the pizza box (upside down) from the ground. I hurried into the house, opting to get my stuff out of the back of the Jeep when Slade returned ... from wherever the hell he went to.

"Asshole," I mumbled, peeling a piece of pizza from the lid of the cardboard box and setting it on a plate just as the back door opened and Jericho rushed me, tail wagging, tongue out.

I squatted down and hugged him before scratching behind his ears. "Where were you when I needed you?" As I slowly stood, Jericho trotted into the living room, and Slade eyed me suspiciously as he tossed his keys onto the counter. "Where were you?"

"Working. Why?"

He'd "been working" many times since I'd met him, but

his job revelation made me pause with his confession. Slade was an assassin. So if he was working ...

"So you just ..." My gaze averted to my plate. I thought I could handle the truth, and I wasn't giving up, but it was going to take some getting used to before I could smile and say, *"Hey, honey, how was your day?"*

"Livy, it's not ..," he closed his eyes and rubbed his temples. "There's more to it than pulling a trigger. I spend most of my time scoping things out. Locations. The target's movements. Routines."

I cleared my throat and brought the piece of mangled pizza to my mouth. "So you didn't just kill someone?"

"What did you mean when you told Jericho he wasn't here when you needed him?"

Smooth subject change.

"Your *friend* Abe was in the garage when I got here."

"Abe?" He narrowed his eyes.

"So you don't know him?"

He shook his head, eyes still squinted. "No. I know him. I just don't understand why he was here. What did he say?"

"He said a lot of not so awesome things. But the highlights are ... I shouldn't move in with you, fucking is fine, but I should 'crawl back to my own bed' when we're done."

He nodded slowly. "I'll take care of it."

"Who is he? Because he's creepy, and he tried to touch me, so I had to drop the damn pizza box on the ground, and now it's ruined, and—"

"Touch you? What do you mean?" He slid off his jean jacket and tossed it on the chair before grabbing my wrist and taking a bite of my pizza.

"I mean this strange, intimidating man who knew my

name reached for my head. I think he was trying to touch my hair because he'd just made mention of it. And I reacted. I kneed him in the groin and planted my elbow in his face."

Slade stopped mid-chew, eyes making a more thorough inspection of me. "Did he hurt you?"

"No."

"Are you sure?"

"Yes. He scared me, but he didn't end up laying a hand on me. He just left, but not before asking me if you taught me to do what I did to him."

Slade's face remained tense and contemplative. "Did you make him bleed?"

I nodded.

He cupped the back of my head and kissed my forehead. "Good girl."

Taking in a slow breath, I wore my bravest mask. I didn't want him or Jessica or anyone to know how close I was to shitting myself and falling into a heap of helplessness like I did the night at the convenience store.

After we ate what we could of the pizza and carried in the few boxes of my clothes and other belongings, I took a bath while he perched in bed studying for a test. I couldn't see him, but we could easily hear each other.

"You changed the subject earlier," I said, sliding a loofa over my shoulder.

"What's that?"

"Earlier, when I asked you about Abe, about your friendship ... how you know him, you evaded me."

"He's ..." A pregnant pause held the air, and I couldn't help but wonder if he was contemplating answering me or manufacturing a lie. "My uncle."

A lie.

Uncle Abe?

I didn't buy it.

"Your mom's brother or your dad's brother?"

"Dad's."

"He seemed quite invested in your life. Your college career. Your roommates. Your sex life."

"My dad died when I was three. Abe was a father figure of sorts. He's just protective."

"Does he know what you do? That you don't need anyone to protect you? Does he know what's in your dungeon?"

"Do you know that I have a test tomorrow and some of us have to study?"

I grinned, pulling the drain on the tub and grabbing a towel while standing. "I'll help you study."

"I don't need your help."

"If you have to study, then you need help." I flipped my hair to one side, squeezing it with the towel. After slipping on my cotton lace-waist panties and a crop top, I tied the towel around my head, brushed my teeth, and stepped around the corner.

He paused his studying to make a full inspection of my body. "I said I have to study."

I shrugged. "My teeth are brushed, and I'm ready for bed. The light doesn't bother me. Stay up as late as you want."

"Do you have something against flannel?"

I chuckled. "If we're going to live together, you need to get used to me being here, wearing what I like to wear to bed, leaving soap rings in your bathtub, and the lid off the peanut butter. And I'll have to get used to whatever it is you do on the regular, the parts of your daily routine."

"I watch porn and jerk off before I go to sleep." He scratched his neck, tipping his chin up.

My eyebrows climbed up my forehead. "O-kay. I …" I had nothing. I knew he said it to get a reaction from me, but I didn't know what reaction he expected, mainly because I had no clue how to react. Clearing my throat, I removed the towel from my head, flipped off the bathroom light, and padded to my side of the bed. "You don't need porn; you have me." I plugged in my phone.

"My own personal porn star?" He closed his laptop over his outstretched legs and lifted his arms, linking his fingers behind his head.

Sitting on the edge of the bed, I grabbed my bottle of lotion and rubbed some on my legs, ignoring his comment. When he didn't say anymore, I glanced over my shoulder while continuing to moisturize. "What's that look?"

After a long pause, he whispered, "Nothing."

"It's something. I've noticed that contemplative look a lot in the past twenty-four hours. Are you regretting this? Me? Here?" I capped the lotion and faced his side of the bed, legs crisscrossed, arms loosely hugged to my waist.

Another slow head shake. "It's just weird."

"Me?"

"Kind of." His lazy gaze stuck to my face, but it seemed far from focused. "You … as in a roommate. You … as in a woman."

"You've never had a roommate? Or lived with a girlfriend?"

"No. Have you lived with a guy before me?"

I nodded. "Well, unofficially. I guess I'm unofficially living with you."

"What does that mean?"

"It means my dad doesn't know. It means I don't get mail here. It means I left a few things at the other house, like my bed and some clothes I don't wear."

"This other guy …" He twisted his lips and narrowed his eyes a fraction.

His curiosity gave me a little high. I didn't want to be controlled by Wylder or anyone for that matter, but a little jealousy wasn't all bad.

"Patrick. Sophomore year. I unofficially lived in his apartment for three months."

"What happened?"

With a one-shoulder shrug, I scraped my bottom lip with my teeth for a few seconds. "A curly-haired brunette happened. I wasn't feeling well, so I skipped my afternoon classes. I just wanted to crawl into bed and die for a few days. My body ached everywhere. I swear even my hair ached. When I opened the bedroom door, Patrick was just … pumping away."

I laughed, a sad one, but I had to stick to the humorous side of the situation to keep my sanity. "She was on the bed … all fours … and he stood at the end with his naked backside to me. And I just watched."

A grin played on Wylder's lips. "Perv."

My faraway stare snapped up to meet his gaze, and I couldn't hide my own grin. "Right? It's when I noticed for the first time just how hairy his ass was. And the girl had a solid future as a porn star. She just kept chanting, 'Yeah baby, yeah baby, yeah baby …'"

"How long did you watch?"

My grin swelled a little more. "Until the end."

He laughed. "Seriously?"

I nodded. "She lurched forward, collapsing onto her stomach, and he ran his fingers through his hair and turned as if he finally sensed my presence."

"What did you say?"

"Nothing. My body ached too much, and I needed to vomit. Lucky for me, brunette girl's fancy handbag was right by the door, so I emptied the contents of my stomach into it, wiped my mouth with the back of my hand, and told Patrick I'd be back for my stuff later. So there you have it. Just another case of me getting my heart broken. Have you had yours broken?"

He shook his head slowly, as if the whole concept was foreign to him.

My smile lost momentum, and my hands fidgeted with the edge of the blanket as I focused on the thread coming loose from the stitching. "You're next. I just *feel* it."

"Next to what?"

"Break my heart."

"Why do you say that?"

My gaze inched up to meet his as he dropped his hands from behind his head, leaving them limp beside him on the bed. "Because I don't know why you weld or what you're making in the garage. I don't know why you got Jericho or your mom's name. I don't know how your dad died or who that woman is who drives the Lexus and hugs Jericho and kisses you. And I don't know why you dropped out of school."

His stone face didn't move for several seconds. "That stuff is important to the wellbeing of your heart?"

I nodded.

"I haven't asked your mom's name or how she died ... and I'm fine."

"Ryn. And she died in a car accident when I was fourteen. We buried her in a soft pink dress that she wore the day she brought me home from the hospital. My dad literally slept on her grave for several days afterward while I stayed with my aunt and uncle. When she met my dad, she had a German shepherd named Gunner. I saw pictures, but I don't remember him. It's what first drew me to Jerry."

"Jericho."

"Fuck you, Wylder. He's always going to be my Jerry."

"Oh, Livy…" he leaned over to set his computer under his nightstand "…we're definitely going to fuck." The second he faced me, his hand grabbed the back of my head, pulling my lips to his.

I reared back. "Tonight, you get charged for sex."

"Then I'm good." He rolled over and shut off the light.

I remained idle, frozen in disbelief as he situated his pillow and pulled the sheet partially over his bare torso, releasing a deep breath while resting his hands on his chest. Not everything in life had to be a game, but I hated feeling like he was in fact playing me … and he was winning.

"Night." I shrugged off my shirt and shimmied out of my panties, resting them next to his head on his pillow, so he'd know, in case he didn't catch what I'd done. Nestling under the covers, I rolled onto my side, putting my back to him.

It took several minutes, but he broke the silence. "Mary." He rolled toward me and his hand rested on my naked hip. "My mom's name is Mary. And I'm welding a wine bottle rack for her because her sister took the one her dad made when my grandparents went to a nursing home. My mom was broken-hearted because my grandfather was a welder and he made it for my grandma. And her sister doesn't even drink wine."

I rested my hand on his and guided it up to my breast. He squeezed it before trapping my nipple between his thumb and finger, giving it a slight tug and sending a jolt of need right between my legs.

"One of my targets ... he had a new puppy. A German shepherd. When he ... *died* ... I took his puppy."

Jericho belonged to a man whom Wylder assassinated. I didn't see that coming. It took me a few moments to swallow that information, but when I did, I moved his hand from my breast to my abs, right at my navel. He tugged on my piercing, and the sensation tickled me a little lower.

"My dad died in the line of fire. I don't remember anything about him ... I was too young. He never married my mom or lived with us."

My fingers ghosted along his arm draped over me before I covered his hand again and moved it lower.

I sucked in a sharp breath when he shoved two fingers inside me, faster and harder than I anticipated. His whole hand cupped me down there, pulling me closer until his erection slid between my legs. I didn't realize he'd removed his boxer briefs.

He fingered me hard and slow, curling them to hit my g-spot.

My hand clawed at his, the intensity almost too much, but I didn't really want him to stop. I just wasn't expecting it to go from a two to a ten in under five seconds.

His hot breath brushed along my ear. "The woman in the Lexus ..."

I panted, digging my nails into his unrelenting hand.

"She's my cousin. Abe's daughter. She cleans up my messes."

"W-Wylder ..." I was so close to seeing all the pretty orgasm stars.

"And *I* was someone's target for a while, so I had to disappear until the threat was neutralized. Are we good now, Liv?" he whispered, and it was so deep and controlled I nearly lost it just from his voice.

His fingers vanished, and his teeth dug into my shoulder.

A controlling hand gripped my leg and lifted it over his hip as he slid into me from behind with a hard thrust.

I was good.

He was good.

Everything was so … damn … good.

Chapter Twenty-Four

Wylder

"SHE BREAK IT?" I asked, sitting across from Abe at our usual table. Usual cafe.

Same grease stench.

Same waitress.

Same fan above our heads making a clicking sound.

He ran his finger along the bridge of his nose. "Nah. Not gonna lie, I wasn't expecting it."

I grinned. "Clearly. She got me too, a while back. Her aunt ... in her fifties ... has been training her in self-defense. A fucking actuary."

"Her aunt, huh?" Abe set his sandwich down and wiped his mouth.

"Yeah." I took a drink of my ice water, staring out the window for a few seconds. "What were you doing there?"

"Just wanted to see her."

"Why?"

"Do I have to have a reason?"

His answer grated on my nerves. "I'm watching her. Keeping her safe. You don't have to worry about it."

"Oh, I'm not worried. I know you're all over her." He smirked.

I kept my reaction neutral. Abe was the man I'd trusted

most in my life. He was also the person I feared the most. I felt pretty sure it was exactly how he intended for it to be.

"She knows you don't have friends. What else does she know about you?"

Shrugging, I glanced at my phone screen and the message from Livy.

Livy: *Surfing. Dinner with the girls. Don't wait up. x*

"Nothing. Why are you so concerned?"

"I'm concerned she's whispering dreams in your ear after sucking your cock, and you're going to lose focus and slip up ... tell her something about you that she shouldn't know."

"Again ... why are we here? Do you have something for me that doesn't involve babysitting?"

He took a bite of his sandwich and grinned while chewing slowly. "Don't worry," he mumbled. "Your babysitting days will be coming to an end really soon."

"How soon?"

Abe reached into the pocket of his suit jacket. "As soon as you take out your next target."

"Why? Is my target a threat to her?"

"Not exactly." He tossed a photo on the table. "It is her."

I stared at the photo of Livy on the beach, carrying her surfboard. Abe had used a serious zoom lens to capture it. "*What* is her?" I asked slowly.

"Your target."

The muscles in my fingers twitched as I forced them to stay slack instead of balling into a fist. My jaw didn't manage to do the same.

"And I'll need a souvenir to send home."

Acid climbed up my throat.

A souvenir … that was code for a body part. I never knew for sure, but I'd always suspected souvenirs were for revenge killings. An eye for an eye. Sometimes it was a finger or even a whole hand. Once it was an entire severed head. I didn't deliver the goods to the family; I just delivered the souvenir to Abe. Honestly, I didn't want to know any more about those situations. Until Livy.

"She's innocent. We don't kill innocent people."

"Aw, son … I was afraid your dick would get in the way."

"I'm not your son," I gritted between my clenched teeth.

"Well, I'm the only father you've ever really had. Is this going to be an issue? You know how this will play out. She doesn't live. If you don't do it, I will."

My gaze lifted from the picture to meet his purely evil expression. "You don't do this anymore."

"I'll make an exception. This one's personal."

"Why?"

"You'll find out when the time is right."

"You've handed me her photo. I think the time is right. And what was the fucking point of protecting her if she's a target?"

"I told you, it's personal. I wanted … I *needed* her to love you. The payback is so much sweeter knowing that she willingly let you crawl between her pretty little legs. She knows, doesn't she? She knows you saved her life behind that convenience store."

I shook my head. "That was you. You had the man do that to her?"

Abe cackled. "I needed your job to feel legit. I gave you the kill you love. You should thank me."

"I'm not your fucking pawn."

"You're whatever I want you to be. Imagine my surprise and pure delight when she enrolled in the same university. Imagine how perfect the timing was that the house you live in now was available right when I wanted you to go back to school. A house just feet from hers. Seriously, fate fucking loves me."

"She doesn't love me." I shrugged.

"She's living with you. Even if I made the stretch to believe that you don't have feelings for her pussy, I know there's no way she'd agree to live with you if she didn't love you. It's a girl thing. I realize you have no social skills, especially with women, so I don't really expect you to realize what you're doing—"

"Just shut the fuck up."

His pie hole shut, but his eyes narrowed. I'd seen that look too many times and nothing good ever came from it. "Watch it, boy."

I bit the hell out of my tongue and swallowed hard.

"Now … you have two weeks. Just in time for the holidays. I'm tempted to say that pretty little head of hers would be my first choice for a souvenir, but I've always left that part—no pun intended—up to you." He stood, tapping his lighter on the table a few times.

Chapter Twenty-Five

Livy

"I T'S JUST SICK," I floated on my board next to Kara and Missy, watching Aiden, my favorite OG (Original Gangster) catch the next wave.

"Um … is that who I think it is?" Missy asked, glancing over her shoulder toward the shore.

I followed her line of sight to my guy and my dog on the beach. He looked completely out of place in his jeans and boots.

"Thought it was a girls' night," Kara said.

"It is." I turned and paddled inward, catching the end of a wave that took me to shore. "I texted you." I grinned, heading up the beach with my board.

"I know." He slipped his hands in his front pockets as I parked my board in the sand and wrung out my hair.

"So what's up? You clearly didn't come to surf."

"I'm crashing your girls' night."

"Crashing?" I narrowed my eyes. "As in joining us?"

"As in taking you home."

"Why?" I reached around and unzipped my wet suit.

"Because Jerry said he wants us to grab takeout and do something like watch a movie."

Pausing with one arm out of my wet suit, my jaw unhinged. He didn't say that. It was his body, but those weren't his words. "Who are you? *Jerry?* Takeout and a movie? What gives? This isn't you. This isn't the guy who complimented me on my lack of neediness."

"Fine. I want to tie you up and bury my face between your legs. Better?"

I coughed a laugh and glanced around to see how many people were in earshot. "You said you were the guy who made sure no one ever tied me up." Pulling my other arm out of my wet suit, I gave him a lifted eyebrow in a question of his own words and new intentions.

"I'm trying really hard to be..." his lips twisted "...amicable and persuasive."

Pushing the wet suit down to my hips, I glanced up. "Amicable? What exactly is the alternative to you being *amicable* with me?"

He squinted against the sun, peering over my shoulder for a few moments. "You're the straight-A student. You tell me, what's the opposite of amicable?"

Crossing my arms over my chest, I trapped my lip between my teeth until he returned his focus to me. "Unfriendly. Hostile. Are you suggesting if I don't go home with you now, things will get unfriendly? Hostile?"

"Affirmative."

"Go home, Wylder. I'll be home later ... or tomorrow." I bent down and kissed Jerry on the head. "Daddy's a little cray cray tonight, isn't he?"

"I'll wait."

"Wait for what?" I trudged through the sand to my bag and retrieved my water, taking a long swig.

"You."

"Yeah, that's what I said. Go home and *wait* for me." I shoved my water bottle back into my bag and grabbed his shirt, pulling him closer until he gave me his mouth for a quick kiss. "Love you. I'll text you if I end up staying at Aubrey's." I turned, heading back to my board while righting the sleeves of my wet suit and worming my arms back into it.

After another hour of surfing, we headed to my Jeep, giggling, and wiped out from a full Saturday at the beach.

"Whoa … stalker much?" Missy nodded to Slade's black Volvo parked on the other side of my Jeep.

"Something's up. This isn't him." I shook my head.

"Here. We've got it." Missy nodded to my board.

I propped it against the Jeep and peeled my wet suit off. Slipping on my sweatshirt, I made my way to his window.

He rolled it down. "Get in. Let one of your friends take your Jeep."

I leaned forward, resting my arms on the door. "What aren't you telling me?" Genuine concern delivered my words.

"Get in, Livy."

"I'm not getting in unless you give me a reason to get in."

He rubbed his temples then dropped his hands to the steering wheel, looking straight ahead. "I'll give you two questions. You can ask me two things … anything … and I'll give you an honest answer."

Desperate Wylder. He took lives. That was his job. He lived in a haunted house. He feared nothing. So why could I feel his desperation?

"Fine. But you answer one right now."

He turned his head toward me.

"Why are you so desperate for me to come with you right now?"

"Because I feel an intense need to protect you."

"From what?"

"Is that your second and last question?"

Gah! I had a million questions for him. No … I didn't want it to be my last question, yet I wanted to know why I needed his protection. "You're scaring me."

"Then get in the car."

Pushing out a forceful breath, I stood straight and walked around to Missy and Kara, helping them finish securing the boards on top of the Jeep. "I need to go with Slade. Can you take my Jeep? Will you forgive me for skipping out tonight?"

"What? Are you serious?" Missy asked, hopping down from the back bumper and unzipping her wet suit.

"What's up?" Kara added.

"It's …" I rubbed my lips together, searching for something that made sense, knowing it was going to be a lie. I hated lying to my friends. "Slade lost a friend."

"What? Oh my god!" Missy covered her mouth. "That's awful."

"Dude …" Kara's eyes widened. "He told you he lost a friend, and you went back to surfing?"

"He didn't tell me what happened. He just asked me to come home. I thought he was being a little possessive of my time since he wouldn't tell me why."

Missy brushed past me.

"Where are you going?" I followed her.

"I want to give him my condolences."

"No—"

Too late.

She knocked on his window. He rolled it down again.

"I'm so sorry to hear about your friend."

"Yeah," Kara added.

I bit my lips together, eyes wide.

Slade's gaze stayed on me for several seconds before flitting to Kara and Missy. "Thanks."

"Let us know if you need anything. We'll get your Jeep back to you in the morning." Missy hugged me.

"Thanks," I released her and hugged Kara.

Grabbing my bag, I climbed into Slade's SUV.

"Who died?" he asked, pulling out of the lot.

"Your friend."

"You didn't believe I had friends."

"Do you?"

"No."

I would have laughed, but he was taking me away from my Saturday night plans with my friends because he feared for my safety, but I had no idea why. And maybe he knew that. Maybe he knew I wouldn't get far enough to ask the real questions. Maybe it was all made up.

But why?

So I asked. I'd get more questions with my bartering skills. "Why do you feel an insane need to protect me? And yes, this is my second question."

"Because I love you."

"That's …" I felt so damn conflicted. Those words coming out of his mouth rendered me speechless every time, but it wasn't the real answer.

"I don't like this game," I murmured, staring out the side window.

"Neither do I," he whispered. I didn't think he meant for me to hear it, but I did.

The second he stopped the vehicle in the driveway, I tried

to hop out, but he grabbed my arm. "I go first."

"You go first where?"

He opened his door. "Everywhere."

On a huff, I followed him and Jericho to the back door. He unlocked the door and reached behind him as he opened it slowly. His hand wrapped around a gun that he slid out of the waist of his jeans.

What the hell …

He had a gun. I knew he had many weapons, but never on him. I held in my gasp, my string of questions, and my fear as he and Jericho stepped inside. I slinked behind them, holding my breath. He turned and held up his hand for me to stay.

Jericho led the way, and they scoped out the main floor before going upstairs while I remained cemented to my spot just inside the back door.

"We're good," he said as he reached the bottom of the stairs and tucked his gun back into his waistband. Not just his waistband … I narrowed my eyes. He had a holster. This wall in my brain kept him separated from his profession.

I'd never seen him take a life.

I'd never seen him hold any of the weapons in his dungeon. Until then.

Something changed when I watched him grip that gun with ease and comfort, when he moved through the house with it pointed ahead of him—on guard yet perfectly calm at the same time.

Slade Wylder took lives, and he did it like an afterthought.

"What's happening?" I whispered, afraid to move an inch.

"I don't know yet." He cupped my neck with both hands, his thumbs caressing my throat, and he kissed the top of my head.

"W-why do you have that gun? Am I in danger? Have you …" I glanced up at him, my hands grabbing his arms as he continued to cradle my neck in his protective hands. "You've put me in danger."

Wylder grunted a laugh and released me. "No." He turned, leaving me frozen in place while he opened the fridge. "Tell me about your dad."

"What? Why?" I squinted. My thoughts spun, making me dizzy as I wobbled on listless legs to a kitchen chair. "What did you do? Why are you carrying a gun? Why did you have to check the house? Tell me what's going on."

"Is your family rich?"

"What?" My face contorted as I shook my head, trying to sort through everything jumbled in my mind. "No."

"Influential?" He turned, opening a bottle of beer.

"No. Why are you asking me this? Whatever this is … whoever is coming after you … it has nothing to do with me. That night at the convenience store was random, not calculated. It could have happened to anyone."

"Has your dad done anything to piss anyone off? Does he have any enemies?"

"No. Slade … *why* are you asking me about my dad?"

He took a long swig and set it down. Then he rested his hands on the edge of the counter and dropped his head. "You said he's a computer geek. What does that mean? Is he a hacker? Does he work for the government? A big corporation?"

"He's a computer engineer. He doesn't work for the government. His job is boring, without influence, and for a midsized company. His hobbies include playing the piano, exercising, overprotecting me, and missing my mom. That's it. What is your point?"

With his head still hanging, he shook it slowly. "The men you've dated ... anything notable about them? Have you ever been with a married man? When you saw Abe, did anything about him look familiar to you?"

"Jesus, Slade. What's happening? I've not knowingly slept with a married man. Nothing about Abe looked familiar. And the most notable thing about any of the men I've dated is my most recent guy is an assassin."

Ignoring my jab, he lifted his head and reached for his beer. After another long swig, he exhaled slowly and pinned me with a hard expression. "Shortly after we met, Abe gave me a new assignment, something I don't usually do, but I do what he says, so ..."

My eyebrows lifted. "So?"

"He told me I needed to look after you. To make sure you were safe ... protected."

Protect me.

I should have felt safe. After all, a man with a slew of weapons was living with me. *Protecting me.* But I didn't feel safe. The only time I'd felt that vulnerable—that exposed—was when I had a knife to my throat while a terrible human tried to rape me.

"How could I be so stupid?" I whispered. "You said it wasn't your job to ... fuck me." My gaze lifted to his. "But I was your *job.*"

"Livy—"

I shook my head, closing my eyes for a few seconds. "That's what happened. That's why you went from clearly hating me to ..." I opened my eyes as tears filled them. "Might as well get a little action, huh? The closer you drew me in, the easier it was to protect me. Oh my god ..." I wiped the tears as soon as they fell from my burning eyes. "We're nothing." My words fell out like someone shot them. Lifeless. Monotone. Numb.

He set his beer down and his boots ate up the distance between us. Hunching in front of me, his hands rested on my hips. "We're everything."

I shook my head, closing my eyes as silent tears spilled out, down my cheeks to my lap.

"Look at me."

I shook my head relentlessly, keeping my chin to my chest, my bottom lip quivering as I clenched my teeth to keep from sobbing.

"Look. At. Me." He framed my face with his hands and forced my head up.

I blinked open my eyes, big tears clinging to my lashes.

"It wasn't my job to touch you the way I've touched you. I couldn't stop myself. I wanted to ... even when I knew it wasn't a good idea. So I did it anyway. And I knew it wasn't my job to love you. Again, I couldn't stop myself. I did it anyway. Protecting you is no longer my job. It's what I do *because* I love you."

I couldn't find words. No matter how much I wanted to believe him, it was impossible to dismiss the arsenal below me, the gun in his holster, and his questions. More than all of that, it wasn't what he did say. It was everything he didn't say.

"Why did Abe hire you to protect me? Protect me from what? From whom?"

"I can't say."

"No." My head whipped side to side as I tried to stand.

He grabbed my wrists. "Livy—"

"Let. Go. Of. Me!" I tried to wriggle out of his hold.

He released me, holding his hands up in surrender while

still kneeling before me as I stood.

"You can't protect me with lies," I seethed.

"It's the only way I *can* protect you. And I'm sorry it sounds so fucked-up, but *that* is the truth. I know it's an unimaginable leap of faith I'm asking, but I need you to trust me and do everything I ask."

"I should call my dad … Jessica …"

He shook his head. "You. I can protect you. I can't protect everyone you drag into this mess. Not until I get things figured out. Please." His hands eased to my hips, eyes pleading as I peered down at him. "Let me love you back."

A new round of tears emerged. "I'm scared," I whispered.

"I've got you." He rested his forehead over my heart, arms encircling my waist.

"Promise?" I eased back into the chair.

He moved several inches forward on his knees, hands finding their way into my hair, lips brushing mine. "Promise."

Chapter Twenty-Six

Jackson Knight

"WHEN'S THE LAST time someone kicked your ass?"

I glanced up from my computer. My twin, Jessica, sauntered into my house with her gym bag. "No one's ever kicked my ass. So the answer to your question is never." I returned my attention to my computer.

"Working? Obsessing? Or stalking?"

"Obsessing? Stalking?"

She took a seat at the dining room table across from me. "Obsessing over Ryn's death, which … for the millionth time … was an accident. Or are you stalking Livy and her new boyfriend?"

I flitted my gaze to hers for a second time. "She told you about Slade?"

"Slade." She grinned. "You know and remembered his name. That's something."

My dead stare remained glued to her until the light went on in her head.

"Of course, you know his name, and you know it well because you're stalking him. I knew it."

"His record is clean."

"Great! Case closed. Well wishes to Livy on her new relationship. Now, let's go spar. My boss was an asshole today. I need to hit someone."

"It's too clean."

She rolled her eyes. "He's in his twenties. Maybe he comes from a nice family. Clean record."

"There's not a father's name on his birth certificate."

"It's not a crime to be raised by one parent."

I nodded slowly. "I know. But he has no social media accounts. And he dropped out of college for three years before going back to finish his senior year."

"Family emergency? Health issues? Second thoughts on his future? Money issues? Seriously, Jackson, you're looking for something that's not there."

"That's my point. He's *too* clean. Not just squeaky clean. I'm talking unrealistically clean."

"So what are you going to do? Go to LA, tie him up, and interrogate him?"

I cork-screwed my lips. "That's not a bad idea."

"Yes." She laughed. "It's a horrible idea. The kind of idea that ruins your relationship with your daughter."

With my thumb and middle finger, I rubbed my temples, staring at everything I could find on Slade Wylder in multiple screens. "The day Ryn died … I was uneasy all day. I couldn't explain it. A sixth sense feeling. I must have messaged her twenty times, checking on her, checking on Livy."

"You said that. It's not unheard of for people to have a feeling that something bad is going to happen, but it still doesn't mean that it was anything other than an accident."

I leaned back in the chair and laced my fingers behind my head. "I've had the same feeling for several days about Livy. You don't know how many times I've considered getting on a plane to go check on her in person. Stay there until the feeling goes away. In the fall, I had the same feeling."

"You did?" Jessica narrowed her eyes, an odd expression morphing her face.

"Yeah. I tried messaging her a million times, and I was ready to head straight to the airport when she texted me back, confirming she was fine."

Jessica rubbed her lips together, forehead tense. "Did you have this feeling before the house fire?"

I shook my head. "Clearly she wasn't in danger. She was at *his* house doing God knows what."

When Jessica didn't jump at the chance to make a joke about all the times I was doing "God knows what" in my twenties, I knew something wasn't right. I sat up straight. "What aren't you telling me?"

She pinched her bottom lip, gaze aimed off to the side. "What can you find on a Stefan Hoover from Nevada? Two kids and a wife. He was killed in LA after attempting to rape a college girl."

"Why?" I asked, my hands already moving over the keyboard to look up his information. "Over a hundred K in credit card and gambling debt. No prior record. But yeah, he was found dead after attempting to rape a girl behind a convenience store in Septem—" My gaze shot to Jessica's.

She swallowed hard.

"This is when I had that feeling."

Another hard swallow as her eyes remained unblinking, like prey would eye its predator.

"Jess." My fists clenched on the table, jaw set. "So help me God, if this was Livy ..." I couldn't even say it. My chest filled with rage and fear of something I didn't want to be true.

"She told me over a month later when I was in LA for

business."

"Why *the fuck* am I just now hearing about this?" I stood, sending the chair backward with my violent outburst.

Jess held up her hands. "Let me explain."

"EXPLAIN?" I took my water glass and pitched it into the wall, glass, ice, and water flying everywhere. "How the fuck are you going to explain not telling me that some guy tried to rape my daughter?" I moved around the table so quickly she flinched, and my sister *never* flinched. "If it were one of your girls, what would you do?"

She stared at my chest, holding her own in posture, but shame filled her eyes. "You know what I would do," she whispered. "She made me promise not to tell you. He *didn't* rape her. Had he … I would not have kept her secret."

"That's fucking great, Jess. You've just kept it a secret that she's in LA, dating some guy I know nothing about, and completely defenseless."

Her eyes shifted upward. "Not defenseless. I've been training her."

I squinted. "Training her? What do you mean?"

"You know what I mean."

"No. I don't. You're her aunt. Period."

Her jaw flexed along with her hands. "You taught her how to punch and run. How to use a bottle of pepper spray."

"Because *that's* what I told Ryn I would teach her. That's it. A normal college student with a normal upbringing. Everything we didn't have."

"Well, after her incident, I decided she deserved a normal adult life. A safe adult life. I decided no man would ever pin her to the ground … would ever leave the kind of scars that never heal."

Emotion crushed my chest. It wasn't the life I wanted for Livy. "How long?"

"Three months."

"That's not enough." I shook my head.

"I'm not done."

I rubbed the back of my neck. "How much? What have you trained her to do?"

Jessica tipped her chin up, lips in a firm line. "I've trained her to bleed."

"Fuck ... Jess ..." I winced thinking about my little girl experiencing the things I experienced, the things Jessica experienced. Even if it was a fraction of it, it was too much.

Jessica tipped her chin up another inch, shoulders back, reminding me of everything she'd survived in her life. "I trained her to get up. I trained her to feel the pain and channel it into one thing ..."

"Her next breath," I whispered the words that were repeated to us over and over.

She returned several slow nods. "This feeling ..."

I shook my head. "It's probably nothing."

"But what if it's something?"

"You mean Slade?"

Jessica shrugged. "Slade. Stefan Hoover. The house that burned down. The cause of the fire was not determined for certain."

"You think it was meant for Livy?"

"No," Jess said as a knee-jerk reaction to keep me from losing my shit. "Maybe."

I grabbed my phone. "She's at Slade's."

"You're tracking her?"

I frowned at Jessica and her stupid question. "I bought her

a new phone after the fire. Of course I'm tracking her. I track her Jeep too. If I could have gotten away with chipping her, I would have." I called Livy and put the phone on speaker.

"Hey, Dad," she answered on the third ring.

"Livy. How are you?"

"Um ... fine. Why? What's up? Is everything okay?"

I listened for odd inflections in her voice, strain, unusual hesitation. "Yeah. Everything is fine. Just wanted to call my daughter."

"O ... kay. Are you sure everything is okay?"

"Absolutely." I shifted my gaze from the screen to Jessica, her face was unmoving—focused on every word, just like mine. "What are you doing?"

"Slade and I just got home from surfing."

"Sounds fun. Do you surf with your friends anymore, or are you glued to a guy?"

"I surfed with the girls last week."

"When are you driving home for Christmas break?"

She paused, hesitated. My eyes locked with Jessica's again.

"Um ... I'm not sure yet."

"Well, when is your last day of classes?"

"Um ... Friday."

"Great. So I'll see you when? Saturday?"

"I'll let you know when I check with Slade."

"Why do you need to check with him? Is he coming home with you? Surely he'll be spending Christmas with his family."

"Yeah, uh ... I'm not sure yet. We haven't really discussed it."

"It's a week away and you haven't discussed it? That's not like you."

"He might have to work over break. And if that's the case,

then I might stay here with him."

"What do you mean stay there with him? Miss Christmas with your family?"

"Well, maybe. It's just one Christmas. You'll get invited to Aunt Jess's, right?"

"Right," I said slowly.

"But I mean ... nothing's set in stone. I'll let you know when I can."

"Yeah. You do that. Let us know when Slade knows his work schedule."

"Totally. Bye, Dad. Love you."

"Liv ..."

"Yeah?"

I wanted to say something. The need clawed at my gut, sending a physical pain shooting up my chest. I wanted to tell her I knew what happened to her—almost happened to her— and how sorry I was for not being there, for not doing more to protect her.

"Love you too." I pressed *End*.

"We need to go to LA."

"Me. Not we."

"Jackson ..."

"*We* don't even know what we're looking for yet. And maybe it's nothing. I'll go check things out and let you know if I need anything."

On a slow exhale, she relinquished a slight nod. "I'm sorry for not telling you."

"Did you tell her about you?"

She nodded. "The PG-13 version."

"When you made her bleed, did she ..." I rubbed my hand over my mouth. It killed me to ask it, but it also killed me to not know.

"She broke my heart. That moment ... when you know that you're changing someone forever. When you've made a mark that will be there forever even if it's invisible. She cried. She begged me to stop."

My face contorted.

Something resembling a smile tugged at Jessica's lips. "But when she found her fire ... it burned so damn bright. She's you."

"She's her mom."

Jessica shook her head. "Her heart is Ryn's, but her soul ... her fight ... is all you."

Chapter Twenty-Seven

Livy

I TRUSTED HIM.

Wylder asked for me to trust him without any more questions, and I did. I said it made me feel weak. He said putting that kind of trust in someone showed unmeasurable strength and bravery.

He escorted me to all of my classes and left Jericho with me until he made it back to the class to get me. I knew he skipped out on parts of his own classes to make sure he was always there. I hated it.

The fear.

The worst kind of fear—the unknown.

Lying to my dad.

Lying to my friends.

The firehouse started to feel like a prison, and Slade started to feel like an actual warden—like I used to feel at home with my dad. We made a few trips to the beach, but not my beach. He wanted us to lie low from my usual hangouts, which meant shitty surfing at best. And just me. He stood guard on the beach with Jericho.

"Still studying?" I asked, climbing into bed in one of his T-shirts.

"Yep."

"Think you know enough to pass?" I grabbed his computer and set it on my nightstand.

He lifted an eyebrow. "What are you doing?"

I crawled onto his lap. He still had on his jeans, no shirt. "I don't like this." I ran my fingers along his abs.

"My stomach?"

With a slight grin that fought through my pain and frustration, I shook my head. "I don't like not knowing. I feel like a child in a classroom with sirens going off, and I don't know if it's for a fire and I'm supposed to run out of the building, or a gunman and I need to lock down in a safe room." I glanced up at him. "I don't like not knowing what I'm supposed to fear."

He ran his hands up my bare legs. "I don't want you to fear anything."

"But I do."

His hands turned, angling up my inner thighs. Pure torture. We hadn't had sex since he deemed things to be on high alert.

"I can't fuck you and protect you."

His words of rejection echoed in my head, but the direction of his hands sent mixed signals, especially when he realized I wasn't wearing panties.

"Wylder ..." I closed my eyes when his thumb grazed my clit.

"What do you need, Liv?" he whispered, as his fingers slid a little farther back, teasing my very wet entrance.

"This ..." I opened my eyes just as those fingers entered me. I pressed my hands to his chest to steady myself, feeling drugged from his touch ... a touch he'd refused me for the entirety of the previous week.

"You like this?" he asked, making slow strokes in and out of me.

"Y-yes …" I closed my eyes, leaning down to kiss him.

He grabbed my chin to push me back, his gaze shifting to the door for a split second. I stiffened, grabbing both of his wrists and twisting my body to see the open doorway. The ghost that wasn't there. At least that I saw.

"I can't." I pushed his hand away from my neck and climbed off his lap. "I want all of you. Not two fingers and a gun on the nightstand." I let my gaze drift to said gun on his nightstand. He slipped it under his pillow at night, but honestly, I didn't think he'd had a minute of sleep since the day he dragged me home from the beach. He ran on coffee and high-caffeine drinks that filled the fridge.

The worry line between his brows deepened for a second before he swung his feet off the side of the bed. After a few breaths of just sitting there, hanging his head, he stood and disappeared downstairs. I leaned against the headboard, pulling my knees to my chest, knowing he'd be back after his final sweep of the house.

Jericho perched himself inside the bedroom door, and Wylder shut it and locked it. "I'm going to shower," he mumbled once my guard dog was in place.

When the water turned on, I pulled down the sheets to get under them. Noticing his laptop still open on my nightstand, I reached over to shut it, just as a message notification popped up in the righthand corner.

Name unknown.

I glanced at the bathroom door before pulling the computer onto my lap and clicking his message screen.

Where's my souvenir?

My heart pounded. Who was the unknown name? There were no previous messages. I clicked onto my name in the message screen.

No messages.

Clearly, Wylder erased all messages.

Clicking back to the unknown name, I let my fingers hover over the keys, shaking.

What do you want?

My pinkie finger rested over the return button for a few seconds, then I hit it, knowing I didn't have long before Wylder would be out of the shower. He didn't take long ones. Two to three minutes was all he allowed himself to be unarmed and vulnerable.

I want you to stop fucking the target and send me the souvenir. Your choice, but I'll give you a bonus if it's her head.

Moments …

That moment. The official moment my existence shattered.

Every dream—gone.

Every inch of trust—gone.

Every ounce of love—gone.

Jessica said I'd feel it; that moment when desperation became the hardest punch, the sharpest knife, the fastest bullet.

I wanted to cry. Inside I sobbed from the pain and the fear. On the outside, I moved my body.

Closed the computer.

Slid on a pair of jeans.

And as soon as the shower shut off, I took the gun and wrapped my hands around the cold grip. It felt heavy and foreign to me.

Jericho stood, making a whining noise. My gaze slid to him as I aimed the gun at the bathroom doorway. Slade poked his head around the corner, his attention going straight to Jericho. Then his attention shifted across the room to me, in the shadows of the corner, pointing his gun at him.

He slowly tucked the towel under to hold it on his waist, water dripping from his hair, rivulets sliding down his torso. "Livy …"

"It's not your job," I whispered past the jagged boulder in my throat.

"What's not my job?"

"Protecting me."

"What are you talking about?" He took a step toward me.

"Don't!" I jerked the gun like a whip. "Don't take another step."

"You're alive. I think that proves I'm protecting you. I'm doing my job. I'm doing what I *want* to do because I love you."

"Lies …" I shook my head, fighting the burning tears waiting to be set free. "You're an assassin. Not a bodyguard. You *kill* people."

The muscles in his jaw flexed. "I kill bad people to protect good people."

"LIES!" My grip tightened as the tears breached the dam, falling fast and hard down my face. "You got a m-message." I could barely see him through my tears. "*I'm* your target."

His gaze shot to the computer on the bed, and it stayed there for several seconds before he closed his eyes and inched his head side to side. "Livy—"

"No! No Livy. No more trusting you. No more anything. I'm going to put all of these bullets in you and make you fucking bleed the truth. For all of the people you've killed. You *lied* to me. You're not a good person who does bad things to terrible people. You're just a sick fuck who hunts humans like an animal. M-my h-head ..." I sobbed as the words from the text replayed in my mind. "Y-you were g-going to c-cut off my h-head." I trembled from the emotions beating me up from the inside out like a malignant cancer.

"Put the gun down, Livy."

"No!"

He frowned, tightening the towel around his waist. "It's not loaded. Put the fucking gun down."

"Liar."

"I'm not lying." He blew out an exasperated breath and glanced at the ceiling. "Pull the trigger if you don't believe me." His eyes shifted, pinning me with his intense gaze again.

"How many?" I said with a shaky voice. "How many people have you killed?"

He lifted a shoulder. "I don't know. I don't keep a count."

Slade Wylder was cold and heartless. And manipulative. I wondered how many women he manipulated before me.

"You're a bastard."

"Fine, but I still love you back."

"STOP saying that!"

"Give me the gun or pull the trigger."

I pulled my left hand from the grip and wiped my tears, quickly returning it to help steady my other hand.

"How much did she teach you? Your aunt? Because it takes a special personality to take another person's life. You're not that person, Liv. You don't take lives. And that makes me fucking love you even more."

"You don't know me," I said just above a whisper.

"No?" He cocked his head to the side. "Then pull the trigger." He taunted me.

He manipulated me.

He touched me intimately knowing he would kill me.

It was worse than anything Stefan Hoover planned on doing to me. Slade took my fucking heart, not just my body, not just a piece of my innocence. He tainted my soul.

"My mom ..." I sniffled. "She told me about the agony of putting her dog down when he was suffering too much. She said her heart knew he had to be put out of his misery. You ... you're a miserable human, and I'm going to put you out of your misery. *I'm* going to take one life to save hundreds of lives. *I'm* going to do a bad thing to a terrible person. *I'm* going to prove to you that *you don't know me ...* and what I am or am not capable of doing." Two more tears escaped as I drew my right index finger toward my palm.

Click.

A hollow click.

I pulled the trigger a second time.

Click.

Third time.

Click.

"Jesus ..." Slade whispered. The most foreign expression took hold of his face.

Shock? Fear? Devastation?

No ... it wasn't any of those things. For a few seconds, I saw a reddening of his eyes, a tiny glimpse of his rawest of emotions.

Betrayal.

He felt betrayed.

I felt like screaming and running. But my cries would've

died inside those walls. And with Jericho by the only exit, I had nowhere to go.

No bullets.

No plan.

No chance.

No hope.

I let the gun drop to the floor, and I held up my hands near my face, curling them into fists.

"I'm not going to fight you, Livy." He released his towel and grabbed his briefs from the top of the dresser, followed by a clean pair of jeans and a black tee.

My stance remained ready to take a punch or throw one. I was going to leave the firehouse that night … or die trying.

"You pulled the trigger." He picked up the gun while sliding his other hand under the edge of the mattress. "Not going to lie, that hurt. Kinda felt like you did shoot me right in the fucking heart." From under the mattress he retrieved a black cartridge thing and shoved it into the bottom of the gun. My heart sank.

The magazine … filled with ammunition.

I had two fists and he had a loaded gun.

"So that's what it feels like?" Our gazes locked as he concealed the loaded gun into the waist of his jeans. "Loving someone without reason? Having your heart broken?" He shook his head slowly just like he released his next breath, blinking several times, hands idle at his sides.

My words were paralyzed somewhere in my body, far from my mouth, because I had two fists and he had a loaded gun. On his computer there was a message offering him a bonus for my head. It wasn't his job to fuck me or protect me. Assassins killed people. *That* was his job. *I* was his job. "Yeah," I finally managed to find the whisper of a voice, blinking out another few tears. "That's what it feels like."

"You still want to fight?" He focused on my hands fisted by my face like an unbreakable statue.

"I want to live … I want to go home."

"This is your home."

I shook my head.

"I'm not going to kill you."

My eyes flitted, gaze focused on where he had the gun. His attention followed my line of sight, and he slowly pulled the gun back out and set it on the dresser behind him.

"It's loaded now. Just for you. Get the gun, Livy."

I remembered loving him, wanting nothing more than his arms around me, the look in his eyes when he was inside of me. My hands remembered what it felt like when he took them and guided me to the car, across campus, or out of the sand at the beach.

The tenderness.

The love.

The smiles.

The whisper of promises.

And all of that just … made me livid.

My heart free falling into Slade Wylder's world.

Vulnerable.

Frightened.

Suicidal.

Stupid, crazy, impulsive heart.

I shoved the lamp off the nightstand. His gaze followed as I landed a fist into his face, a knee to his ribs … another jab to his face, his nose, his groin. He did nothing more than let his body move naturally with the force of strikes. I drew blood from his nose, his lip, the corner of his eye … I drew blood from my knuckles, channeling the pain into my next breath.

With each hit, I counted my breaths. I waited for him to fight back, but he didn't. He also didn't go down. A dead expression took over his face. I couldn't recognize it. Nothing I did was new to him. He was like Jessica—fearless, focused, and conditioned to take *everything*. It was like someone took his life long ago without actually stopping his heart or stealing his breaths.

I stepped back, straightening my fingers slowly. They were covered in blood and pulsing to the beat of my heart. Throbbing. Aching. "Wh-who did this to you? Who tortured you?" My eyes shifted up to meet his face.

It bled, but his eyes remained two dark holes like pieces of coal, no life. He didn't answer.

On the nightstand, his phone vibrated with a call. I glanced at it and then at Slade while slowly grabbing it. I slid the bar to the right and pressed speaker.

"Livy …" Abe's voice rose from the phone. "What did you do with my boy?"

My eyes narrowed.

"You're wondering how I know. Aren't you? Easy … he doesn't respond to his messages. Ever. I just send him things to prod him into action, to remind him that I'm always watching. Now … what did you do with my boy?"

Slade made no attempt to speak, no attempt to move, not so much as a blink.

"Why …" The word tore from my throat, barely audible by the time it reached the air. That was it. That was all I wanted to know. Why did someone want to take my life? Not on a whim. A plotted assassination. "Why me?"

"If you did anything to Slade …" His voice carried an edge.

I blinked at Slade again and again. Why didn't he speak? If it were my uncle trying to see if I was safe, I would have yelled and pleaded for help. I would have said *something*.

"Why me?" I repeated. In my mind, it was the only question that deserved an answer.

"Because your dad is the reason Slade grew up without a father … the reason I no longer have a brother."

My head shook. He had the wrong person. Not my dad.

"Jackson Knight, formerly Jude Day."

My head continued to shake as my attention shifted to Slade's face. He held me captive with just his presence, but the look in his eyes morphed from resignation to something darker.

"No …" I said.

"A soldier in the dismantled organization called G.A.I.L—Guardian Angels for Innocent Lives. Jude Day was trained to protect the innocent by removing threats. Just like Slade."

"No …" I whispered as Slade's forehead tensed along with his jaw, hands curling into fists.

"Yes, Livy. Daddy Dearest was a trained assassin … just like Slade. He took more lives than your pretty little head can even imagine. On his final killing spree, he put a bullet between my brother's eyes out of revenge. And he left a little boy without a father … he left me without my brother."

"Y-you don't know my dad."

"No, sweetheart … *you* don't know your dad. He's an animal that needs to be put down, but not before he suffers … the way I've suffered without my brother, the way Slade suffered without his dad, the way Mary suffered as a single mom. That's three. Three lives destroyed. So I'm taking three lives to even the score. Well ... two. I already took one."

"Dad ..." I choked on his name. He killed my dad.

"Not yet. He'll be the last ... after he knows I took his world. And let's be honest ... it will be a mercy killing. I honestly didn't think he would survive after your mom's *accident.* Did you know he slept on her grave for days while you were with your aunt? I watched him. I fed off his suffering. It felt so fucking good, but not as good as it's going to feel when I deliver you, well, part of you, to him."

The phone fell from my hand as waves of pain gripped my body, shaking me to the core. My breaths came one right after the other so quickly it felt like I wasn't getting any oxygen at all. It wasn't an accident. Abe killed my mom. Or ...

I stepped back until the wall caught me as Slade studied me. Was he just an extension of Abe? The killer giving all the credit to his handler? I began to crumble, sliding down the wall. "Y-you killed my m-mom ..." I glared at Slade and hugged my bloodied hands to my chest as my butt hit the floor.

Slade reached behind him and grabbed the gun. I jumped when he pulled the trigger, shattering his phone on the floor and ending the call with Abe while my ears rang from him firing the gun. "I didn't." He lifted his gaze from the gun to me, his tone eerily calm. "But it sounds like your dad put a bullet in my dad's head, and that's a problem, Liv."

I didn't—I *couldn't* believe that about my dad. Some black ops group? An assassin? Then again, I thought about Jessica and her skill set that I knew nothing about until the day she fractured a piece of my innocence with her fists.

Clarity blurred.

Colors faded.

Reason and purpose for my own existence started to wither like a starved plant after months of a summer drought.

Nothing in my life was what it seemed to be just weeks earlier. Twenty-one years of lies. If you didn't know where you came from, it was hard to know who you were—are.

"We have to go. Get up." He aimed the gun at me, jerking it in an up motion like the threat of dying mattered to me at that point.

It didn't.

He retrieved a bag from his closet and set it on the bed. Pulling out his holster, he secured it around his waist and filled it with the gun in his hand and another gun from the bag along with extra ammunition magazines. Then he covered everything with his shirt and nodded at me. "Get. Up."

I didn't.

Slade grabbed my arms near my shoulders and lifted me from the ground. When I didn't force my legs to keep me standing, he tossed me on the bed. I felt so numb, so empty, so lifeless.

I didn't fight him when he guided my arms around my back and tied my wrists.

I didn't fight him when he heaved me over his shoulder and carried me downstairs with Jericho in tow.

I didn't fight him when he tossed me in the back seat of my Jeep, gagged me, and put a black cloth bag over my head.

Jericho sat next to my head. The door closed. Minutes later, the back door opened, and the vehicle dipped with the weight of whatever he was loading into it. I closed my eyes, hearing only the residual high-pitched ringing in my ears as I prayed for death, the welcoming arms of my mom, and an existence free from the ugliness.

Chapter Twenty-Eight

HOURS LATER, ROUGH hands startled me from my sleep or coma … whatever state of pre-death I fell into on the long journey. Pain radiated from my abdomen to my ribs when Slade once again hoisted me over his shoulder. Gravel crunched beneath his boots, and that was the only sound I could hear.

The creak from wooden steps replaced the gravel. A familiar loamy and mossy scent seeped through the cover on my head. We were in the woods.

Screen door screeched.

Thunk. It slammed shut.

More wood creaked beneath his surefooted steps. He deposited me on something lumpy like an old sofa, the waft of musk replacing the outdoorsy scent. I started choking as my need to cough, the gag in my mouth, and the bag over my head stifled my breathing. Slade removed the bag and untied the gag in my mouth.

I coughed until my throat burned, raw and dry. My ribs ached, but not as much as my shoulders, arms, and wrists from the tie around them. Squinting against the light from the floor lamp, the rustic cabin came into focus. Dirty windows framed in cobwebs revealed nothing more than complete darkness shrouding the cabin in all directions. It must have been early morning before sunrise.

Slade hunched in front of me. "Here." He held a water bottle to my mouth.

I took one swig, desperate for something to sooth my throat. He offered another sip, and I took it, holding it in my mouth for a few seconds before I spat it in his face. It streaked the blood crusted on his face. *I* did that to him. And maybe he would kill me and decapitate me, but I made him bleed first.

Drawing in a slow breath, he stood, steely eyes set on me. He turned, jerking his head for Jericho to hop on the sofa beside me. Then he disappeared around the corner to what I assumed was a kitchen. Water ran for several minutes before he returned with a wet towel and a cleaner face.

Pulling a knife from his holster of weapons, he squatted in front of me again. I stiffened, emotions surging up my chest, constricting my throat, and burning my eyes. Visions of Stefan Hoover pressing a knife to my throat as he pulled down my panties flashed in my head.

Slade flinched and eased his head side to side a fraction as he murmured, "I'm not him." He leaned forward snaking his arms around me and cutting the tie on my wrists. Grabbing the wet towel, he wiped the blood from my hands.

I tried to keep from grimacing, from showing my weakness, but they were raw and swollen. "Did you know?" I whispered. If he didn't kill my mom, did he know that Abe did? Did he know everything when he met me?

The palm of his hand pressed to mine as he gently erased the blood with the rag in his other hand. "No."

"Did you know any of it? Did you know about my dad?"

"No."

"Then … what are we doing here? Is this where it ends?"

He glanced up at me, stilling his hand. "Yes."

I swallowed hard and nodded as he stood, slipped his knife

back into its holder, and pulled out a gun. He eased into a wooden rocker, resting the gun on the arm under his hand as he leaned his head back and closed his eyes. I started to shift on the sofa and Jericho growled.

Just like that ... I was the enemy. It didn't matter how many treats, hugs, and ear rubs I gave him. He was loyal to his master when it mattered most. Inching back, I rested my head on the cushion and hugged my knees to my chest before closing my eyes again.

When I woke again, it was in desperation to pee, and the sun was just starting to illuminate our surroundings.

Trees.

Just as I suspected.

Jericho watched me, unblinking, as if he hadn't slept a second, and the rocking chair sat empty.

"I need to pee." I rested my hands on the edge of the sofa to stand. Jericho growled again.

Slade stepped around the corner with a coffee mug in his hand. He nodded to Jericho. "Bathroom."

Jericho stood, and I took it as a sign that I could too. Easing to my feet, I kept my attention on the dog, not the man dragging out my death for no good reason. Jericho led me past Slade, through the tiny kitchen to a small hallway with a half bathroom on the right. I tried to push the door shut before Jericho came inside, but he was too fast, taking a seat by the pedestal sink.

On a huff, I shut the door and slid down my jeans and underwear. I grumbled, "Fucking dog," under my breath. Jerry leaned forward and rested his snout on my knee, giving me puppy dog eyes.

And I just ... lost it.

Tears.

Sobs.

A complete meltdown.

I barely got myself wiped and my jeans pulled up before I fell to my knees and wrapped my arms around Jericho. "D-don't l-let him k-kill me …"

He whined a bit and slid to a down position, letting me emotionally bleed out on the bathroom floor, hugging him. As my sobs started to subside, the door opened. I scrambled to my feet, facing the corner by the toilet while my fumbling hands zipped and buttoned my jeans before wiping the tears from my face.

Slade could take my life, but I sure as hell wasn't going to give him the last shred of my dignity too. Feeling him looming over me like a pollution-filled rain cloud, I sniffed one last time and turned.

"You're a monster," I mumbled, brushing past him.

"A monster who loves you."

My motions screeched to a halt with my back to him. He didn't say that. No fucking way he said that to me. Slowly, I turned.

Whack!

I hit him again, reopening the cut on his lip along with one on my knuckles. "You are nothing more than a bastard with the soul of Satan. A monster of the worst kind!"

He brushed his middle finger across his bloodied lip before swiping his tongue along the cut. "This bastard with the soul of Satan, this monster of the worst kind … loves you."

Whack!

I hit him in the exact same spot again. My hand screamed as his head whipped to the side where it stayed as he closed his eyes and clenched his teeth.

"Your uncle killed my mom! You don't get to love me!"

He wiped more blood from his mouth. "Your dad killed my dad. So you don't get to hate me!" His voice boomed louder than mine.

"Well, I do!" I kept my fists clenched. "I hate you! I hate you! I—"

In a nanosecond, he grabbed my face and smashed his bloodied mouth to mine, brutally kissing me.

I clawed at his hands and his arms, trying to wriggle out of his grip, trying to turn my head away. He backed me into the wall by the bathroom door. His bruising hands on my face were just as punishing as his lips and his thrashing tongue. The metallic taste of his blood flooded my mouth. When I managed to jerk my head out of the kiss, I spat in his face again ... giving him back his blood.

It landed on his upper lip and he licked it off like an animal. Then his hands released my face and cuffed my wrists. He jerked them above my head, painfully restraining them in one hand. I thought he was going to try to kiss me again. And I prepared to bite off his fucking nose if he got close again. Instead of offering me another pound of flesh, he reached behind him with his free hand and pulled something out, but I couldn't focus fast enough. He raised it above my head, and the familiar sound of a zip tie accompanied the cutting grip on my wrists.

"What are you doing?"

He grabbed my cuffed wrists and dragged me toward the front room.

"What are you doing?"

He shoved me onto the sofa and plucked out another tie,

binding my ankles in under five seconds. "Restrain me. Tie me up, Wylder ... that's what you wanted. Remember, Liv? You wanted to practice staying calm in the eye of a fucking storm. Well, here's your chance."

"Just kill me, you monster!" I yelled at his back as he retreated to the door, heading out to the Jeep.

Chapter Twenty-Nine

Jackson Knight

I LANDED AT LAX a little after eight in the morning and was on my way to Slade's house in a rental car by eight thirty. Ten minutes out, Jessica called me.

"Hey, I just landed, and I'll be at his house in ten. I'm not letting her know I'm here yet. I need to check some—"

"Jackson," she interrupted with an edge of impatience.

"What is it?"

"I left Reagan a message last night. Asked her to dig a little deeper into anything suspicious with Stefan Hoover. And she just called me. His gambling debt has been paid off, and he didn't have life insurance, but his house has been paid off too. Want to know who paid for everything?"

"Jess ..."

"Pull over, Jackson."

"Just tell me."

"Pull over, then I'll tell you. Then we'll make a plan."

"Jesus ..." I took the first exit and pulled into a gas station. "Tell me."

She paused for a few seconds. "Abe McGraw."

The muscles in my jaw ticked for a few seconds. "I should have killed him years ago. Fucking loose end." I ran a hand through my hair and cupped the back of my neck.

"There's more. And I need you to *think,* not react."

"Say it."

"Reagan found something in Abe's file. The surveillance you requested for two years after Knox died? It showed him with a child. Not worth mentioning since a child isn't a threat. But … it wasn't his child. Reagan saw him dropping the boy off at school. She researched the boy with the school's records. His mom is Mary Wylder."

I shoved the car into drive and sped out of the parking lot.

"Jackson, Slade received a ten-million-dollar inheritance from Knox. He's Knox's son."

"I have to call her."

"Jackson, wait! There's—"

"Not now." I disconnected the call and called Livy. It went straight to voicemail. Weaving through traffic, I glanced down at my phone to see the location of her Jeep. It looked about an hour outside of LA. I assumed she was hiking with her friends as she often did when they didn't surf. If luck was on my side, Slade would be home.

Alone.

I parked up the street close to Aubrey's old house. Then I strolled down to his driveway with a black Volvo SUV parked in it, feeling relieved that he was home and Livy was an hour away, safe with her friends.

Knocking on the front door, I stood to the side, just out of sight.

No one answered.

I walked around back and tried the side door to the garage, but it was locked. Tugging my shirt up to cover my elbow, I broke the glass and unlocked the door. Welding and exercise equipment occupied the space. Next, I tried the back door. It too was locked, so I broke another window. Before I stepped into the house, I noticed drops of dried blood at my feet.

As soon as I stepped into the kitchen, I slid open the drawers until I found a knife. Inspecting the downstairs and then the upstairs, I searched for him, but he wasn't there. The lamp in the bedroom was broken on the floor and a bullet had taken out a cell phone. I couldn't tell if it was Livy's or not. Heading back downstairs, I called Jessica.

"He has her. An hour away."

"Jackson … he's been trained. That's what I tried to tell you."

I stopped when I noticed the kitchen rug that had been under the table was missing, but there was a trapdoor in plain sight.

"Trained?" I flipped the table onto its side with a crash and threw open the door before switching to speaker phone so I could use the flashlight on it to climb down into the hole.

"He's trained to—"

"He's an assassin," I muttered, seeing all the weapons on the wall, feeling more desperate than I'd felt in my whole life. And I'd been put in a lot of desperate situations.

"Reagan found huge transfers from Abe to Slade. She thinks Abe is working again."

"G.A.I.L was dissolved."

"She thinks he's working on his own or with a smaller group. Freelancing … with Slade as his favorite weapon. Abe is Slade's handler, and I think Livy's the target."

I gathered as many weapons as I could haul in one load. "He did it, Jess. He killed Ryn."

"Jackson—"

"Don't you dare tell me I'm wrong."

"I don't think you're wrong. What are you going to do?"

"I'm going to get my daughter."

"I can come—"

"It will be over before you get here." I ended the call and shoved my phone into my pocket before climbing out of the basement, loaded down with everything I'd need.

Chapter Thirty

Livy

AFTER BRINGING IN the last of the arsenal, Slade grabbed some water and took a seat in the rocking chair again.

"What are you waiting for?" I asked in a monotone voice while gazing at the guns, ammunition, and grenades.

"Abe and Jackson … Jude."

Jude Day.

I'd never heard that name before. Not from my dad, not from my mom or Jessica. What if Abe had the wrong guy? It had to be an identity mistake.

"Tell me about G.A.I.L."

He shrugged, staring out the front window while clenching a gun resting on his leg. "Can't. Never heard of it until today."

"Do you really think my dad killed your dad?"

"Yep."

I flinched, but he never looked in my direction. "How can you be so certain?"

"Because I checked your Jeep for a tracking device before we left. If your dad was in my line of work, he'd sure as hell track his daughter's vehicle."

My phone? Maybe. But not my Jeep. "Did you find one?"

"Yep."

"And you removed it?"

"No." He twisted his lips. "I need him to find us."

"Are you going to kill him?" I could barely get the words out.

"Not sure yet. But I know for a fact that he's on his way here with every intention of killing me." After a few seconds of silence, he slid his gaze to me. "Not that you give a shit."

I frowned. "Why do you think that?"

"Because you tried to kill me three times."

"So that you wouldn't kill me first."

"Why would I kill you?" He squinted at me.

"Because it's your job."

"Abe hired me to protect you."

"Then he hired you to kill me!"

"But I didn't!" He shot up from the chair, gripping his weapon and pacing the floor while he rubbed his neck with his other hand, chin dipped to his chest. "As soon as I found out, I came to the beach. I took you home to protect you from him because he knew ... he *knew* I'd crossed a line and I wouldn't kill you. He's testing me knowing that I'll fail. So he knows he has to be the one to do it. *That's* why I'm protecting you."

"I don't believe you."

Jerking to a stop, he rested his free hand on his hip and stared up at the ceiling. "Of course you don't fucking believe me. You pulled the trigger three goddamn times!"

"So then why don't you just kill me and get all of this over with?" I yelled.

He kicked the rocking chair with his boot, splintering the wood and sending it crashing against the wall. "Because I LOVE YOU!" he roared, anger erupting like hot lava from every inch of his tense body. "I would walk through the flames of Hell for you. I would let someone torture me to protect you.

I would *die* the worst fucking death in the world for you." His breaths surged from his heaving chest as his eyes reddened. "I love you …" He clenched his jaw, holding onto his emotions that threatened his eyes. "Even if you can't love me back."

Dead.

Slade Wylder killed me with his words. No … he tortured me with his words, with his love. Maybe he had militant control over his tears, but I didn't have that kind of control over mine. They fell in unrelenting waves down my face.

"Wylder—"

Bang … Bang … Bang … Bang.

I jumped as Jericho instinctively placed his body in front of mine.

"Bathroom now." Slade slung the strap of a machine gun over his shoulder. "Abe just shot your Jeep tires to announce his arrival. Get in the bathroom with Jericho *now!*" He bent down and cut the ties around my wrist and ankles and grabbed my arm, jerking me to standing before shoving me in the direction of the bathroom.

I did as he said and locked the door, not that it was going to protect me from Abe if he had a gun.

I listened for more gunshots or dialogue exchange.

Nothing …

Wylder

I HID JUST behind the front door threshold, peeking around the corner and through the half-screen door at Abe, but he was just out of shot on the driver's side of Livy's Jeep.

"Leave your dick out of this, son, and just give me the girl.

Or even just part of her. I'm good with you keeping a souvenir too."

I said nothing. I was trained to say nothing. By. Him.

Assassins weren't negotiators. A predator's greatest assets were patience and silence. One time, I stood with a gun and my eye glued to the scope of it for over seven hours waiting for the shot. As long as I had a pulse, I knew I'd stand silently and patiently to protect Livy.

"Your father loved Livy's grandmother. They were childhood sweethearts. Sunny was the love of Knox's life. She moved on when he took another tour of duty, but she never loved her husband the way she loved your dad. And he always knew it. Jackson found out, and he just couldn't handle it. So he killed Knox. That's the blood running through Livy's veins. Are you really going to fight for that? You willing to die for that? If we don't make him pay ... justice will never be served. And the only way to get justice is to take everything from him, the way he took everything from you, from Mary, from me."

I leaned my head back against the wall and closed my eyes, gripping the gun with both hands.

"He's coming. Jackson. I'm sure he'll be here soon. I had eyes on him, and he was at your place this morning. We both know he's tracking her Jeep. But something tells me you planned on that ... hence the reason you brought her here in it and not your vehicle. He's the best at what he does. Even now ... he'll take you out from a hundred yards away with one hand tied behind his back and blindfolded. And that's not even his specialty. He's good with his hands. If he gets within five feet of you, he'll disarm you and snap your neck before your brain has a chance to tell your finger to pull the trigger."

Taking a deep inhale, I let it out slowly, staying perfectly still.

"Don't get me wrong. You're good. Someday you might even be better than him, but not today. He's smarter. And you have his daughter. I'm certain we're about to see a version of Jackson Knight … Jude Day … that no one has ever seen before. So put a bullet in the girl's head and take your place at my side. It's where you belong. *We* are family."

Maybe what he said was true. Maybe it was a lie to scare me. Maybe it was all a game to get in my head.

What we did agree on … Jackson was on his way, and I wasn't on Abe's team, and Jackson wasn't going to be on mine. There would be a fight for Livy, and I couldn't allow that. Sliding down the wall, I adjusted the strap of the rifle, shifting it to my back. Then I army crawled to the kitchen toward the bathroom so Abe didn't see me through the windows or the solid bottom half of the screen door. Once around the corner, I stood and turned the handle to the bathroom door. It was locked.

"Livy," I whispered, gently tapping the door. "Open the door."

The knob clicked and I turned the handle, easing it open. She and Jericho were on the floor, her eyes swollen from all the tears.

"Come here," I said softly, holding out my hand.

She stared at it for a few moments, arms hugging her knees to her chest. Without looking me in the eye, she took my hand and let me pull her to standing.

I grabbed her face forcing her gaze upward. "You need to go out the back door. Go into the woods with Jericho. Don't stop; keep going until you get to a main road. It's going to be a few miles down the way." I pulled a burner phone from my pocket and handed it to her. "Call your friends. Call the police. Call anyone you can trust, but no matter what … don't turn around. Don't come back here."

"My dad …"

I shook my head. "He's not here, but he's on his way. Abe is outside. It's going to be too dangerous for you. Abe wants you and your dad dead. I want Abe dead. And your dad will kill anything that tries to get in his way of getting to you."

Before she could respond, I took her hand and checked around the corner before leading her and Jericho to the back door, easing it open slowly and surveying the backside of the cabin. "It's clear. Go."

Jericho led the way, going down the three steps and stopping to wait for Livy.

She clenched the phone in her hand, staring at it for a few seconds before giving me those brown eyes to adore one last time. "Wylder," she whispered.

"Go, Livy." I didn't let my heart sway my determination to get her to safety. I gave her an emotionless expression and a firm command.

"Wyld—" she started to speak again.

"Three shots. You tried to kill me three times. Now get the fuck out of here before I change my mind, put a bullet in your head, and let Abe kill your dad."

She took in a shaky breath, dropped her gaze, and turned. I watched my whole fucking world disappear into the trees, wearing my favorite T-shirt while following my best friend.

Chapter Thirty-One

Jackson Knight

I PARKED A mile away and jogged through the mountain terrain to Livy's location. Abe would know I was coming, and if Slade had even a fraction of the training that Jess and I had received by his age, then he, too, would know I'd be coming for my daughter. So I made my way there knowing they were baiting me.

They'd be waiting for me. They'd been waiting for me for years.

Stalking.

Preying on my family.

And it was going to end even if I had to lose my own life to keep her safe and avenge the death of Ryn.

From the insane number of weapons in Slade's basement, I knew he'd be heavily armed. Stopping fifty yards out, I used the pair of binoculars I stole from the basement to scope out the situation.

"Fucking amateur," I mumbled catching sight of Abe hunched down beside Livy's Jeep with a semi-automatic rifle clenched in his hands. I would have taken his ass out right there on the spot had I known the exact location of my daughter. I couldn't risk it if Slade had her. Setting him off by killing his uncle before I had Livy under my protection wasn't an acceptable option.

I continued to survey the area, looking for the slightest movement, a shadow in the window … anything.

Nothing.

Holding a gun in one hand and a knife in my other hand, I trekked closer to the cabin. Why was Abe outside as if he was stalking his own nephew? Something didn't feel right, but time wasn't on my side. Pushing that uneasy feeling aside, I veered around to come in from the opposite side of the Jeep, but I still was uneasy about Slade and his whereabouts with Livy. Changing the plan, I trekked a bigger circle to the backside of the cabin. If I could get Livy, I'd use two bullets and head home with my daughter.

If…

Easing up the backstairs with two swift steps, I listened at the door, but I heard nothing. Off to the side, I turned the handle slowly, praying the stupid thing didn't creak when I opened it.

Once inside, I inched my way down the small hall, checking the bathroom before entering the kitchen with my gun pointed forward and my knife readied in my left hand. My movements stopped when a set of dark eyes locked on me along with the third eye … the barrel of a gun.

Slade stood to the left of the screen door, a peculiar situation. If they were working together, their set up was shit. He said nothing.

I remembered those days … eyeing my target for hours if necessary, never saying a word, no matter what. Fortunately, I played by a different set of rules. I was no longer an assassin. Just a dad picking his girl up from a cabin outside of LA.

"Livy?" I said her name calmly, using my best father-ese.

Slade said nothing.

"If I don't hear her voice soon, I'll have to assume she's dead. If she's dead, this will be the worst fucking day of your life because I won't kill you. I'll spend the next month right here with you and that fuckup hiding by the Jeep, torturing you until your heart gives out because you just can't handle any more pain. And even then, you'd only know a fraction of the pain I've felt since you took my wife. Now ... where is my daughter?"

It was like looking in a goddamn mirror. Not only did my daughter find a guy who had an eerily physical resemblance to me in my twenties, she found a guy who didn't flinch, blink, or so much as swallow. It was hard to put the fear of God in someone's eyes when they didn't believe in a god. Slade clearly didn't believe in a god, and he wasn't afraid to die.

"She's not here, is she?"

I took a step forward, gaining an odd admiration for the young man staring me down like I was nothing but a fly buzzing around his head. I wondered what his number was. We all had a number. Mine was five. I let my prey get within five feet of me before I'd strike. Most others had bigger numbers like eight or ten.

Not me. I liked to draw them in so close I could feel the warmth of their skin, hear the exchange of their breaths, and kill them with my bare hands.

I took three more steps, reducing the distance to about six feet, keeping my body just to the left of the window, but still to the right of the screen door—out of Abe's sight.

One more step.

Slade's left hand lifted, pointing two guns at me. Five ... what were the chances that the kid's number was five like mine?

"If she's not here, I can't let you live." I shrugged. It wasn't my fault. Everyone needed rules. Mine were pretty simple.

"Daddy?"

<hr />

Livy

SLADE'S GAZE SHIFTED from my dad to me as I took slow steps down the hall toward the kitchen. They stood five feet apart, guns pointed at each other.

Jericho stayed right at my side.

"Hey, baby. I just have a few things to wrap up. I have a score to settle for you and your mom. Why don't you wait for me in the bathroom," Dad said like he was asking me what I wanted for dinner.

Slade said nothing with his mouth, but the look on his face conveyed anger. He was angry at me for not following his instructions.

"Please put the guns down. He didn't kill Mom. Abe did it." My feet continued toward the two men.

"Doesn't matter. He was going to try to take you away from me. Weren't you?"

Wylder gave him nothing. A goddamn iron expression—fearless and steadfast. Why didn't he plead his case? He didn't kill my mom. He didn't know anything about it.

Dad grunted, cocking his head to the side at Slade. "You actually think you love her? Is that why she's still alive and that fuckup is outside?"

Still ... Slade said nothing. Did nothing. Not a blink.

"Well, you'll have to come through me to get to her." Dad

slid the knife from his left hand into the back of his cargo pants and retrieved a gun from the same spot, handing the gun to me. "Livy, take this and wait in the bathroom. If anyone but me opens the door, pull the trigger."

"Dad …"

He dropped the gun in his other hand. "Don't worry, sweetie. I'm giving him the advantage. Two guns to no guns. Now take it and go."

My attention stuck to Slade. He made the tiniest nod of his head and slid both guns back into the holster. "Go," he whispered, eyeing my dad.

I backed up slowly, my heart torn apart, my world on the edge of imploding. As soon as I shut the door. I heard the unmistakable sound of flesh and bones colliding. The grunts. *Crash!* The *thunk* of bodies falling to the floor and against the walls, rattling everything else in the house.

"Stop," I whispered, shaking my head and releasing a new round of emotions. "Stop …" I said a little louder before opening the door.

My eyes homed in on Slade's back against the kitchen floor as my dad took a menacing step toward him preparing to plant his boot into Slade's ribs. Slade swiped my dad's leg, bringing him to the ground. His fists brutally planted into my dad's face, sending blood splattering along the floor. My dad's hand cuffed Slade's throat and they rolled, giving my dad the advantage on top of Slade. I couldn't tell if Slade was breathing. He gripped my dad's wrist with one hand while his other hand flew in a hard fist toward my dad's jaw.

"Stop! STOP!" I ran out of the bathroom as their bodies rolled again.

My dad pulled a knife as Slade lumbered to his feet, his

271

attention and his bloodied face pointed toward me. His eyes landed on my chest, widening like someone infected fear into them. The next few seconds happened in a blink. My gaze started to follow his. That was when I noticed a red dot, like a laser right over my heart. As I glanced up, the world around me erupted into chaos. Slade dove at me. My dad lurched from his position on the floor and buried the blade of his knife in Slade's leg. He grunted. Retrieving another gun from his holster with one hand, he pointed it behind him while grabbing my shirt with his other hand and pulling me to the ground. Two shots fired at almost the exact same time. Pop. Pop.

Slade fell to the ground at my feet as my dad's body flew forward, shielding me. A breath later he glanced over his shoulder and climbed off me.

"NO!" I cried when I saw blood saturating Slade's shirt. As soon as I rolled him over, his left hand stretched across his body, slowly reaching to cover the gunshot wound on his right side. "Wylder!" I pressed my hands over his as if together we could stop the bleeding.

My head lifted and I saw a new monster. A different monster.

My father.

He took the front porch steps with brooding confidence. Abe was on the porch, shot in the leg. Slade shot him as he threw himself in front of the bullet meant for me. The monster's boot landed in Abe's face, making him grunt and moan. I couldn't even see his actual face. It was like my father shattered his nose and mangled all the skin around it.

Abe groaned.

The monster rammed the heel of his boot into Abe's hand,

eliciting a howl as his fingers broke. He knew … I think he'd always known Mom's death wasn't an accident. And in that moment the monster inside of him needed revenge.

"My wife. You took my *life*. You took my daughter's world." He kicked him in the side of the head.

I sobbed, turning away, unable to watch my father torture another man. Tears ran down my cheeks, dripping onto Slade's chest.

Grunts, gasps, and gurgling from Abe's chest filled my ears, interrupted only by the thud and cracking noise of the new monster's hands and boots slowly killing him. I thought I knew … I thought I understood my father's pain after Mom died.

I didn't.

"Daddy …" I whispered, squeezing my eyes shut, feeling at my very core the depth of his pain, like if he broke every one of Abe's bones, it would bring Mom back. I wanted him to stop because a very selfish part of me didn't want to believe my father could take another person's life so brutally. "Please stop …" I knew he couldn't hear me. Maybe my pleas weren't for him to stop. Maybe it was my heart begging for the pain to stop—the pain of losing a piece of my father, the pain of losing my mom all over again, the pain of the man who lassoed my soul only to suffocate it before fracturing it and bleeding out beneath my hands.

That warm blood continued to gush out of control between my fingers and his. "No …" I cried. "Don't you dare die. Don't you dare."

Jericho whined, nestling at Slade's head, resting his snout on his shoulder.

"It's not over. You don't get to say when it's over!" I

sobbed.

"Livy, it's time to go." Dad rested his hand on my head, stroking my hair like he did when I was young, like he did after Mom died. "It's time to let *him* go. There's nothing we can do."

"No ... no ..." I sobbed, interlacing my bloodied fingers with Slade's.

His eyes blinked heavily, and I felt him squeeze my fingers too. "I'm sorry. I'm so so sorry." I pressed my forehead to his, my tears falling to his face.

Sirens sounded in the distance because of me. I did call for help, but I also went back to the cabin. I followed half of Slade's instructions. He wouldn't have been on the floor, fighting for his next breath had I followed all of his instructions.

"Livy. Now! We have to go." Dad pulled at my arm.

I yanked away from his grip, resting my forehead back on Slade's. "I knew the gun wasn't loaded when I pulled the trigger. I knew. I promise I knew ..." More sobs ripped through my chest.

"Liv-y ..." Wylder said in two weak syllables as he closed his eyes.

They stayed shut. All remaining rigidness in his body released ... it surrendered. He surrendered.

"NOOOOO!" My hands released his hands, and they covered his cheeks, smearing his blood everywhere. My lips pressed to his. "Noooo ..." I breathed into his mouth, trying so hard to give him more breaths. "I love you back ... I love you back ... I love ... you ... back ..." I wept as my dad tore me from Wylder's lifeless body and cradled me in his arms. "Jerry ..." I said through my sobs. Abe's mangled, disfigured, and bloodied body passed through my blurry peripheral vision as Dad hauled me down the porch steps.

My father must have carried me forever. By the time he set me in the back seat of the rental car with Jericho, my tears had dried. So had the blood on my hands. I should have walked away. That day I found the weapons in the dungeon, I should have kept going.

Had I just walked away and let him disappear to protect himself ... to protect me ... he would have lived.

Chapter Thirty-Two

Livy

Five Years Later

"THERE'S MY FAVORITE patient." Dr. Jones hugged me.

"Graduation day, huh?" I grinned taking a seat on his sofa as he sat in a side chair.

"You graduated from therapy years ago. I just like seeing you."

I smiled.

"When are you moving?"

"Tomorrow." I rubbed my lips together while unwrapping a stick of peppermint gum. I held out the pack to him.

He shook his head as his eyebrows lifted a fraction. "Wow, I had it in my head you weren't leaving for another few weeks."

"I'm assisting Timothy Morten on a huge case that goes to trial next month, so they want me there as soon as possible to help prepare."

"We're going to miss you."

My eyes rolled. "Sacramento is less than two hours away."

"And Darren?"

I chewed my gum slowly and shrugged. "He's staying here."

"You're breaking up?"

"Not sure. We're both feeling very casual about it. If absence doesn't make the heart grow fonder, then I'd say we're breaking up. If we can't stand to be apart, he'll consider looking into finding work there."

"I see."

"What's that look?"

"No look." He shook his head.

I laughed. "I think I know you better than you know me at this point—at least I know when you have a look. You're judging my relationship with Darren."

"I don't judge. Not my job."

I sighed. "I know. If I loved him. If we were serious ... every night apart would feel like too much. Is that still how you feel when you're not with Jess, when one or the other of you travels alone?"

"Yes. But not every person needs the same thing out of a relationship. Some people thrive on independence and space. Some married couples don't even live together. Long distance relationships can definitely work. And like you said, it's less than two hours away. Weekends will be very doable."

"I *am* independent. I like my space. Even with Slade, I valued my time surfing with friends, or just time alone. My dad is that way. Before Mom died, he thrived on having space. Mom would sometimes tell me that Dad needed a minute. Of course I thought it meant an actual minute. It was more like an hour at least." I grinned. "Besides ... I have Jericho. I'm never alone."

"Have I mentioned that it's okay if you find happiness even if it's not quite the same? Not quite right? Because it might not ever feel the same."

"I know." It took years, but I got to the point that I could talk about Slade and not tear up. I could talk about him and feel a sense of peace and gratitude. He saved my life twice. "Some loves are once in a lifetime."

"Yes, Livy."

"I'm looking forward not backward. I've accepted my past, and I think you said that's what I needed to do in order to welcome my future. So I've accepted the secrets ... my father was an assassin like the man I loved. It's not who they were; it's what they did. My dad lived to find a new life. Slade did not. But I'm here. And I'm young. I deserve happiness. I deserve love." I shrugged. "I just don't know yet if it's with Darren."

"Follow your heart, Livy. And maybe what your heart desires the most right now isn't a serious relationship. Maybe your heart desires a courtroom. Working hard to make partner in a firm someday. Or ..."

I bit back my grin. "President Livy Knight."

He leaned forward resting his elbows on his knees while shooting a wink at me. "Or that."

THE NEXT DAY, my dad followed me to Sacramento to be there when the moving company arrived and helped me get settled. He usually ignored Jericho. Apparently, Mom's dog Gunner didn't like my dad. That might have been part of it, but most of it was Slade. Dad hated that I insisted on keeping such a big part of the man who was hired to kill me. Still ... before he headed home to San Francisco, he rubbed Jericho's head and told him to take care of me. It was the first time he made any sort of recognition that Jericho was not only special to me; he was, in fact, my protector.

I had twenty-four hours to get settled before my first day on the job at the most prestigious law firm in Sacramento ...

maybe in all of California. They had won some of the biggest environmental lawsuits in history: most notably, a multi-billion-dollar one against a petroleum giant and another one against a company that had been knowingly poisoning people with its coating for nonstick pans.

"Relax ..." I said, blowing out a breath before stepping on-to the elevator that took me to my new firm on the eighteenth floor.

A bright-eyed woman with dark skin and straight black hair greeted me with a warm smile from behind a sleek glass desk the second I stepped off the elevator.

"Hi. I'm—"

"Livy Knight. I'm Rosalie. We've been expecting you. Welcome. Follow me."

Before I could get out another word, she led me down a wide hallway to a conference room with a full glass wall, a long table, leather chairs, and a monitor on the only wall that wasn't glass or windows to the Sacramento skyline. The familiar face of Timothy Morten, who personally drove to San Francisco the previous month to recruit me, smiled, as did his partner, Trisha Brattebo. We chatted via video after Tim's trip to San Francisco.

"Go on in. Good luck."

I smiled at Rosalie. "Thank you."

"Livy, come in. Sorry to throw you in the deep end before you get to see your new office, but Mr. Wright will be here soon."

"Have a seat." Trisha gestured to the chair next to her. "Nice to see you in person."

"You too." I tried to control my nerves while taking a seat, thankful they didn't offer to shake my embarrassingly sweaty hand. "Who's Mr. Wright?"

"Floyd Wright." Trisha curled her wispy auburn hair behind one ear and gave me a conspiratorial look.

"Floyd Wright as in Off Grid Transportation?"

Timothy chuckled at my shock, and I cringed as my immaturity stood on full display. Of course, environmentalist, activist, billionaire Floyd Wright would have used Timothy and Tricia for his legal needs. They were the best.

"Yes. That Floyd Wright. We were supposed to meet tomorrow, but he had a change in his schedule for security reasons. Sadly, his activism has put him in danger." Timothy nodded behind me. "There's his team now. He's on his way up."

I glanced behind me. Two men and a woman, all in black suits, inspected the area, including all of the offices.

"Team?" I again showed my shock or ignorance.

"Security," Tricia added.

I nodded slowly.

"I wanted you to sit in on this with us just to observe and to meet Floyd. You could be working with him in the future."

My bladder screamed. I needed to pee. The rush of nerves quadrupled with the news of sitting in on a meeting with *the* Floyd Wright on my very first day. I reached into my purse to fish out a breath mint. My mouth suddenly felt like the desert.

"Floyd, good to see you again," Tim said before I could get the mint popped into my mouth. I dropped it back in my purse and lifted my head, plastering on a smile like I wasn't shaking to my bones.

I thought it couldn't be more intense and surreal—*me* in the same room as Timothy, Tricia, *and* Floyd.

I was wrong.

The man standing at the door, guarding it in a suit with a crisp white shirt, perfectly knotted tie, and neatly trimmed beard was … *him*.

A ghost.

An illusion.

A lie.

He was dead. He died. I watched him close his eyes, taking his final breath.

I mourned him.

I spent years in therapy.

I slept next to his dog every night.

Things were said. Introductions were made. Yet, I heard nothing more than echoes of sound until Tricia touched my shoulder. "Livy, are you okay?"

It was then that I realized everyone was standing and shaking hands except me. Tearing my gaze from the ghost that gave me an emotionless expression, at his post like a wooden soldier, I pressed my hands to the table and tried to stand. "F-fine."

"Whoa … are you sure?" Tricia grabbed my arm as my knees started to buckle the second I attempted to stand.

I told myself it wasn't real.

"Do you know Alex?"

My gaze ripped away from *him* and landed on Floyd. He appeared smaller than the man I'd seen in pictures. Still, a handsome man in his forties with thick salt and pepper hair and irresistible dimples accentuating his warm smile.

"Alex?" I muttered, feeling on the verge of passing out.

Floyd glanced back at *him*. "Alex. My head of security. Or maybe you're just like all the other women who find him rather pretty to look at." He chuckled. "I used to be young and handsome like him."

Tim laughed. "Didn't we all."

"No." I shook my head slowly, forcing my gaze to stay on Floyd. "I don't know Alex. I'm … uh …" I shook my head quickly to regain some sense of composure as I held out my hand. "I'm sorry. I'm Livy Knight. It's a true honor to meet you."

"Livy is our newest associate. Top of her class. Did some work in San Francisco with Tim's old partner, and Tim personally drove to San Francisco to steal her. We didn't give her a heads-up that she'd be thrown into the deep end on her first day by meeting you." Tricia covered for me, and I was so grateful.

I was also grateful when she poured me a glass of water and shoved it into my hand.

"It's a pleasure to meet you too." Floyd shook my sweaty hand.

"Well, time is money." Tim winked at Floyd. "Shall we?" He nodded to the seat opposite him.

I eased into my chair and risked another glance at *Alex*.

After a few seconds, he blinked. The man I remembered could go forever without blinking.

The meeting lasted just over an hour. I heard nothing except my heart pounding against my aching chest. I felt nothing but pain swelling in my stomach and throbbing in my head as I tried to make sense of *him*.

Living.

Breathing.

Haunting me in every way possible.

And just when I didn't think the punch to my gut could hurt anymore, the meeting ended and everyone stood. The ghost at the door gave a hand gesture to one of his team members in the hallway, and my gaze locked onto his hand. His left hand. And the silver band on his ring finger.

He was married.

The man who loved me back ... the man who protected me.

He died.

He came back to life.

And he married another woman.

Nothing ... *nothing* had ever felt so fucking painful. Not Jessica's fists landing on my face and ribs. Not the night a man tried to rape me. Not even the day I thought he died.

My mom's death. It felt like that.

Unexpected.

Unimaginable.

Un-fucking thinkable.

I'm happy you're alive.

I'm happy you're in love.

I'm happy you're happy.

My mind tried to latch onto something positive. Mind over matter.

But I couldn't.

I couldn't be happy that he was alive and with anyone but me. Maybe that made me a terrible person. Or maybe that made me twenty-six, heartbroken, and human.

Love was supposed to be many beautiful things. And it was. But at the core of love, there existed this really selfish need. I refused to believe that if you truly loved someone you'd set them free. No. You didn't set them free.

You held them.

You nurtured them.

You made their happiness yours.

His hand dropped to his side as Floyd headed to the door after saying goodbye to everyone, including me. I think I smiled or nodded, but I can't remember. *He* curled his fingers and ran the pad of his thumb over the ring. My focus shifted up his body, and it latched on to his gaze. He knew what caught my attention because his gaze quickly averted to Floyd.

In seconds, they were gone.

"Let's show you your office. I remember what it felt like on my first day at a big firm. I'm pretty sure I was as nervous and pale as you." Tricia nodded toward the door.

In one hour, my hopes were resurrected from the dead only to be demolished by a little round band.

Chapter Thirty-Three

I HADN'T HAD a drop of alcohol.

Not one. Not ever.

My dad ruined that for me. He no longer consumed alcohol, but I couldn't erase the man he was—absent and barely living—after Mom died. When I lost Slade, I thought about drinking, finding something to numb the pain.

I didn't.

When I passed my boards, I didn't celebrate with alcohol like the rest of my friends.

I surfed.

I hiked the hills of LA.

I sparred with my dad and sometimes Jessica.

I focused on searching for a job.

After seeing that ghost, I picked up a bottle of wine and headed back to my apartment.

"Hey, Jerry." I managed a tiny greeting. Even Jericho had to think something was wrong with me. I usually greeted him with infectious enthusiasm.

Not that day.

I set the wine and my purse on the counter. "Let's go potty, babe." I fought an onslaught of tears, the same ones I'd been fighting all afternoon.

Wylder was alive.

And he was married.

When we reached the front of the building, I let him guide me to his favorite pissing spot, actually his favorite tree. I couldn't blame him for having a favorite tree. I always had one in school.

Jericho marked the tree and ran—top speed run in the opposite direction down the sidewalk.

"Jericho!" I yelled, turning in that direction, shocked that the dog who never needed a leash just bolted.

My heart couldn't take anymore. Yet there *he* was, hunched down, receiving kisses from Jericho. A long-awaited reunion. Breaking my heart wasn't enough. He had to come for his dog, stepping on that barely beating organ behind my ribs and grinding it into dust, like a black boot snuffing out a cigarette on the concrete.

Slade slowly stood and walked toward me with Jericho right at his side, as if he never left. As if he never died. He no longer wore a black suit. Instead, he wore jeans and a white tee, looking like the man I loved years earlier.

Six feet apart, we stood idle, a standoff to see who would speak first. I gritted my teeth and willed my emotions to stay in check. As usual, he won. I *had* to say something before I exploded.

"He's not yours. He's mine now. You died. You abandoned him. And I know a pretty good fucking attorney if you try to fight me on this." Anger wrapped around every word like barbed wire. I felt the words cut from my throat, and I hoped he felt them just as brutally.

"He's yours. Always."

Fuck you ...

I didn't want him to be nice. I didn't want him to be the version of him I fell in love with at the beach in the back of a sprinter van.

But he was. And I hated—yes *hated*—him for it.

Swallowing hard, I shifted my attention to Jericho. "Let's go."

When I turned, that boot stomped on my heart again as he said to Jericho, "Go."

The loyal German shepherd wanted to stay with his master, but Slade was giving him to me. I hated that too. Jericho became this consolation prize.

You can't have me, but here's my dog.

Once I recovered from tripping over my emotions, I continued to the door of my apartment building. Jericho followed, but so did Slade.

"Can we talk?"

I grunted a laugh, taking fast strides toward the elevator. "We have nothing left to say. I said it all, the day you died." My finger incessantly pushed the button for the doors to open. When they did, I stepped inside and waved my card in front of the reader.

"Well, I was choking on my own blood, so I didn't get a chance to say everything I had to say."

Crossing my arms over my chest, I focused on the digital numbers instead of him. When the doors opened, I spewed my parting words while exiting it. "You've had five years. You've exceeded the statute of limitations on that."

I opened my door, and he pressed his hand to it, holding it open for Jericho and himself.

"I need you to leave. I don't ever want to see you again." Keeping my back to him, I marched to the kitchen counter and opened my cheap bottle of wine with a knife since I didn't have a corkscrew.

"You don't drink," he said, standing in the middle of my living room, sucking up all the oxygen.

I poured a generous glass into an eight-ounce water glass. "You haven't seen me in five years. You don't know anything. I drink. I fuck other people. I pay for vet bills and dog food. And I'm a lot stronger than the girl you knew. So I suggest you get the hell out before I make you bleed."

He pressed his lips together, his gaze following Jericho as he paced the space by his food bowl. "I know you're stronger. I know you pay for vet bills and food. I know that you *fuck* other people. And I also know that you don't drink."

I took three big gulps and failed my attempt to not react with a sour face. Wine tasted like shit, or at least the bottle I purchased was nothing more than over-priced piss. "There ... see that. Me drinking. Now you know. You can leave now."

"I'm proud of you."

I stared at him with no response. His pride was something I no longer needed.

"Morten and Brattebo ..." He whistled. "That's impressive, Liv. I have no doubt Knight will one day be up on that wall."

I returned a series of blinks. That was it. That was all I had for him. "You need to leave."

He narrowed his eyes a bit. "Why?"

"Because I'm not taking the bait. I'm not going to ask you how you lived..." my anger built as my volume escalated "... where the fuck you've been for five years..." my fists clenched as the words came out through gritted teeth "...who the hell is *Alex*, and how could you abandon Jericho!" I pitched my glass of wine at him.

He bobbed casually to the side as it hit my coffee table and shattered, red wine everywhere. I should have gotten a white wine.

"So just GO THE FUCK HOME TO YOUR WIFE!" My fingers stabbed into my hair as I lost the control that had been hanging by a tiny thread all day. I no longer cared what he thought as tears broke free from my burning eyes.

Jericho whined, ears alert and eyes wide.

Wylder gave him a tiny head shake as if to let him know it wasn't his fight. And again, his hand balled into a fist as his thumb rubbed that circular promise of forever. Some other woman took his heart and it. Hurt. Like. Hell.

"Livy …"

"No." My head whipped back and forth over and over again. "You're not allowed to say my name. You're not allowed to look at me like this…" I wiped my cheeks and held out my tear-stained hands "…like this affects you." Choking on a sob, I tucked my newly cut, shoulder-length hair behind my ears. "Are you here for a thank-you? F-fine …" I sucked in a shaky breath. "Thank you for saving my life twice. Take Jericho. We'll call it even. Just disappear and never come near me again."

I didn't mean it. If he took Jericho, I would have to quit my job to accommodate my full-time grieving.

"I'll leave."

I nodded, forcing my chin to stay tipped up, jaw clenched.

He made his way to Jericho and hunched down again to scratch behind his ears, kissing him on the head. "Continue to take care of her. Nobody does it better than you," he whispered.

I choked on another sob and turned my back to him as emotions racked my body. When he opened the door, my mouth moved on its own accord, words pouring out before my brain had time to censor them or keep them from finding life outside of my head. "Do you have k-kids?" My hand covered my mouth as my eyes squeezed shut, wringing out more tears. Someone stole my dreams. Did she take *all* of them? Were there little Wylders running around?

"Bye, Livy."

The door clicked shut.

Fucking ghosts.

I MADE IT a full week, preparing for the trial of the decade, before I got the nerve to ask Tricia about Floyd and his security detail. Popping into her office with an armful of documents she requested, I set them on her desk and gave her an apprehensive look.

"What is it, Livy? Just ask it." She didn't glance up from her computer, hands vigorously moving across the keyboard.

"Floyd lives in Malibu, correct?"

"He has many homes, but yes, he has a residence there. Although, as of late, he's been spending most of his time in Austin."

"Texas?"

She grinned, pausing just long enough to give me the duh look.

I frowned. "For your information, Texas doesn't own the only Austin. There's one in Arkansas, Colorado, Nevada, and I think maybe Utah too. I'm sure there are others as well."

"Okay, smarty-pants ... I give. Why the curiosity about Floyd's residence?"

"Nothing. Well, actually, I was just wondering about his security detail or the really rich men like him who have security. Does he have multiple details in different locations? Do the same people travel with him? If that's the case, it would make it really hard to settle down and start a family, right?"

She slipped off her silver framed glasses and shook her head. "I'm sorry. Why are we discussing this?"

My lips quirked to the side for a few seconds. "The guy. *Alex*, the head of his security detail ... I was staring at him last week, but only because he looked familiar, and it's been driving me crazy. I can't figure out how I know him, so I just wondered where he lived. Maybe it would jog a memory."

She slipped back on her glasses and returned her attention to the computer screen. "I don't know. My guess is that he travels with Floyd, lives with him wherever he's at."

"But he had a wedding band on his left ring finger. Do you think his family travels with them?"

She peered at me over the frames of her glasses. "How observant of you to notice his wedding band." A smirk accompanied her wide-eyed inspection of me.

Behind a fake smile, I tried to hide my disappointment from her lack of information. "Well, my good observations are just some of the reasons I'm here."

She snapped her wrist in a shooing motion. "Yes, well ... go. Observe. Research. Bring me something that will nail these bastards to the wall in court."

"I'll do my best."

"Oh ... Livy ..."

I turned. "Yeah."

"Floyd will be here next week for another meeting. Maybe you can find the information you're looking for then."

I nodded once.

Information? I didn't need any information. My morbid

curiosity had an insatiable hunger, and as usual, nothing good came from it.

The following week passed painfully slow. My lack of sleep didn't help. If I wasn't at the firm until the early hours of the morning, I was tossing and turning in bed with nightmares of Slade with his wife and two kids. Both girls. I didn't know why I imagined him with girls; I just did. Maybe because I imagined us having one of each, and I wasn't ready to give *her* that too.

When someone else lives your life, part of you dies.

Slade wasn't the ghost anymore. I was the ghost.

Chapter Thirty-Four

A WEEK LATER, I wore a tailored-fit, gray sheath dress with capped sleeves and the hem brushing my knees. Black heels. Wavy hair up in a ponytail with long bangs framing my face.

I wasn't invited to be a part of the meeting with Floyd that day. Tim buried me in work for the bigger case. However, I made a point to need a refill on my tea a few minutes after I noticed Floyd and his security detail arriving. They met in Tim's office instead of the conference room, and Slade waited just outside of the closed-door office along with one other guy on the opposite side of the door. I meandered past Slade and the other guy, keeping my head down and focused on my phone like I didn't even notice him.

But I *felt* him.

I felt his eyes on me. I felt him everywhere.

The trip to the break room was a mistake. *He* was a mistake. I chased a monster. I fell for him. And he gobbled me up and spit out my soul, hollow and lifeless.

As soon as I got to the break room, I pressed my back against the wall out of sight from him or anyone else. Drawing in an uneasy breath and chasing away the emotions that threatened to steal my composure, I closed my eyes and blew out that breath in tiny increments. "Let him go, Liv ... let him go," I whispered.

I remained in the break room for nearly thirty minutes until I got the nerve to walk back to my office before anyone questioned my absence. Again, I buried my face in the screen of my phone as I approached Tim's office and the two men parked outside of it.

"Livy?"

I turned a few feet before reaching the man I needed to avoid. Tricia approached me, jerking her head toward Slade. "Didn't you have a question for him?" She smiled at Slade. "Alex, right?"

My gaze fell to my feet, next to my heart that had been on the ground since the day he appeared from the dead.

When I didn't hear his response, I assumed he gave her a nod.

"Livy thought you looked familiar. Right, Livy? She was dying to know where you lived, hoping to make a connection."

I wasn't *dying* to know, but I was dying as she exposed me right in front of him. I forced my gaze up to meet his. His neutral expression gave away nothing.

Clearing my throat, I formed a pained smile. "At first … you looked familiar. But now that I get a closer look, I realize it's not you. And his name wasn't Alex. And he wouldn't be standing where you are. He'd be inside one of these offices. You see … he was on his way to law school. I always imagined seeing him in a suit for the first time at graduation. But he never graduated. Or maybe he'd have worn a suit to a job interview for a prestigious law firm like this one. Or at his wedding."

My chin tipped downward again for a few seconds before finding the courage to gaze into those haunting eyes again. "Did you wear a suit at your wedding?" I whispered past the suffocating emotion gridlocking my throat.

He didn't get a chance to answer. Tricia laughed. "Okay, now you're sounding weird, borderline harassing the guy with too much information about your friend that's not him." She rested her hands on my shoulders and guided me toward my office.

"Gray ..." he said, stopping my footsteps along with Tricia's.

She turned, but I didn't.

"I wore a gray suit to my wedding. White shirt, pink tie. It was raining that day ... felt symbolic of my mood ... of my life. A friend married us. Two witnesses, no family or other friends. I've never worn that suit again."

"Alrighty then. Interesting story." Tricia chuckled and she released my shoulders and whispered in my ear, "I stand corrected; he's the weird one." She brushed past me. It took a few seconds for my legs to resume carrying my body to my office.

That night I attempted another bottle of wine, a white one. I didn't like it either. Maybe I wasn't a wine person or maybe alcohol wasn't the answer. Exercise seemed like the more palatable and healthy option, so I took Jericho for a run to the park with his tennis ball and a launcher. A few smaller dogs were there, but they left soon after my beast of a dog started fetching his ball. I needed something like fetch to keep my mind occupied—a repetitive task that would keep me on track and not thinking about *him*.

Even when he wasn't at work ... he was there. His ghost invaded my new place of business. I still saw him standing in my living room every time I glanced at the red wine stain that didn't come out of my rug.

When I tossed the ball again, he invaded my life again, walking toward me. He wasn't real. He couldn't be real. Then Jericho ran to him, *again*, and I knew he was real in the most painful and cruel way imaginable.

Alive … and married.

"Hi," he said, sauntering toward me with the ball that Jericho dropped for him. My traitor dog right at his side.

I rubbed my lips together. That was the greeting he got from me—an obscured expression.

"Did you really know … that the gun wasn't loaded?"

He heard me that day. He heard what I said just seconds before he died. Before I thought he died.

I owed him no apologies. I thanked him for saving my life—twice—and he married someone else. We were even.

"No," I said with confidence.

"You thought I was dying, so you lied?"

I crossed my arms over my chest and flipped out a hip. "Sorry … are we keeping track of lies? If that's the case, you lose. Don't even get me started on all the lies you told to cover your ass. Including the one where you were hired to *protect me*. So yeah, I thought the gun was loaded. I pulled the trigger to kill the man who was hired to kill me. Call it lack of trust or self-preservation, I don't care. But you can't fault me for that."

"Your dad killed my dad." He narrowed his eyes a fraction.

"Your dad raped my aunt. So fuck you, Wylder … Slade … Alex … whatever the hell you're calling yourself."

He winced.

I lifted my eyebrows. "Ah … I see. No one ever told you that your dad was a rapist? Well, wake up. You turned us into a war over the sins of our fathers. But *my* father killed truly bad people. He didn't rape women. He didn't take out innocent family members as revenge. But that's in your blood. Revenge is the reason your father raped my Aunt Jessica. He called it training, but that's not training. That's just a sick, fucked-up mind."

After a few long moments of no reaction, staring at the ground between us, he slowly lifted his head. "Well, now you know."

"Know what?" I canted my head to the side.

"Why I didn't come for you."

"Don't," I said in a thick voice as I shook my head. "It was our love story. Not my dad's, not your dad's. I loved the monster. I came back for you. I. Came. Back. For. You. And for five years you let me believe you were dead. You …" I swallowed and told myself I would not cry. He didn't deserve any more tears. "You didn't love me back."

"I took a fucking bullet for you!" With his hands shoved into the pockets of his jeans, he leaned forward, shouting the words in my face.

"You…" the tears did their own thing, not caring whether he deserved them or not "…*married* someone else. It hurt less when you were dead."

He nodded slowly, pain stealing his practiced no-fucks-given face. "Well, you're the one who didn't follow my instructions. You're the one who must have called for help. Had you just done what I fucking told you to do, maybe I *would* be dead."

"Oh …" I coughed a laugh. "And that's a good thing? Saving you was the *wrong* thing to do?"

"I was an assassin. A man died where they found me that day. I had two choices … prison or a new life. New name. New everything."

"Choices?" I shook my head. "How do you choose anything but prison?"

"Ask your dad."

His words paralyzed me. It felt like the day I found out my computer engineer father was an ex-assassin. No more secrets. My dad promised me … no more secrets. "What does that mean?"

"His connections weren't completely severed after he married and started living the boring suburban life. He knew the right person to make it happen. I had one hour to make the decision the day I was supposed to be discharged from the hospital. I could go to prison or I could be extracted and moved to a secure location in preparation for my new life. I just … I didn't think my new home in Texas and my new job with Floyd Wright would one day land me in a conference room with you."

My lips parted as his words fought for space and meaning in my mind. "My dad knew?" I whispered. "My dad knew you were alive?"

"What would you have chosen for me, Liv? Prison for life? Or life without you?"

"Your mom …" I shook my head.

"She thinks I'm dead. I have a grave and headstone next to my dad's and uncle's. It was the only way. She could visit my grave or visit me in prison. So I guess the question is … how many people have you told? Does your dad know you've seen me? Friends? Your boyfriend?"

My gaze shot to his. "How did you know I have a boyfriend?"

He stared at the toe of his black boot as he dug it into the grass. "It was part of the deal. I get to know what's happening in your life. I get video and pictures of you."

"W-what?" I felt violated and betrayed. "Someone spies on me so you can what? Fantasize about the life you'll never have? Do you look at these pictures and videos before or after you fuck your *wife*?"

He winced. "It's not like that."

"Then what's it like? At what point did you decide to fall in love with someone else? Was it when I found Gavin *two years* after you died? Did someone show you pictures of him kissing me outside of the theater? Was it video of me leaving his place the next morning? Did you happen to see my face? The tears running down my cheeks because it was the worst night of my life? A painful one-night stand. It was the moment I let myself truly accept you were gone. I hated his hands on me because they weren't yours. I hated his kiss. I hated myself for pretending that I enjoyed it. You made me hate my life ... my existence. And the whole time you were watching me? The whole time my dad knew I was grieving a living man? Livy's happy. Livy moved on. Time to go find someone else?"

"That's not how it happened."

"I ..." Swiping my tears, I shook my head. "I don't want to know how it happened. I don't want photos or video of your life with *her*. It sucks ... it hurts to feel so much hatred toward any human being, especially one I've never met. But I hate her. I hate her because she took my life. She took *you*. And you were supposed to be mine!"

"Liv ..." Redness filled his eyes, such a rare side of the monster I loved.

"I hate you too ..." I turned and started jogging home with Jericho at my side. When we reached the apartment, I peeled off my clothes and stood in the shower with nothing but ice-cold water washing over my body until everything began to feel numb, until the tears subsided, until reality blurred.

Shutting off the water, I remained idle in the shower, shivering, my breaths jumping in my chest like little staccatos as my teeth chattered. Jericho sat in the doorway and whined. Grabbing my towel, I slowly dried my goose bump covered body and slipped my arms into my satin robe.

I couldn't remember a time when I'd ever felt that alone.

No Slade.

My dad betrayed me.

Jessica wouldn't understand because she was the victim of his dad's brutality.

I had no one.

Grabbing a blanket, I curled up on the sofa. Jericho cried a bit more in concern for me before he jumped onto the sofa and lay at my feet.

Black ops.

People high up who could fake Slade's death and give him a new identity to keep him out of prison.

Someone spying on me for five years.

My dad's connection to all of it.

It was all too much.

Knock. Knock. Knock.

I eased to sitting, tightly wrapping the blanket around my shoulders. My bare feet shuffled to the door. Peeking out the peep hole, I frowned, wondering how he got up to my floor without an access card. A stupid question. He averted jail. Gaining access to my apartment had to be an afterthought.

I pressed my head to the door for a few seconds. The answer was no. No. I couldn't do it anymore. No more talk. No more explanations. There was nothing he could say to make things right. As I turned to head back to the sofa, the door opened.

I closed my eyes with my back to him. He had a fucking key to my apartment.

"If you don't leave, I'll call the cops. Call it payback ... Karma. Now go." I drew in a shaky breath and stared out the window.

The door clicked shut, but I felt him behind me.

Close.

Too close.

"I've always been yours."

My chest tightened. Why did he have to do that to me? It was cruel.

"No," I whispered.

"Yes."

I shook my head.

"Yes."

"No ..." I said with emotion building in my tone as my fists tightened around the blanket.

"Yes, Livy. I'm—"

I shrugged off the blanket and planted my fist in his face. His head whipped to the side and blood bloomed along the corner of his mouth. Sliding his tongue out to lick it, he faced me again. My hand no longer hurt. I wasn't the weak girl trying to fit the shoes of a fighter anymore. I was a warrior, broken by *him* and rebuilt by Jessica and my dad.

He eyed Jericho briefly, giving him the look that said, *stay,* before his gaze returned to me. "I'm still yours."

Whack!

My fist landed on his jaw. Again, his head whipped to the side. As he turned to face me a second time, he moved his jaw back and forth.

"Put your fists up, you fucking monster. I'm not done making you bleed."

"Good girl. Give me your pain."

I was *not* his good girl. Those two words had me seeing red.

I gave him my pain. Another jab to his face, my knee in his stomach. My leg swept his, taking him to the ground where I straddled him and hit his face until the skin on my knuckles mixed with the blood from his face.

"I hate you!" My fight weakened into nothing more than my fists pounding his chest as he remained absolutely still with his hands limp at his sides, not fighting back one bit, taking everything and surrendering to every breath of my pain.

Hugging my bloodied hands to my chest, I closed my eyes and sobbed.

He didn't move for the longest time, as if he knew what I needed even if I didn't know anything at the moment other than I hated life.

Inching his way to sitting, he rested his hands on my legs straddling him. I felt his warm breath on my face.

Minty.

Familiar.

Torturous.

"Yours," he whispered as his hands framed my face.

"You belong to her," I said in defeat with broken words and without opening my eyes.

"I belong to you."

"She's your wife."

"You're my whole fucking world."

I opened my eyes to the bloodied face I'd created.

His lips pressed to mine. As he moved them slowly, I tasted

the metallic blood along his lips.

He wasn't mine, but I was his.

Our kiss deepened, and I moaned as his tongue slid into my mouth.

He wasn't mine, but I was his.

As his mouth took everything I had to give him, his hands ghosted from my face to my shoulders, pushing off my robe. My fingers reacquainted themselves with his hair while his mouth sucked in a nipple. I seethed when his teeth dug into it, tugging it like he was on the verge of losing control.

He wasn't mine, but I was his.

"Wylder …" I closed my eyes, arching my back.

He released my nipple. "Shh … don't say anything." He took my other nipple and tugged until I groaned from the clash of pleasure and pain.

My hands left his hair and curled at his shoulders and back, pulling up his shirt one inch at a time. He shrugged it off and attacked my mouth again, all control lost.

He wasn't mine, but I was his.

Flipping me over onto my back, he hovered above me, controlling my mouth as I worked the button and zipper to his jeans. It was *so* wrong. But nothing about *us* ever really felt wrong except when we were apart.

Wrong …

He lifted onto his knees for mere seconds to push down his jeans and briefs to his thighs as I waited, naked on my wadded-up robe, hating myself for not being able to stop what was about to happen.

He wasn't mine, but I was his.

Smearing blood from his face up my torso and over my breasts to my neck and face, he lowered his body and pushed into me with one hard thrust.

No condom.

No questions.

No regrets.

I was a monster too.

Two monsters fucking like nothing or no one else in the world existed. Monsters held no accountability. They were selfish. And they feared nothing ... not even death.

I was his ... and *he was mine.*

Chapter Thirty-Five

Wylder

*Y*OU CAN NEVER *see her again.*
   You will always be dead to her.
Slade Wylder is dead.

Had I chosen prison, she would have lived knowing I was alive and forever taken from her.

So I chose to force her to let me go without choice.

I chose to watch her move on with her life, a special kind of torture that I felt like I deserved. Jackson Knight felt it was fitting as well. I knew he loved her; it was its own special variety of sick love, as most parental love is ... overprotective, controlling, suffocating.

My father was a controlling, sick bastard who deserved to die.

My uncle shared those same traits, and he, too, deserved to die.

I didn't think Jackson Knight deserved the same fate, but he also didn't deserve one drop more than I promised him.

The marriage. That was the one secret I was not allowed to compromise. He vowed to personally remove my soul from the earth if I ever told anyone. It was his safeguard.

If you ever come face to face with her, she can never know.

At five in the morning, she tiptoed from the bathroom to

her closet, wrapped in a towel, hair wet but combed straight. I reached across the bed and turned on the nightstand light.

She whipped around, eyes wide, hands tightening the towel around her body. "Sorry. I … I have work."

I sat up, rubbing my eyes with the heels of my hands before scrubbing the rest of my face. "I know. I have to go too."

"Yeah." With her back to me, she dropped her towel and slid on black panties and a matching bra. "Who protects Floyd when you're…" she glanced over her shoulder and rubbed her lips together to contain her smile "…up to no good."

I scratched my jaw and neck. "I lead his travel team. When he's on the go, I'm there. When he's home or secured in a hotel, I'm allowed to roam and…" I grinned "…be up to no good."

As she stepped into a fitted blue skirt and zipped it in the back, she glanced up at me, her lips the opposite of a suppressed smile. "I slept with a married man," she murmured.

I wanted to lift the weight of the world from her shoulders, but I couldn't. "There wasn't a lot of sleep involved."

She attempted a weak smirk while sliding on a gray satin blouse and buttoning it.

"Come here." I eased my legs over the side of the bed and spread them. My hands reached for her waist as she took hesitant steps toward me, gaze sweeping along my face.

"You're a mess. Don't get blood on my work clothes."

I nodded slowly as my hands slid from her waist to her ass, and she rested her hands on my shoulders. "I love you, Livy."

She swallowed hard. "But you love her too."

Tension gripped my face, tightening my brow as my gaze slipped from hers to her partially buttoned blouse. "I love *you*, Livy."

"But ..." I could tell from her shaky voice that emotions were gathering in her eyes, and I couldn't go there. I couldn't look up.

Taking her hand, I lifted her wrist to my lips and pressed a kiss to it. "No buts, Liv ... no buts ..."

Her hand moved to cup my jaw, fingers teasing my short beard. I closed my eyes.

"What now?"

I guided her back a step so I could stand. "Now you go to work." After pressing my lips to the top of her head, I brushed past her toward the bathroom.

Livy met me at the door when I came out of the bathroom after my shower, wearing only a pair of jeans. "Here." She handed me a shirt. One of my old shirts. "Since your other shirt is soiled with blood." Pivoting, she sauntered back to the kitchen in her heels, looking sinfully sexy in that tight skirt and legs that made me weak in the knees. "I don't have coffee. Ten different flavors of tea, but no coffee." She shrugged, taking a sip of her tea as I pulled on my shirt.

"Did you take anything else of mine or just this shirt and my dog?"

Her grin hid behind the mug. "Shirts, sweatshirts, your denim jacket. A couple guns and a few knives."

I lifted a single brow, unable to read her well enough to know if she was serious.

"And your boyfriend is okay with it?"

Her smile faded as she lowered her mug to the counter, cupping it with both hands. "I can end it with a call. Can you say the same?"

I shook my head.

"Wylder ... Alex ... whatever ..." She gazed at the steam

rising from the tea. "I need to know. Do you have children?"

I paused, not intending for my pause to be an assumed yes, but as tears filled her eyes, I knew that's exactly what she thought.

"Oh god …" She covered her mouth and closed her eyes, shaking her head several times before dropping her hand. "You have a family. That's … that's not okay. What I did was not okay. It was wrong last night, but you have a *family*. You don't …" She batted away a stray tear. "You don't do this to your *family*."

I made my way to her, pressing my chest to her back, hands snaking around her waist as my mouth dipped to her ear. "What bothers you more? The idea that I have children and I cheated on my family? Or the idea that I have children and they're not *ours*?"

"It's not fair to ask me that." Her hands covered mine over her stomach.

"I have one child."

She stiffened, holding her breath.

"A boy."

Nothing. Not one breath, not one sound.

"His name is Jericho. He's ten, but he lives with his mom."

It took her all of two seconds to turn around and fist my shirt. "You're such an asshole." She narrowed her eyes.

"I am." I grabbed her face and kissed off every ounce of lipstick, leaving her breathless and red from my whiskers. "I'm going back to Austin today. Talk to your dad."

She pulled back. "What does that mean?"

"It means … talk to your dad." I kissed her forehead and stepped back, making my way to the door. "I'll take Jericho out. You're going to be late if you don't get going."

When I opened the door and whistled to Jericho, her high heels clicked furiously along the hard floor toward me. She threw her arms around my neck. "You're not coming back, are you? This is goodbye, isn't it?" she whispered, voice thick with emotion.

It. Fucking. Killed. Me.

I hugged her waist, lifting her off the ground and burying my face into her neck. "Talk to your dad."

Chapter Thirty-Six

Livy

I COULDN'T GO back to San Francisco, not with my work-load. So I asked my dad to come to Sacramento that weekend.

Wylder? He left. No contact information. Nothing more than a sad smile, a kiss goodbye, and a final "talk to your dad."

When I opened the door, mid-morning Saturday, Dad smiled and held out his arms. I returned a frown, pivoted, and shuffled back to my kitchen to finish washing my dirty dishes from the previous days.

"That's not the greeting I expected when you texted me to visit you." He shut the door.

I resumed scrubbing the dishes in the sink with my back to him. "Slade's alive."

"What?"

"No!" I whipped back around, hands fisted at my sides, dripping soapy water onto the floor. "Not *what*, like you didn't hear me. Not *what* like you can't believe what I just said. The correct answer is: When did you find out, Livy? I'm incredibly sorry for lying to you for five years. It broke my heart to watch you grieve him for so long. But I did it because ..." I lifted both hands, palms up, eyes wide and expectant. "Fill in the fucking blank, Dad!"

My dad was militant in his control. Nothing phased him, at least that he showed to me. I couldn't bully him, and I knew it. That didn't stop my anger. That didn't soothe the pain.

He twisted his lips and canted his head. "Because he lived. He could live in prison or live a new life. But he couldn't live with you. His uncle didn't work alone. Slade wasn't his only soldier. The police wanted him in prison for the death of his uncle. The other people who worked with him wanted him dead. And they weren't going to give up until he was in fact dead. So what did you want me to do? Let him die? Let him come for you so you died too? Let him go to prison? Let *me* go to prison?"

"The truth! I wanted the truth."

Dad nodded slowly. "I see. And what were you going to do with the truth? Be with him?"

"Yes!" I pressed my hands against the side of my head, furious at his ability to stay so calm while I crumbled like an avalanche, violent and reckless.

"Do you know what would have had to happen for you to be with him?"

"Yes. You would have had to tell me he was alive. That you relocated him to Texas."

Dad chuckled. His aloofness fed my anger. "No, Livy. You would have had to die too. Faked your death. Funeral. Gravestone. Everything."

"So ..." I shrugged as frustration bled through my voice.

"Slade's mom thinks he's dead. For his safety and hers, she will always have to believe he is dead. She will never see him again. When you die, fake or real, you never see your family again."

"You and Jess did."

"We were rare exceptions."

"Why?"

"Because I killed Slade's dad."

I swallowed hard.

"Let him go. He's alive. That should mean something. That should be enough."

I shook my head. "It's not enough. If you found out that mom was alive, but you couldn't be with her … would that be enough?"

He flinched a bit. "Livy …"

"There's no way you would let that happen."

"Liv—"

"No. You don't know what it's like to feel like you have to say goodbye forever to the same person twice! And you definitely don't know what it's like to have the person you love come back from the dead and be married." Tears filled my eyes and my voice cracked. "H-he's m-married."

He took a step toward me and I stepped backward, shaking my head. "I don't need you to comfort me. I don't need to sit on your lap while you coddle me and tell me everything is going to be okay. I just need to know why he told me to talk to you. What does that mean? What isn't he telling me? What aren't *you* telling me?"

"We're not having this conversation."

"YES!" I smacked my palm on the counter. "We are having this conversation."

"No …" he said with an uncharacteristic loss of control to his tone. "We are not talking about this. I am not letting you die. I am not letting you go."

It dawned on me, even then … five years later … I needed to die, to take on a new identity to be with Slade. I would not get to see my dad or the rest of my family *ever* again.

"His wife …"

Dad scratched the back of his neck and sighed but said nothing.

"He wouldn't say anything about her, except he wore gray on his wedding day and it rained. And it fit his mood. He wants *you* to tell me about his wife. Why was he not happy on his wedding day?"

Nothing.

I hugged my arms to my stomach. "Does he love her?"

Dad shrugged. "They've been married for almost five years. He might love her."

"Five? Almost *five* years? The incident at the cabin happened just over five years ago. He didn't fall in love and get married that quickly. Who the hell is she and why is she married to the man that I love?"

Another flinch from my father. He never could swallow the truth—and the truth was, despite everything, I loved Wylder to my soul.

"She needed a new life too. Single people relocating as a couple are less likely to be noticed, to be found."

"Did he know her?"

Dad shook his head.

"He married a stranger? Like an arranged marriage?"

"Yes."

Five years.

He'd been with her for five years. As friends?

"What's she like?"

"Livy—"

"Jesus, Dad! Just tell me what she's like!"

He deflated. "She'd just turned eighteen when they married."

My stomach clenched.

"She's smart. A lot like you, actually. She likes to surf and drive fast cars. She's a vegetarian and an environmentalist. You'd like her."

"I hate her."

I didn't. But I wanted to hate her.

Another grimace from him.

"Is she pretty?"

"Don't do this."

"Answer me." I kept my emotions in check. Wylder loved me. I knew that. Still … he'd been married to her for five years. A girl that was like me.

"She's young enough to be my daughter. I don't focus on her like that."

"Am I pretty, Dad?"

"Of course."

"Is. She. Pretty?"

He stared at the ceiling for a few seconds. "Yes, Livy. She's pretty."

I had nothing more to ask. Nothing more to say. I just had … nothing.

"Let him go."

"Maybe they don't find us. Whoever you're afraid of finding him and hurting me. Maybe they don't find us. I've seen him. He was here. And we're fine."

"He was here? In your apartment?"

I nodded.

His jaw tightened. "Where is he now?"

"Texas."

"Did he find you?"

I shook my head.

"Chance encounter?"

I nodded.

"Good. Let him go."

"What if—"

"No, Livy! There's no fucking what-if's here. It was incredibly stupid of him to come to your apartment, knowing damn well someone could be watching you."

"Why would someone be watching me?"

"Because you were with him. You lived with him. If there's the tiniest doubt in anyone's mind that he's not dead, *you* are the place they will look to find him."

"I'm fine. He was here twice, and I'm fine."

"Livy, you don't understand. These people are patient. They will not take you out on a whim. They will wait until you're married. They'll watch you build a life of happiness, and then they will take it from you one piece at a time. Abe could have made an attempt on my life years ago, but he didn't. He waited until I had the best damn life, and then he killed your mom and let me suffer for years, patiently waiting for me to recover just so he could take you away from me too."

More tears released down my face. What did Wylder want from me? Was our night together a goodbye that felt better than the day I left him for dead? Did he expect me to leave my family forever—to die and take on a new identity? Quit my job. Lose everything I'd worked for over the previous twenty-six years?

"So this other woman, his wife, she's acceptably disposable? It's okay if they find him and take her? Kill her?"

"Yes. She's an acceptable risk because she agreed to it, knowing the risks. She nearly died. She lost all of her family.

Every day is borrowed time for her. No family around to miss her or worry about her. Alex is her family now."

Alex.

I hated hearing him call Wylder Alex.

"Livy, he's alive and well. He has a good job. A nice home in the suburbs. And he's protecting a young woman who lost everything. You have a dream job. You have family. You have a boyfriend if you don't mess it up. I'm sorry … I'm truly sorry you ever had to find out. And I don't know what it's like to lose the same person twice. But I know your strength. It's your mom's strength. Use that strength to move on. And let time take care of the heartache. Look at me. I was a mess. But here I am, still in one piece. I made it through the pain, and you will too."

Chapter Thirty-Seven

THE PAIN.

It took my dad years to make it through the pain. Five years after losing Wylder the first time, I still felt the pain.

Every.

Single.

Day.

And there I was ... getting ready to start the whole process over again.

Wylder was the one. My choice was to lose the one or lose all of my family. It shouldn't have been a choice at all.

I would keep my family and return to my life before Floyd Wright brought Wylder back into my life. He would protect the woman he married. It made sense to my brain, but my heart didn't understand. My heart looked at it differently.

So I worked. I researched and observed Timothy and Tricia deposing experts and witnesses. The trial came and went. I felt history being made and witnessed justice at its finest. A win for our clients. A win for us. A win for the environment.

Life should have been good, but it wasn't.

I broke up with my boyfriend. It didn't feel right after what happened with Wylder.

I joined a gym since my escapes to the beach were rare occasions instead of my usual form of exercise.

I went out with people from work to make friends, celebrate wins, and not think about *him*.

Yet, nothing worked. I thought about Wylder all the time.

"Haven't seen Floyd Wright around here lately," I said, casually sipping my tea in the break room while making small talk with Timothy as he waited for the espresso machine to disperse another dose of caffeine. It had been nearly four months since I'd seen Floyd or Wylder.

My dad said to move on. So ... I tried to move on.

"I referred him to another firm."

"Oh?" My head jerked back a bit.

"We were up to our ears in the Solis case, and it deserved this firm's full attention. And Floyd's issues require someone with honed skills in international law. I dabble, but it's not my area of expertise. Wealthy men like Floyd should and usually do have a whole team of lawyers to meet specific needs. I was a little surprised he didn't already have someone else." Tim shrugged, lifting his cup to his mouth.

"That ..."

Is crushing. Heartbreaking.

How was I supposed to ever see Wylder again? I had no contact information for him, not even his new last name. Maybe it was a sign. Time to let go again. Not just again ... *forever*.

I cleared my throat. "That makes total sense. It is surprising a man like him wouldn't already have someone who specialized in international law."

Tim nodded and smiled before slipping around the corner toward his office.

"You look like you've lost weight," Meghan, Tricia's secretary, eyed me as she walked toward the fridge.

I shrugged. "What can I say? They've been riding me hard.

I've had very little sleep."

"Hope you're going home for Thanksgiving so your family can put some meat back on those bones."

On a chuckle, I shook my head. "We're a pretty athletic family. My workouts are intensive. It's hard to keep weight on that's not muscle."

"Now you're just bragging." She rolled her eyes at me, just before I winked and headed to my office.

"Call on line two, Livy." Dani smiled at me as I walked by her desk. "An *Aunt Jessica.*"

I slid my cell phone out of my pocket, looking for a missed call. There wasn't one. Sitting at my desk, I picked up the receiver. "Jess?"

"Hi, Livy."

"Why are you calling my work number? Is my phone not working?"

"Your dad monitors your cell phone."

"He does what?"

"It's not important. We need to—"

"No. I'm pretty sure my dad violating my privacy is very important and illegal."

"Your dad has made a living doing illegal stuff. That's not why I called. I need you to listen. He'll be out of the shower soon."

"Where are you at?"

"His place. We sparred and now we're going out for dinner since Luke is out of town for a conference. Just. Listen!"

I narrowed my eyes. "Okay. I'm listening."

"I was using your dad's computer to check on something at work, and he had a notification pop up. A notification about you. I managed to erase it to buy you some time, but he'll eventually come across the information."

"What are you talking about?"

"He gets notifications about your medical records and the—"

"He's hacked into my medical records?" My face soured as anger climbed up my neck. He knew no boundaries.

"Livy! I don't have much time. I heard the shower go off. You're pregnant. Please tell me it's Darren's baby."

I said nothing because I knew I didn't hear her correctly.

"Livy?"

"I ... I'm not pregnant."

"The blood test you had two days ago says otherwise."

"Then it's the wrong person's records. I'm on the pill. I haven't had sex in four months."

"Have you had your period in the past four months?"

"Of course."

Wait ...

I had no fucking clue. I didn't have regular periods. And when I started training so intensely with Jessica and my dad after the Abe incident, I would often skip periods, sometimes several months.

"You're sure?"

"Pretty sure."

"You don't keep track?"

I rubbed my temples. "No ... I ... they're irregular and all over the place. But I promise you, I'm not pregnant. I broke up with Darren. I haven't seen him since I moved here."

"To be clear, because I'm going to have to hang up in less than a minute, you haven't had unprotected sex since you moved to Sacramento. Correct?"

"I'm. On. The. Pill."

"Condom, Livy! Did you have sex without a condom?"

I swallowed hard. "Yes."

The line went dead, and I assumed my dad had emerged from the bathroom and she had to disconnect the call. It was a routine physical. I had no complaints. They were going to run an STD test after I confessed I'd had sex without a condom with someone who wasn't my partner. The doctor said a pregnancy test would be a good idea, but I'm pretty sure I declined it.

Confidentiality ... or so I fucking thought. Of course I was pissed off at my dad, but I didn't have time to give his massive invasion of my privacy the attention it deserved because Jess thought I was pregnant.

I was not pregnant.

No way.

I *know* I didn't ask for a pregnancy test. The doctor must have ignored me, adding it to the lineup of STD tests. When did a fetus become an STD?

Fetus ... baby ...

Nope. It had to be a mistake. I. Was. On. The. Pill.

Not to mention, it really did take an act of God for me to have a regular period, which meant it had to take an act of God for me to get pregnant.

God wasn't that cruel. He had better things to do than facilitate the meeting of an egg and sperm in me after all that I'd been through in my young life.

With shaky hands, I brought up the number for my doctor, a hot doctor Tricia recommended when I asked for a referral.

"Hi. This is Livy Knight. I need you to give me my test results from my appointment Monday. I don't see anything posted to my app."

"What is your date of birth?"

I clenched my teeth.

Just tell me if I'm pregnant!

I gave her all my information and waited on hold ... and I waited ... and I waited.

"Sorry, there's a glitch in the app. You can go onto our website and access all of your test results there."

"Am I pregnant?"

"I'm sorry. I'm not allowed to share any information with you over the phone."

"Can you at least tell me if they ran a pregnancy test? Because I didn't ask for one."

"Again, all tests and results can be viewed if you log in to our website. And your doctor will be calling you soon to discuss them."

I ended the call without a goodbye. Then I went to their website and logged in to my account, with no clue how to quickly find my answer.

"Shit ..." There it was right there on the screen.

I ... was ... pregnant.

Chapter Thirty-Eight

SIX POSITIVE HOME tests later (because those official medical lab tests could not be accurate), I conceded ... I was pregnant.

I didn't want a child, not like that. Not by myself. Not if my life could possibly be in danger.

"You don't have to keep it." Jessica handed me a cup of tea the day before Thanksgiving. I went straight to her house before I went home.

Dad knew.

He didn't say the actual words. He texted "get your ass home."

I ignored him for five days, packed my bag, and drove to Jessica's house.

"It's Alex's baby, isn't it?"

I winced before blowing the steam. "Why do you have to call him that too?"

She shrugged, angling her body at the opposite end of the sofa. "It's been his name for five years."

"You knew." I tried to hide my disappointment, but it was hard to do.

"I knew. And I would have told you had I thought it was safe and in your best interest ... emotionally."

I stared past her, out the window to her view of the bay. "I love how everyone thought they knew what was best for me ...

a grown woman."

"I've made some impossible decisions in my life. I've had people keep secrets from me in my 'best interest.' So I'm not going to waste my breath trying to convince you that you shouldn't be mad, hurt, and disappointed."

"Did you meet his wife?"

She nodded.

"Should I hate her?"

Jessica chuckled. "You slept with her husband and got pregnant. If their marriage was a typical marriage, I'd say she'd have every right to do physical harm to you. But I honestly don't know what their marriage is right now. Five years with a stranger makes them anything *but* strangers. She's pretty and likable. He's handsome and a man ... with needs."

"Wow ... you are a ray of sunshine on my life right now."

"Livy, I won't lie to you to save your feelings. Your life? Your sanity? Yes. But not your feelings."

With a sad smile, I met her gaze. "Is it fair to him to keep the baby if we can't be together? If he can't be part of his child's life?"

"Well, that's a loaded question. So many assumptions. First is assuming you tell him about the baby. Second is assuming you tell him and choose not to be a family."

My eyes narrowed. "I don't have a choice."

"Yes." She took a small sip of her tea. "You do."

I shook my head. "That's not a choice. Leaving this life ... my job, my friends, my family ... it's not a choice."

She inhaled a long breath and released it slowly. "Family. That's something you have to really think about. In twenty ... thirty years ... who will be your family? What happens when your dad dies? When I die? And you have this child or children and they have children of their own. *They* will be your family. And as much as it rips my heart out to imagine not having you in my life, it equally breaks my heart to think of you clinging to the past instead of looking to the future."

I felt the burn starting in my eyes. "It would be like ... I died." My words broke at the end as I rapidly blinked away the tears.

Jessica had her own emotions building in her eyes. "I know, sweetie. I've been in your shoes."

"Do you think you made the right choice?"

She bit the inside of her cheek for a few moments. "I made *a* choice. There wasn't a right or wrong choice. There was a painful, agonizing choice, but it was never going to be right or wrong."

I nodded several times.

She stared at her wedding photo on the wall to our right. "I guess if I had anything to do over again, I might have not made the choice alone."

AFTER TALKING WITH Jessica, she forced me to go home and face my father. I took the longest route to home, waited in my car for nearly thirty minutes, and finally got the courage to go to the door just as the sun started to set.

It was unlocked—clearly he was expecting me.

"Hey." I set my bag by the stairs as he glanced up from the piano, pencil behind his ear. He liked to compose his own music.

"Hey." He sounded defeated, so unlike my strong father. The last time he sounded like that was after Mom died.

I dragged my heavy feet to the piano and sat next to him,

facing the opposite direction.

"I want to kill him. And I mean that in the most literal sense. And here's the thing … I could do it and not go to prison because he's already dead."

I closed my eyes. "I love him. You know that. I made a conscious decision to love the monster if that was the only way to keep the man. *You* made the decision to keep me away from him because you knew …" I couldn't finish because I wasn't sure if the words preparing to come out were the truth. Not yet. I didn't know my truth yet.

"I knew what, Livy? That you'd choose him over me? That you'd choose him over all of your family? That he could whisk you away one minute, cheat on you the next, and you'd have no choice but to stay in a life … separated from your family and friends … forever."

"He would never do that."

"Livy … I taught you better than that. No human is one hundred percent trustworthy. You have to invest in you first. Always you first."

"What about the baby? Shouldn't I invest in my baby? His or her future?"

"Jesus …" He scrubbed his hands down his face. "You have choices."

"Abort it? I can't! I haven't seen Wylder in over four months. So I don't know why I don't feel pregnant or look pregnant, but I'm past the point of getting an abortion. And I don't want one!"

"Fine. Keep it and raise it on your own. Or adoption. Or a million other choices that don't involve …"

I opened my mouth to finish his sentence for him, but I couldn't do it either.

Choices that don't involve him losing a child in a way that would feel as painful as losing his wife.

My eyes burned so badly as my face contorted, and I choked out a sob as I leaned against my rock. "I-I don't know w-hat to d-do ..." It hurt so badly because the pain went both ways. He would feel like I died, and I would feel like he died. A forever goodbye. I didn't know if I could do it. "I w-wish Mom were h-here to t-tell me what to d-do ..."

He wrapped his arms around me, one hand pressed to the back of my head, guiding my face into his chest as I cried. "For the first time ever, I'm glad she's not here because this would kill her."

"I l-love you s-so much ..." My hands fisted his shirt. "I c-can't do it. I can't s-say goodbye."

He pressed his lips to the top of my head. "And I can't make this decision for you. Not this one. I'd rather lose you than have you hate me for asking you to choose me."

I didn't care for life at that moment.

Pregnancy was supposed to be a joyous occasion, not a death sentence.

Love was supposed to heal all wounds, not rip apart souls.

I didn't know what to do, so I let myself have a timeout. I let myself celebrate Thanksgiving with my family, as if I didn't have a choice to make, as if I didn't have a baby in my belly, as if I didn't miss Wylder to the deepest part of my heart.

Then ... I asked for a few personal days, and I got on a plane to Texas with an address Jessica gave me as she whispered in my ear, "You have to know."

Chapter Thirty-Nine

ALEX OBERMEIER AND his wife Melinda lived in a conservative ranch just outside of downtown Austin. They had an actual white picket fence, a basketball hoop on the garage, and a curved walk to their red front door beyond a lovely porch with a swing. I sat in my rental car across the street wearing sunglasses and a baseball cap for three hours before a black truck pulled into the driveway. He climbed out and my heart hammered into my ribs, wanting out to chase him.

Loosening his tie as he walked toward the house, the front door opened for him. A long-haired brunette flashed him a huge smile and stepped outside to beat a rug against the railing. They stood on the porch for several minutes talking.

She grinned and nodded as he talked. And when she responded, he threw his head back and laughed. I couldn't recall a time he laughed like that for me. After she finished shaking out the rug, he took it from her, and she slipped her arm around his waist, leaning up to kiss his cheek.

I died.

I knew it was a mistake.

Jessica was right. Five years was a long time to be with someone in the same house and not risk developing feelings for them. The reality was … she'd known him and been with him a lot longer than I had been with him.

Time should not have mattered, not with love. But in that

moment, I felt certain the woman who had time on her side was the woman who would spend forever with him.

I had Slade Wylder. He died.

She had Alex Obermeier, and he was there, married to her, living under the same roof, laughing, kissing, and huddling together after a long day.

I wasn't sure how long I stared at the red door, the picket fence, and the manicured lawn. Probably a good half hour. Just as I reached for the button to start the car, the front door opened again.

I pulled the bill of my hat down and scooted lower in my seat as he strutted outside wearing different clothes—his usual jeans, tee, and boots. He came closer, but I anticipated him stopping at the mailbox.

He did not.

I completely ducked my head and held my breath, hoping he wouldn't focus in on the strange woman hiding in a rental car across from his house.

Tap. Tap. Tap.

"Fuck …" I blew out a breath and risked a glance at the window.

"Open the door, Livy."

It had been over four months since I'd seen him. My heart wasn't ready for him to ask all the questions I knew he was preparing to ask me. But I didn't have a lot of options, so I unlocked the door.

He opened it. "Scoot over."

"I'm leaving."

He glanced around before meeting my gaze again. "Scoot. Over. Now."

I unfastened my seat belt and crawled into the passenger

seat as he slid inside, shut the door, and sped off down the street.

"She's beautiful," I said softly after a few minutes of thick silence.

"She is."

I tried to hide my reaction, like he'd slapped me across the face. There were no more words to say. It was like I got on a plane to Texas just to confirm that he was attracted to his wife, which meant he was fucking his wife, which meant he had genuine feelings for her. And I was the knocked-up mistress.

After a silent fifteen-minute drive, we pulled off the road and drove down a long lane to a huge mansion surrounded by acres of grass and horses.

Halfway down the lane, he veered off into a grassy area facing another white fence and a view of three horses grazing.

"Where are we?" I managed to ask.

"Don't worry about it."

"Floyd's house?"

"One of them. He's not here." He hopped out and walked to the front of the sedan. Then he stopped and eased back until his butt hit the hood of the car.

When I realized he wasn't going to turn around and look at me or come open my door, I climbed out of the car and headed straight to the fence, resting my arms on the top rail. "Do you love her?" I asked, feeling brave with him a few feet behind me.

"I care for her."

"That's not an answer."

"It's the only one I have, Liv."

"You weren't coming back, were you?"

"No."

My lips parted to let out the pain in a silent exhale. "Why?"

"Because I played all of my cards. It was your move."

"So you knew? You knew the only way we could be together was if I died. If I left my family. If I chose you and only you."

"Yes."

I closed my eyes, one tear managed to escape, but I quickly wiped it off my cheek. "And your wife? What would happen to her if I chose you?"

"She would remarry."

Shaking my head, I released a painful laugh. "How terrible. How insensitive. What if she loves you? What if you love her?"

"She would remarry." He sounded so unaffected.

I turned. "You make her sound so disposable. Like her life and her feelings don't matter."

He blinked several times before crossing his arms over his chest and staring at his boots. "When you think your life is over and someone steps in and gives you a second chance, you feel this ... relief. This gratitude for simple things like sunrises and oxygen to breathe. She's just happy to be alive. Have a home. A job. A second chance."

"And you." I quickly batted away another tear. "I saw her smile at you. I saw you smile at her. And you laughed. You never laughed like that for me."

He glanced up. "Don't."

"Don't what?"

"Jealousy isn't a good color on you."

My teeth gritted. "You're such an asshole. I don't know why I came."

"You came to tell me that you're pregnant with my baby, and you don't know if you're going to leave your life to let me be part of my child's life."

"H-how did—"

"I told you. I know your business."

"My dad?"

He shook his head.

"Jessica?"

"She knew you'd chicken out if you saw me in my new life. Is that what you were getting ready to do before I came back out of the house? Were you going to leave without giving me a chance to plead my case?"

I shook my head, biting my lips together while trying to focus on him though blurry tears. "It's not that simple."

"It is that simple. It's as simple as if I asked you if after you give birth, if you'd be willing to give me and Melinda the baby to raise while you went back to your life. If you'd be willing to never see your child or be part of their life."

I flinched. "It's not the—"

"It *is* the same fucking thing!" His angry hands ran through his hair. "The only difference is I wanted this baby ... I actively tried to get you pregnant. I didn't want there to be a decision for you to make. I wanted you to choose me because we're meant to be together and have a family and a *life*!" His eyes shined with tears, and he lost control. "I've felt so fucking lonely for as long as I can remember. But with you ..." He rolled his lips between his teeth and managed to keep the tears from releasing as he swallowed hard. "With you I felt like I belonged somewhere. With you I felt human even when I knew I was a monster. But you ..." He rested his hands on his hips and forced his gaze upward unable to finish his thought. And he blinked, releasing big, fat, wet emotions down his face.

I knew what he was trying to say. I knew it all too well. "I loved the monster because I loved the man first."

He nodded, bravely giving me his emotion-filled gaze. "I need you more." He swallowed so hard my own throat felt the pain and suffocation.

More …

He needed me more than my dad or Jessica, or my friends, or Timothy and Tricia … or anyone else needed me.

Family. Who is my family?

The world was too unreachable. *Everything* was too unattainable.

So I couldn't have the world, and I couldn't have everything. That was life. I had a baby in my tummy and a man who loved me. Losing the rest would hurt like hell for a very long time.

The decision wasn't right or wrong.

It wasn't easy.

And it was so very far from fair.

But it was necessary.

When my incessant thoughts dragged out in silence, he turned his back to me and dropped his chin, interlacing his fingers behind his neck. "It's too much to ask."

I took cautious steps toward him and pressed my lips to the center of his back. "It is too much to ask, but if you love me, you'll ask it anyway."

When my hands snaked around his torso, he covered them with his and whispered, "Choose me, Livy."

Chapter-Forty

Jackson Knight

WE BURIED LIVY Knight between her mom and some guy named Jude Day beneath a hill not far from the Golden Gate Bridge. Friends and family mourned her tragic death—a shark attack that left only part of her body and half of her surfboard.

Jessica wiped real tears because the reality of the situation was … Livy was gone. I left my sobbing daughter collapsing in the arms of a man who everyone swore was just like me. She tried to claw her way free for one more kiss, one more hug, one more time of nuzzling her face into my chest.

"You're emotionally dead," Jessica said after everyone left the cemetery, leaving just the two of us staring at the empty casket being lowered into the ground. "You will never see her again, and yet … not one single tear."

"She's all I have left. I think you underestimate what I would do to have her in my life. Like you underestimated what I would do to keep you safe, to save your life."

Jessica shook her head. "You'd have to take down an entire army. Kill probably a dozen people still loyal to Abe and Knox. And they could be anywhere. You're going to hunt all of them down? Kill all of them?" She grunted a laugh, punctuating the insanity of it all.

I leaned down and kissed her head. "Please stop underestimating me. Now ... go home with your family."

As I made my way toward my car, she called, "Where are you going?"

Without stopping, without looking back, I murmured only to myself, "I'm going to kill them. All of them."

Epilogue

Wylder

"WHERE ARE WE?" Livy (Emily James) opened her tired eyes as the small plane landed, coasting up to the shore.

It took months to plan her death, months to plan the death of Alex Obermeier. That meant months apart.

Months of not being with her at her doctor's visits.

Months of not hearing the heartbeat of my child.

Months of the most torturous patience.

Then we spent another month apart as we were moved to multiple temporary locations (separately) while it was determined if anyone was following us ... suspecting we were still alive.

At seven-and-a-half months pregnant, we were transported to the same airport to be reunited and then put on a sea plane for the final leg of our journey to a new life. With a doctor who would stay with us until the birth of the baby, we took an hour flight to an island off the coast of Livy-would-never-know. And that was where we were to live out the rest of our lives.

"It's home." I unfastened her seat belt and kissed her belly while I was in the vicinity.

"It's an island."

I chuckled, taking her hand to guide her off the small plane as the doctor grabbed her bag and followed us along with

Jericho. "Good observation, Mrs. James."

"What island?" She slipped on her sunglasses as our feet hit sand.

"Our island."

"What does that mean?"

I took her hand and led her toward the two ATVs that had been delivered a few weeks earlier along with all of our new belongings. "It means I bought an island for us. It's small. No one else lives here. All of our supplies will be delivered once a week. And we'll never have to do stupid shit like work or wait in traffic."

"Can I be president of our island?" She climbed into the passenger seat of the first ATV.

I leaned in and kissed her slowly for a few seconds before pulling away and smiling. "No. Our island doesn't have a president. It has a queen."

"We're a monarchy." She grinned.

I helped the pilot and the doctor with the bags, tossing them in the back of the second ATV.

"Up." I nodded to the seat for Jericho to hop up there as the doctor climbed into the driver's seat and grinned at Jericho and his reluctance. Hope Faber (previously Gemma Blair) was weeks away from finishing her fellowship to become an OB-GYN when her father was killed by Abe, and she was shot and left for dead.

After years of rehabilitation, she fully recovered, all while taking on a new identity far away from friends and family who all assumed she did in fact die. Jackson sent her to bring his grandchild safely into the world.

It was a ten-minute drive to the only structure on the island, our house.

"Eddie ... it's stunning ..." She leaned forward, head swiveling in every direction as we pulled to the small drive of our small two-bedroom bungalow on the beach. The island was tiny, so basically everything was on the beach.

Referring to me as Eddie, my new name, surprised me. I assumed I'd always be her Wylder.

Before I got the ATV in *Park*, she jumped out and ran to the side of the house and straight to the beach. "The waves! Oh my gosh! I can surf these babies!"

"I've got this." Hope giggled as she pulled out the bags. We had very little with us, most everything else had been delivered earlier.

Jericho followed me to the beach as Livy kicked off her sandals and lifted her sun dress, running to the water. "No surfing with my baby still inside of you."

She ignored me, wading farther out until it reached her belly, soaking the bottom of her dress. "I'm going to surf for the rest of my life." She turned and gave me the first *real* smile I'd seen on her face since the day I carried her away from her father, sobbing and crying, *"It's not fair."*

It wasn't fair.

It was life.

"And you…" she drudged through the water back to the beach "…will hunt and fish."

"Oh, I will, huh?" I grinned, sliding my arms around her.

"You bought me an island," she whispered, shaking her head as the first real sparkle of life came back to her brown eyes.

"I bought you an island. It seemed like the only fair thing to do since you won't be president." I pecked her lips. "Let's go inside. I'm starving and you should be too."

WYLDER JAMES CAME two weeks early, weighing in at six pounds, eight ounces and one hundred percent perfect.

I didn't know how to be a dad. Livy said fathers have two jobs: to love and protect.

That I could do.

I wasn't sure any father had ever loved their son the way I loved Wylder. And I knew it the second he first looked at me.

Livy called them moments.

"Moments ..." Livy (because she was forever my Livy) said as she breastfed our son and drank tea in a lounge chair under a palm tree as the sun set.

"What moment this time?" I asked, carving an odd figure out of a piece of driftwood.

"This one. I like it, but it's incomplete. It's bittersweet. It's everything, but with an asterisk. Your mom has a grandson, so does my dad. One they will never see."

"Maybe."

"Maybe?" she parroted.

"Your dad doesn't seem like the kind of guy who would really let his daughter go *forever*."

"What are you saying?"

I offered another shrug, focusing on what looked like a dolphin taking shape. Or a wood turd. "I'm saying ... I think your dad isn't ready to let me win quite yet." I squinted one eye and gave her a quick glance.

Hope.

Hope did a lot of things. In that moment, it breathed life into my wife. It gave her back her most genuine smile. Hope came with no promises. It offered no solutions. It fought the good fight and knew when to let go. And I knew the most likely scenario was that she would never see her father again.

But life was too fucking short to lose hope.

She stretched her leg out and dug her toe into my side until I grinned, keeping my head down and focusing on her birthday present taking shape. "I love you."

I set the knife and wood down. Then I grabbed her foot and kissed my way up her leg, over her soft belly, stopping to kiss Wylder on the cheek before continuing up her neck and to her ear.

"I love you back."

⌁

Livy

AFTER PUTTING NINE-MONTH-OLD Wylder to bed, I peeked out the window at my husband sitting in the sand next to Jericho, gazing into the dark night and endless miles of ocean. He did it every night. I never asked why or what he thought about. His dark, mysterious side is what first drew me to him, so I let him have his moments, his time alone.

Retrieving a piece of paper and pen from the kitchen drawer, I sat at the table and wrote him a note.

What did you think of me the first day in class?
When did you know you loved me?
How often do you think about your mom?
Do you really think I'll see my dad again in this lifetime?
What went through your mind when you saw me after five years apart?
When should we give Wylder a sibling?
Do you have a stick of gum?
XO Your Livy always

I left the note by the door and retired to the bathroom for a soak in my tub. After I shaved and shampooed, I leaned my head back and closed my eyes. Minutes later, something hit the top of my head. After a quick glance around and no signs of anyone, I spotted a paper airplane on the floor next to the tub. Stretching my arm over the edge, I nabbed it and unfolded it— my note to him.

What did you think of me the first day in class?
I thought you were pesky.

When did you know you loved me?
The morning after my gunshot wound.

How often do you think about your mom?
Several times a day.

Do you really think I'll see my dad again in this lifetime?
Yes.

What went through your mind when you saw me after five years apart?
It hurt like hell. Worst fucking pain of my life. I thought death would have been better.

When should we give Wylder a sibling?
When you're done reading this.

Do you have a stick of gum?
Of course.

XO ~~*Your Livy always*~~ *Your world—always.*

My mom used to say goals are the future we'll never have, dreams are the future we're too afraid to have, and reality is what you never could have imagined.

Before I saw him, I smelled peppermint.

"Pesky? Really?"

Wylder chuckled, ripping a piece of gum in two and sliding half into my mouth before shoving the other half into his mouth and shrugging off his shirt. "Like a fly."

I grinned, holding my words while so many thoughts swirled in my head. He slid off his jeans, leaving him in nothing but his boxer briefs as he leaned against the vanity and crossed his arms over his chest. My love for him ran to the center of the earth and infinitely into space; it never failed to bring tears to my eyes.

My lover.

My protector.

My world.

My monster ...

"I wasn't chasing you, in spite of what your ego thought." The corner of my mouth twitched. "I liked the unknown, the mystery, the enigma that was you and your dog on campus. I wanted to know why you chose to live in a haunted house. Your asshole attitude wasn't an attraction. It was a small speed bump."

"Wow ..." His eyes widened. "I say pesky and your comeback is all of that?"

Still ... after all that time, I couldn't let him win. I pulled the drain and stood, blotting my wet body with a towel as his appreciative gaze caressed me.

"Wylder ..." I whispered.

"Livy," he replied just as softly.

"You're the most beautiful thing I ever could have imagined. And leaving my family was hard, but choosing you was easy."

His gaze fell from mine. One—there was *one* thing that brought out his guilt, maybe a hint of insecurity.

Me.

He would always feel guilty for asking me to choose him. So I played the one card, the only card that mattered.

"How far would you go for me?" I stepped out of the tub onto the mat.

He lifted his gaze and pushed off the vanity, taking two short steps to me. "The ends of the earth."

I grinned. "I think you've already done that." *Everything* Wylder did for me, even when I didn't trust him, was out of love.

He nodded slowly, ghosting his hands over my hair to my face, cupping it with a gentle touch. "Now ... I think you mentioned something that requires copulation."

Before my giggle fully released, he kissed me, stealing my gum, my heart, my soul ... my world.

All because I had no control over my stupid ...

Crazy ...

Impulsive heart.

The End

Acknowledgements

Thank you to my readers who have embraced this whole series and its spinoffs. I could write these characters forever.

To the world's best assistant, Jenn ... what can I say? You always exceed my expectations. Thank you for being all the things. Thank you for being a sounding board and giving me amazing abs.

Thank you to my brilliant and patient alpha readers and editing team for making my words shine so brightly—Max, Monique, Leslie, Kambra, Sian, Sherri, Cleida, Amy, Bethany, and Shabby. LOVE YOU!

Thank you to Nina and all the amazing women with Valentine PR. It's a true pleasure to work with you. Special thanks to Kayti for the blurb love.

Sarah Hansen, thank you for a beautiful cover.

Paul with BB e-Books, you are always awesome.

To the bloggers and bookstagrammers who take my words and bring them to life with stunning graphics—you make my heart swell with so much love. Thank you for sharing your art.

Special thanks to my community of author friends who encourage me along the way. It's an honor to be in this world with you, always celebrating in each other's successes, no matter how big or small.

Tim, Logan, Carter, Asher, and Swayze ... thank you for being my world.

Also by Jewel E. Ann

The Life Series
The Life That Mattered
The Life You Stole

Jack & Jill Series
End of Day
Middle of Knight
Dawn of Forever

Holding You Series
Holding You
Releasing Me

Transcend Series
Transcend
Epoch
Fortuity

Standalone Novels
Idle Bloom
Only Trick
Undeniably You
One
Scarlet Stone
When Life Happened

Look the Part

A Place Without You

Naked Love

Jersey Six

Perfectly Adequate

jeweleann.com

Receive a FREE book and stay informed of new releases, sales, and exclusive stories:

Monthly Mailing List

jeweleann.com/free-booksubscribe

About the Author

Jewel is a free-spirited romance junkie with a quirky sense of humor.

With 10 years of flossing lectures under her belt, she took early retirement from her dental hygiene career to stay home with her three awesome boys and manage the family business.

After her best friend of nearly 30 years suggested a few books from the Contemporary Romance genre, Jewel was hooked. Devouring two and three books a week but still craving more, she decided to practice sustainable reading, AKA writing.

When she's not donning her cape and saving the planet one tree at a time, she enjoys yoga with friends, good food with family, rock climbing with her kids, watching How I Met Your Mother reruns, and of course...heart-wrenching, tear-jerking, panty-scorching novels.

Made in the USA
Columbia, SC
17 February 2021

33094226R00192